Titles by Whitney Lyles

FIRST COMES LOVE
HERE COMES THE BRIDE
ROOMMATES
ALWAYS THE BRIDESMAID

Anthology

CATCH OF THE DAY
(*with Beverly Brandt, Cathie Linz, and Pamela Clare*)

First Comes Love

Whitney Lyles

BERKLEY BOOKS, NEW YORK

THE BERKLEY PUBLISHING GROUP
Published by the Penguin Group
Penguin Group (USA) Inc.
375 Hudson Street, New York, New York 10014, USA
Penguin Group (Canada), 90 Eglinton Avenue East, Suite 700, Toronto, Ontario M4P 2Y3, Canada
(a division of Pearson Penguin Canada Inc.)
Penguin Books Ltd., 80 Strand, London WC2R 0RL, England
Penguin Group Ireland, 25 St. Stephen's Green, Dublin 2, Ireland (a division of Penguin Books Ltd.)
Penguin Group (Australia), 250 Camberwell Road, Camberwell, Victoria 3124, Australia
(a division of Pearson Australia Group Pty. Ltd.)
Penguin Books India Pvt. Ltd., 11 Community Centre, Panchsheel Park, New Delhi—110 017, India
Penguin Group (NZ), 67 Apollo Drive, Rosedale, North Shore 0745, Auckland, New Zealand
(a division of Pearson New Zealand Ltd.)
Penguin Books (South Africa) (Pty.) Ltd., 24 Sturdee Avenue, Rosebank, Johannesburg 2196,
South Africa

Penguin Books Ltd., Registered Offices: 80 Strand, London WC2R 0RL, England

This book is an original publication of The Berkley Publishing Group.

Copyright © 2007 by Whitney Lyles.
Cover art: *Bride* by Jan Cobb; *Clothesline* by Andy Crawford/Getty Images.
Cover design by Annette Fiore.
Interior text design by Kristin del Rosario.

PRINTING HISTORY
Berkley trade paperback edition / July 2007

Library of Congress Cataloging-in-Publication Data

Lyles, Whitney.
    First comes love / Whitney Lyles.
        p. cm.
    ISBN 978-0-425-21535-7 (trade pbk.)
    1. Marriage—Fiction. 2. Pregnancy—Fiction. I. Title.

PS3612.Y45F57 2007
813'.6—dc22

                                        2007008605

PRINTED IN THE UNITED STATES OF AMERICA

10 9 8 7 6 5 4 3 2

For my daughter,
Charlotte,
who fills my life with smiles,
and gives me so much to look forward to.

Acknowledgments

Many thanks are in order. First, to my wonderful agent, Sandy Dijkstra, whose encouragement always lights a fire beneath me. Then to Tova Sacks, who gave my idea the green light. And for my supportive and talented editor, Kate Seaver, whose sharp insight helped fine-tune this book. I thank them all.

Also, a big thank-you to the SDLA team, especially Elise Capron, and all the friends and family who have stood behind me.

From the bottom of my heart I have a tremendous amount of gratitude to two very special mothers. Without the help of my mother, Martha Lyles, and my mother-in-law, Carol Dodds, this book wouldn't exist. Many thanks, not only for their support but for the love they showed my new baby while I was writing. I couldn't have done it without them.

Also a special thanks to my mom for the last-minute reading. I loved hearing her laughter from the other room. And thanks to Dad for all his encouragement and for helping Mom while she helped me.

I am, once again, forever grateful to my husband for all his support and all that he does. Finally, endless thanks to Charlotte for being such a good baby while I was completing this book, and whose smile alone can kill stress in an instant.

Part One

It's a Fine Line

·1·

Egging On

At some point in every woman's life she faces a moment of sheer panic, a moment when she realizes that everything is about to change. Perhaps it happens in high school when she drinks whiskey with ten friends in a movie theater parking lot, then realizes her parents are seated two rows behind her in the theater. It might be in college when she thinks she's found the love of her life, then walks in on him with another woman. Maybe it's when she's engaged and she looks down at her ring, only to find it's missing. However, there is no realization more startling than an unexpected pregnancy.

As Cate Blakely sweated in a hot-pink rabbit costume, the idea that she might be pregnant shot through her veins like nails. For the past week she'd been shoving the thought of her overdue period to the back of her mind the same way she turned her cheek when their yard looked like a scene from *Greystoke: The Legend of Tarzan*. Why the idea had smacked her while celebrating Easter in Scottsdale, Arizona, with her husband's family, she had no idea.

Maybe it had something to do with all the screaming children that ran across the lawn, using every opportunity they had to smash raw egg on one another. Or perhaps it was the fact that she just wanted out of the rabbit outfit, and checking to see if Aunt Flo had arrived seemed like a good reason to ditch the getup.

For the first time in her life she felt as if being pregnant wouldn't excommunicate her from her heavily Catholic parents. The feelings she had now weren't the same as the anxiety she'd felt when she'd been dating Ethan and her period had played a stressful game of hide-and-seek. She was married to him now. For the first time in her life it was *okay* to be pregnant—socially acceptable, and something her mother would greet with a wardrobe sized zero-to-three months. Then why was she scared to death? This was a different kind of fear. This was a *holy shit, I might not be ready for this* kind of fear.

She'd be responsible for another life. A small human being that would throw up on her, wake her every two hours during the night to latch onto her breasts like a pair of pliers and then grow into a rebellious hormonal teenager who would crash her car and throw raging keg parties when Ethan and she went to Hawaii.

Through the gigantic headpiece she wore she heard a muffled crunch against her leg. She looked down upon the small face of a felon in the making. A bucktoothed blond monster, Keith Junior had come into their lives when Ethan's cousin Denise had begun dating his father. What Keith Junior's father had done to the boy's hair could be considered child abuse as far as Cate was concerned. Keith Junior, too young to have good taste, couldn't be held responsible. His hairdo was the kind that made people flinch when they sat behind him in a theater. It was the kind of style that provoked shared glances of disgust, something appreciated by only a handful of people—the same people who lived for professional wrestling and thought mullets were still in. Cate was willing to bet that even most of these folks probably squirmed at the sight of Keith Junior's hair.

The child's small head was shaved down to stubs. What remained should've been snipped off and burned. A long, curly tail spidered down the nape of his neck. Rat was the first image that came to mind each time Cate noticed it.

She reached down to wipe the yolk from her leg and Keith Junior smashed another egg against her gloved hand.

"Hey! Stop that!" Her voice was distorted from behind the mask.

She watched as he flew into peals of laughter and his bucktoothed sister, Ashlyn, joined in. Looking at them made her even more worried about her missed period and tender breasts. She definitely wasn't ready for this.

Ethan's aunt was supposed to hard-boil the eggs. Instead, she'd accidentally let the kids color raw ones. His aunt couldn't tell which eggs were raw and which were hard-boiled. Most of the kids ran around the yard with raw eggs in their baskets. They'd decided that smashing the eggs on the lawn, the patio, and anyone who had their back turned was more fun than searching for the plastic ones filled with candy and coins. Raw egg covered a good portion of Aunt Caroline's yard.

Cate had decided not to move around much for fear of stepping one of her furry feet in the mess. The worst part of it was that some of the children had confused the raw eggs with the boiled ones so they pelted eggs across the yard like they were baseballs. In some ways wearing the costume had been a blessing. It had saved her from getting a concussion.

"We know you're not the Easter bunny," Keith Junior said.

"You're that skinny girl with lots of shoes and a dumb dog," Ashlyn chimed in.

"Who said that?" Cate asked, breaking the rule that the Easter bunny wasn't supposed to talk.

"See!" Ashlyn pointed. "You're not him! You're that lady."

Lady? Sure, twenty-nine qualified as being a lady. However, hearing little kids call her one made her feel old. Ladies joined the PTA. Ladies wore one-piece bathing suits. Ladies had kids.

Keith Junior eyed the basket of Cadbury eggs that she held. "Now give us some of those." His tone was firm. "Or we'll tell everyone who you are."

Cate scanned the yard for the two people responsible for Keith Junior and Ashlyn—Ethan's cousin, Denise, and her boyfriend, Keith, whom Ethan and Cate secretly referred to as Scary Dad. Several other children raced around the lawn, pegging each other with eggs. She watched as Ethan's grandmother dodged one, then gasped as it hit the window. Several of Ethan's relatives quit sipping mimosas to watch in horror as cracks spidered down the glass.

"Someone needs to stop this!" his cousin, Heide, shouted. She went to look at the window and stepped a pointy heel directly into a pile of raw egg.

Denise was in the opposite corner of the yard wearing a hat that could've inspired an entire episode of *What Not to Wear*. Covered in fake pastel flowers that appeared glue-gunned to the rim, the hat rested on her head like a straw toilet bowl. To complete her look she wore a yellow tank top and matching silk shorts with white sandals, all of which should've been thrown into a bag labeled *Theme Parties* fifteen years earlier. Scary Dad stood next to her, eyeing the yard suspiciously.

Why Denise had ever begun dating Keith Bubich was a mystery or *pure desperation* as Ethan had called it. Scary Dad, a divorcé and father of two children, worked as a parking lot attendant in an airport long-term parking garage downtown. He was the guy who sat in the booth, took the ticket, punched in the total on a small screen, then buzzed open the little lever that allowed customers to leave after they'd paid an astronomical amount in parking fees. From what Cate knew of him, she figured he probably wasn't the type of guy who cut breaks for those who lost their tickets or accidentally pulled in and then decided not to park there. He was, frankly, scary. He rarely spoke, smiled, or laughed. At thirty-seven, his interests included video games and polishing a set of tools no one had ever actually seen him use. He'd voluntarily put a bumper sticker on his gas-guzzler that read, "I don't give a FUCK what you think." A real gem, that Keith.

She looked at his chunky thighs sticking from shorts, the tasseled loafers on his bare feet that exposed a shocking farmer's tan up his ankles. His bald head and dark mustache reminded her of Anton LaVey, and she wondered how on earth the man had managed to score women.

"Give us the basket of candy," Keith Junior said. She looked at him through the slits on her headpiece. He had a tail, for crying out loud.

"Why don't you guys go look for some eggs? There are still tons out there, and I hear there is money in some. You guys can buy something better than candy."

"It's only coins. There's no bills," Ashlyn said. "We want the candy."

She wanted to shout for joy as she watched Ethan head across the grass toward her. He stepped in a pile of raw egg then paused to scrape his shoe over the grass. As he did so Keith Junior grabbed the basket. His grip was strong and Cate heard the handle rip.

"Hey," Ethan snapped as he approached. "Get outta here."

Startled, Keith Junior fled. His tail bobbed over his neck.

"I can't believe his father lets him run around like that," Cate whispered.

Ethan shook his head. "I know. What weirdos." They watched as Keith Junior smashed a hard-boiled egg against his own head, eggshell falling over his tail like confetti.

What if she had kids like these?

"Thanks for doing this," Ethan said. "I still feel so bad that you were the one to draw the rabbit from the hat."

All the adults in Ethan's family had drawn from a hat to see who would be the unlucky soul who had to play Easter bunny this year. Cate had sort of felt like she should be exempt from playing Easter bunny since she'd only been a part of the family for five months and wasn't really familiar with the Blakelys' traditions, but she decided to be a good sport and went along with it. Of course, she drew the rabbit.

Ethan had offered dozens of times to swap places with her, but she wanted to fit in. Furthermore, she'd been a kindergarten teacher for seven years. She figured entertaining kids for a couple of hours in a bunny costume wasn't a big deal. Carrying the prize basket and letting dozens of kids fueled on sugar highs climb over her in desert heat had nearly melted her.

"Good news," he said. "Aunt Caroline's trying to end the egg hunt. Someone just threw a dozen raw eggs in the pool, so you can go change now."

"Don't I have to pass out the prize candy after the kids collect all the eggs?"

He shook his head. "It's too hot. Get outta that thing."

"I missed my period." Standing in ninety-degree heat in a rabbit costume with most of Ethan's extended family in earshot was hardly the ideal time, but she couldn't help it. She was dying to tell him.

She hadn't expected him to look tortured. "What do you mean?"

"I mean, I've always been a little irregular but I've never gone two months straight without one."

"Yes, you have."

She laughed. "How would you know?"

"Haven't you?"

"Not two months." For some reason, seeing him worried made her a little less anxious. If she didn't remain calm and collected, Ethan might crumble.

He ran his fingers through his curly dark hair. "Maybe it's just . . . I don't know . . . are you sure?"

"Yes, and my boobs hurt. Bad. Sometimes they hurt before my period. So I don't know, maybe it's a false alarm."

"We've used protection." A toddler ran between the two of them, howling as chocolate dripped from his face. They both paused to look at the wet ring of what appeared to be urine around his bottom.

"There was that one time," she whispered. "When you were out of condoms. Remember?" It seemed like a strange conversation to have when children were running from every corner of the yard and his grandmother and parents were lurking.

"So let me get this straight. You're telling me that you might be pregnant?" he said.

"Well, I'm not sure, but I'm a little worried."

"Holy shit," he said right before a blue egg hit him square on the forehead. It was raw. Slowly, he lifted his hand to his brow and wiped away runny yolk. "I can't believe this."

·2·

The Line

Ethan's sighs were stronger than the air-conditioning in his Ford Explorer. The heavy breathing that had come from his side of the car since they'd left Scottsdale two hours earlier was making her nervous. Now heading past Gila Bend, his knuckles looked white and his face so pale it appeared gray. She wasn't prepared for a child either, but he seemed so worried that she was starting to wonder if he *ever* wanted kids.

"Ethan, are you o—"

"What about your insurance? We don't even have you on a normal insurance plan yet. Does our insurance even cover baby birth?"

"It's called maternity care. And I don't know. I just signed up for catastrophe insurance."

His eyes actually lit up. "Catastrophe?" She watched as his knuckles relaxed on the steering wheel. "Well, then we're fine."

She stared at him.

"What?" he asked.

"Ethan, for crying out loud. It's a child—our child—and I don't think one reckless moment of passion qualifies as a catastrophe."

After she'd gotten married last fall she'd left her teaching job to help Ethan with his catering business. His partner, Sean, had left the company to open his own restaurant, and Ethan had offered Cate the opportunity to join him in a self-employed career. There had been many reasons that had influenced the decision. More free time and flexible hours were just a couple. Mostly, the freedom of being one's own boss would be compatible with taking care of a baby. With the flexibility, they could raise a family.

The business was doing fine, but it was the off season and things had been a little slow, so she'd signed up for the cheapest insurance plan offered through the small group program Good Time Catering was contracted with. Overall, she was healthy and rarely visited the doctor so an inexpensive plan that covered a couple of routine check-ups and emergencies seemed like the most practical route. She'd never imagined a potential, unexpected pregnancy might present itself so soon.

"And we just bought the new car," he reminded her. "We can't afford to take on any more expenses."

"Look, we don't even know if I'm pregnant. My cycles have always been all over the place, so maybe it's just a false alarm."

"Have your boobs always hurt like this, too?" The way he asked seemed fragile, as if he were a child venturing into a realm unfamiliar to him.

She shook her head. "No. But don't worry. Okay?"

For most of her life she'd been afraid she wouldn't be able to have kids. Her cycles had always been a little off, and she'd experienced cramps that had put her in the fetal position on the bathroom floor. Her mother had always assured her that irregular cycles ran in the family. Nonetheless a fear of infertility had started when she was young and had haunted her for most of her childhood.

Perhaps it had stemmed from her first meeting with her parents' friends, the Otats, when she was still playing with dolls. A nice couple, the Otats were her parents' age and in her child's mind she'd been under the notion that everyone who was married had kids. "Why don't they have kids?" she'd asked her mother.

"They can't have children," she'd whispered even though the Otats had left.

"Why?"

Connie shook her head. "No one knows."

"No one knows? Isn't there a reason? There has to be a reason."

"They think it's something with Lynn, but they've never found out for sure."

"Something? Like what?" She'd never heard of this before. Not being able to have kids? There had to be a valid reason. As far as Cate knew there had never been an explanation as to why Lynn Otat couldn't conceive, and Cate had spent most of her childhood harboring fears that anyone could be inexplicably stricken infertile.

Then there had been that dramatic miniseries, *Baby M*, the true story of a totally neurotic surrogate mother, played by JoBeth Williams, who tortured a desperate couple with her indecisiveness. She'd watched *Baby M* in the sixth grade. Ever since the made-for-television movie had debuted the media had been filled with stories of in vitro fertilization, sextuplets, international adoptions, and sperm banks. There were thousands—maybe even millions—of people who had trouble conceiving. Not to mention her close friend Leslie Lyons, who'd revealed a month ago that she'd been trying to get pregnant for over a year without success. They were looking into it and still weren't sure what the problem was.

So shouldn't she be thrilled if she was pregnant?

She looked out the window. Instead of seeing desert landscapes of pristine sand dunes and bright cactus flowers, she looked at Denise and Scary Dad driving past them. Every time the lane next to Ethan's

Explorer opened up, Keith's truck roared past and his young children performed obscene gestures through the skinny window of the extra cab. Cate watched as Keith Junior pressed his mouth to the glass and puffed out his cheeks like a blowfish. Ashlyn flipped them off. The child's bird screamed inexperience. Her finger stuck from her balled fist like a pencil. Oblivious, Denise enthusiastically waved from the passenger seat.

Cate waved back, wondering how it was possible that her head didn't itch from the hat yet. After the way Denise had treated Cate ever since Ethan had proposed, Cate wasn't a huge fan of her. Cate had never been sure what exactly had provoked Denise to act like a nuisance during the events that led to their wedding. Denise had not only been the bridesmaid from hell, but she had also befriended Ethan's annoying ex-girlfriend, Janet, and brought her along to several of their wedding events. It had seemed as if Denise felt threatened by Cate. Denise had practically been orphaned as a child and had spent many years living with Ethan's family. Cate had always wondered if Denise felt as though Cate were stealing her attention. It sounded childish and ridiculous, but there was no logical explanation for the way Denise had behaved.

Shortly after the ceremony Denise must've had a crisis of conscience because she'd been much friendlier toward Cate. She'd never come out and apologized for bringing Ethan's ex-girlfriend around on a regular basis—including their engagement party—or laying a guilt trip on Cate the day before the wedding over a pair of cheap shoes, but Denise had been extra nice since the I do's. Cate had figured all the sweetness had been Denise's way of apologizing. As far as Cate was concerned, the apology was accepted. It might be impossible for anyone to be best friends with Denise. The girl was her own worst enemy.

She was the type of person who would offer to pick up something you needed at the grocery store and then make sure you paid her back to the penny. If you were short ten cents she'd lose sleep over it. She was the type of frustrating little soul who argued just to argue. If you heard it was going to be sunny the next day, Denise was adamant that rain was on the way. If you said Michael Jackson sang "Thriller," and she thought it was Stevie Wonder, well, then it was Stevie Wonder and that was the end of it. She was maddening at times. However, Cate still thought she could do better than Keith. Beneath her tough exterior there was a thoughtful person inside. Cate hated to see her settle for someone like Keith.

"Do you think they'll get married?" Cate asked as Ashlyn began to scratch the glass with her middle finger.

Ethan shook his head. "No. Her last name would be Boob Itch."

"Denise Boob Itch. Or it could be Boo Bitch."

Ethan laughed and she was relieved to see his shoulders soften and his hands relax a little.

"How did she get wrapped up with that guy anyway?" she asked.

"It was that country-line-dancing thing she signed up for."

Cate knew this. Denise had tried to convince anyone who had ever claimed a pair of cowboy boots or mentioned the Dixie Chicks in conversation to join her.

"I know you have a pair of cowboy boots," she'd said to Cate.

"Those are UGGs," Cate had said.

Denise had finally taken it solo. "No, I mean how did she fall for him?"

"She's desperate." Ethan held nothing back. "You've known her for years. She's not exactly the type of chick who gets a lot of guys."

It was true. She'd had one other boyfriend before Keith and a few dates. Ever since Keith had thrown one spark of attention in her direction all she could talk about was Keith. Keith this and Keith that, and Keith is so great and listen to what Keith did and so on. They'd all waited in anticipation to meet wonderful Keith and when they had it had been awkward as most moments with Keith were.

"I feel sorry for her," Cate said. "I know she's not exactly a babe magnet but she could still do better. I just don't think she has the confidence."

He nodded. "I know, but she's kind of a beating. I think she scares normal guys away."

Before Ethan, Cate had dated a few idiots—none as bad as Keith—and she'd always had the sense to cut off the relationship. "Keith is the type of guy who is a *learning experience*. Someone who teaches you what you don't want from a relationship. He's a growing pain. Definitely not marriage material."

"Someone married him before." Ethan glanced at both kids, who were now licking their window. He sighed again. "*That*"—he nodded toward the kids—"is what we have to look forward to."

"Hey," Cate said. "Stop this. I mean, I hope I'm not pregnant but eventually I do want kids and you've always said you do, too. So quit acting like our lives would be ruined if we had a baby."

He squeezed her knee and glanced at her with his big blue eyes. "I'm sorry," he said. "I'm just nervous. I do want kids. I just . . . I don't know . . . the thought of actually having one right now is a little scary."

"I know." She wished they had made up an excuse to ditch Denise and Keith. Their original plan had been to stop at Wal-Mart on the way back to San Diego. They'd kill their overwhelming curiosity by purchasing a pregnancy test and taking it right there in the ladies' room at Wal-Mart. It wasn't the most sentimental of plans and finding out that she was bringing a life into the world in the restroom of a desert superstore had never been a part of her motherhood fantasies, but neither she nor Ethan liked suspense. They didn't think they could make it seven hours back without knowing if they would be parents.

They were just about to make a clean getaway from Aunt Caroline's when Denise had popped her head in Cate's window like an ax murderer during a critical part in a horror movie. Cate wished Ethan had taken the cue to throw the car in reverse and screech from the driveway as if their lives depended on it.

The sight of her sunburned face beneath the brim of her hat had startled Cate.

"You guys leaving?" she asked.

Ethan had turned the key in his SUV and air-conditioning blasted from the vents. "Yeah," he'd said. "We'll see you in San Diego."

"Hey, why don't we caravan back? That way we can stop at McDonald's and stuff together. It will be fun!"

Ethan and Cate had exchanged a panicked *you come up with something* glance. "Um" was the best they could do.

"It will be safer," Denise had said. "If you get a flat, we'll be right there. And I'm sure Keith would like to have dinner with you guys."

"He would?" Cate had immediately tried to cover her shock. "I mean, he would. I just figured he'd want to rush back with the kids and everything. I'm sure they have bedtimes."

The thought of eating with Keith and the two kids while wondering if she was pregnant sounded as appealing as eating with a group of death row inmates. "Actually, we really have to head back so we probably won't be making too many stops," she'd said. "We only had our house sitter come until this morning, and Oscar starts to dig if he's left too long."

"Well, we can just go through a drive-thru. We don't even have to get out. It would just be nice to have someone along, in case something happened. You never know . . ."

So they'd been trapped in a caravan with Denise and the Boob Itches, and their plan to stop for a pregnancy test had been ruined. They had to wait until they got home to take a test, which was probably just as well.

"Now *I'm* worried about my insurance," Cate said. "What if we're not covered? I think my sister said her C-section and hospital stay were twenty thousand dollars before insurance."

He reached for her hand. "Hey, don't worry about it. I'm sorry I brought it up." Then he pulled her hand to his lips and kissed it. "Everything is going to be fine."

"How?" she asked. Minutes earlier she'd been the calm one while Ethan had been ready to drive them into a saguaro cactus to end their impending destiny of parenthood. "This is much worse than I thought," she said. "Do you know how screwed we'll be if we don't have insurance? We could go bankrupt."

"Listen, we'll figure out a way to take care of everything. Have we ever lost control of a situation in the past?"

She thought of Oscar. "Yes. Our dog."

"True. But it's not our fault that he's inbred. Listen, don't worry. Worst-case scenario, we refinance the house. We can take up to fifty thousand out. We're not going to starve or become destitute. We'll be just fine. *Our family* will be just fine."

Something about hearing him say *our family* made her a little excited.

"We said we wanted to wait a year after we were married. So it's been five months. It's not the end of the world," she said. "It's wonderful if you think about it. It's just happening a little sooner than we'd planned, is all."

He nodded. "You're right. We were going to start trying later this year anyway. It's just a little frightening when it comes as a surprise."

"Everything happens for a reason, and think of Leslie and cousin Val and all the people who can't get pregnant."

"Yeah, we'd be really lucky."

The car felt cold and she turned the air conditioner down. "What would you want?"

He thought for a moment. "One of each would be nice, but I guess a boy first."

She didn't have a preference. "What names do you like?

"I like Jed. Or Cruz."

"For names?"

"Yeah. Those are the names of boys who would never get beat up." What was most troublesome about this conversation was that it seemed as though he'd actually spent some time thinking about it. He wasn't kidding. "Those are cool names."

"We are not naming our son Cruz. Cruz Blakely? Or Jed."

"What did you have in mind?"

"For a boy? I like Evan and Ian."

"Evan and Ian?" He looked as if he'd just taken a bite of bad sushi.

"What's wrong with those names!"

"I hate the name Ian and Evan sounds so girlie. I'm not having a boy named Evan."

She stared at him. "You'd rather name your child Cruz than Evan?"

"I also like Luke."

"I like Luke. Luke Blakely? I like it."

By the time they pulled into San Diego it was dark and they'd already named their son Lukas Walter Blakely. Walter was Ethan's middle name and his grandfather's name. Girl names were still up for grabs.

· 3 ·

The Moment of Truth

Cate felt like she'd been sitting in the car for three days when they pulled into San Diego. Her face felt oily, her hair dry, and her clothes worn. She wanted a hot shower and her bed. However, there was no way either one of them would sleep if they didn't take a pregnancy test.

They found a grocery store that was still open. Only one checker with dark circles beneath his eyes stood behind a register. The emptiness made the bad instrumental music seem loud, and shrilly notes dragged from the speakers. They passed a few other late-night shoppers as they headed for the Feminine Needs aisle. She was still dressed for the desert and the store felt cold. Spring nights were chilly in San Diego anyway, but it seemed as if the grocery store was especially cool. She folded her arms over her chest.

Even though she was married and buying a pregnancy test shouldn't feel like a big deal, it still did. It felt private. Maybe it was because the last time she'd taken one she hadn't been married. It had been a false alarm when she'd been engaged to Ethan, and her fears at that time had involved never speaking to her parents again and planning a shotgun wedding.

They spent a few minutes looking at the different brands of tests and ended up picking the most expensive one.

"This isn't something we want to fool around with," Ethan said. "We want quality here."

"These things aren't cheap," she said, looking at the fifteen-dollar price on the shelf. "Do we need anything else?" she asked. She kind of wanted to bury the test beneath other groceries so it wouldn't stand out on the conveyor belt like a screaming notification that she might be expecting a child. Ethan shrugged. "Water? I think we're low on cat food."

Their hands were full by the time they made it to the register, and Cate was relieved to see the checker was the only person in the area. He looked sleepy and she wondered if the sight of her pregnancy test would make his eyes bulge from his head, if he would suddenly be wide awake at the sight of something other than milk and bread.

He looked at them and yawned.

Cate threw a pack of gum onto the conveyor belt then shoved her hands in her pockets. Where there had been no one earlier, suddenly their aisle looked like a line for flu shots in October. A couple of college students loaded three cases of beer behind their Only Response, and a man with enough TV dinners and Diet Rite set his stuff behind them. An elderly woman was next and after her stood a pregnant lady with a bottle of Tums the size of a jug. Cate felt as if her pregnancy test stood out as loudly as a singing horse.

She waited patiently as the checker breezed through their cereal, cat food, and water, finally reaching for the test. She expected him to look at the test, then look at them, but he picked it up just as if it were any other boring item he'd dragged over his scanner a million times. She was just starting to realize what an overly self-conscious weirdo she was when a beep from the register startled her. She watched as he scanned the test again. Then again. And again, until finally he shook his head and held the item up to the light to examine it.

"Only Response, pregnancy test," he mumbled. "I know I've sold one of these before."

"Oh shit," someone behind her whispered as the cashier punched in a bunch of numbers from the box on the register. She thought for sure the item would clear, but the register beeped louder.

She watched as he flipped the box in his hands. "There is no price on this," he mumbled. He yanked a walkie-talkie from above the register. "I need a price check on aisle eight. Price check on aisle eight."

"Sorry," Cate said. They accepted her apology with annoyed stares.

By now two other people had joined the line, and their groans were loud enough to make her cheeks turn warm. She caught sight of a man wearing bedroom slippers and holding two huge plastic gallons of water behind the old woman. He took the Lord's name in vain before he set his stuff on the floor. She looked up at Ethan who nervously rubbed her arm. She realized that she was sweating.

It seemed like an eternity before a teenager holding a broom appeared. The checker tossed him the test. "I think home pregnancy tests are on aisle four," he said. "In between the tampons and Monistat."

The college students snickered and Cate decided she'd rather have blood drawn than buy a pregnancy test. They finally figured out the price, paid for the test and groceries, and scurried from the store without making eye contact with anyone.

"That was torture," Ethan said as soon as they were in the car.

"He may as well have aimed a spotlight on us and announced over the loudspeaker that we might be pregnant."

"No kidding. Pretty much every single person in the store knew."

They didn't say much on the ride home. On one hand, the thought of having a baby was probably one of the most exciting things she could imagine. She'd wanted to be a mother her entire life and now the opportunity was finally here. On the other hand, if the result was negative it would come as a huge relief. They weren't ready for the medical bills and she wasn't sure if she was comfortable with sacrificing her freedom.

Aside from their honeymoon in Kauai, they'd done little traveling together. They'd discussed spending three weeks in Europe and revisiting Hawaii. She'd imagined them eating bratwurst and drinking beer in Germany, riding a gondola in Venice, and touring the Von Trapp mansion in Austria. Images of soaking up sun with a view of Bali Hai were suddenly replaced with standing in the kitchen at three A.M. with bad hair and spit-up down the front of her nightgown while she tried to heat a bottle and hold a screaming infant. Or what about the days she spontaneously buzzed off to a movie or the beach? Trying on size-two jeans in a dressing room, free of a stroller and baby bag, would be faded memories. She may never be able to fit into size two again. That was the other thing. She'd get fat. One of her closest friends, Beth, was due in a few months and she'd already packed a whopping forty pounds on her five-three frame.

However, there had been a glow about Beth ever since she'd gotten pregnant. She took in soft swirls and supersized fries from McDonald's with delight, as if forty extra pounds was worth every second of her pregnancy. Every time Cate hung out with Beth, Cate had witnessed moments when Beth would get caught in her own little world, staring dreamily at her belly while gently rubbing her hands over her basketball-sized stomach.

She looked at Ethan. His knuckles were tight and pale on the steering wheel again. He looked preoccupied, but it was hard to tell what he was thinking. She rubbed his shoulder.

"How do you feel?" she asked.

"I'm fine."

Their little 1921 bungalow was dark when they pulled up. The roses that had been pruned to bare branches back in January were starting to return. Countless buds would soon bloom and light up their green lawn. Just under a thousand square feet, their house may have inspired the eighties cartoon *The Littles*. Though they'd done a ton of work renovating the place, they were already outgrowing it. They rented a large kitchen and office space in the Golden Triangle but most of Cate's work for the catering business was conducted from the extra bedroom. Where would they put a baby? With the cost of living in San Diego County there was no way they could afford to leave their neighborhood in Escondido.

Oscar began howling in the backyard when he heard their voices. Cate was hoping to slip into the house without being noticed by the dog so they could take their pregnancy test in peace. But they'd have to let him in now. He'd wake the whole neighborhood.

Their cat, Grease, yawned when they entered. He stretched his white body, released a loud meow, and immediately ran to Cate. When Grease wanted attention he had ways of letting her know. He rubbed every inch of his body against her legs. She leaned down and picked him up and he immediately began purring.

Ethan plopped the groceries on the counter, then reached for the test.

"Don't you think we should let Oscar in?" she said. The dog had quit howling and was now scratching their back door so loud she thought he might rip it from its hinges.

"We'll never be able to take the test while he's inside."

"What about the door?"

"It'll be fine." Ethan tore open the package. Cate set Grease on the kitchen counter and read the directions while Grease rubbed his head over her arm. "I guess I just pee on this for three seconds and then we wait five minutes? It says results should appear within two, but no longer than five. One line means no. Two lines mean yes."

"Maybe I should find my old stopwatch." Ethan shuffled through their junk drawer.

"We'll just use the timer on the microwave."

"Well, what about when you're peeing on it?"

She laughed. "Ethan, I can count three seconds."

"Make sure you count one-one-thousand, two-one—"

"I know. Do you want to come in with me and count?"

He shook his head. "I'll wait."

She went into the bathroom and paused to look at herself in the mirror. She couldn't believe she was doing this. In five minutes she'd know if she was going to be a mother. Maybe she was flattering herself, but she still thought she looked so young. Her blonde hair hung to her shoulders and she'd had her hairdresser cut choppy, edgy bangs with a razor. She was far from the short shag hairdo that went along with driving a minivan and setting up playdates.

She followed the instructions and looked to see if any lines had appeared before she left the bathroom. Within seconds one dark line appeared in the test window. She held it up to her eyes as she approached Ethan. If another line was going to appear, it was taking its time. It seemed as if the control line was only getting darker. Ethan immediately set the timer for five minutes.

"Turn the lights up," she said.

He pushed the dimmer switch as high as it would go before hovering over the counter where she'd set the pregnancy test. They both stared, waiting for any sign of a line to appear—any hair of pink to crease down the test strip. She took her eyes away only to look at the timer.

"The instructions said that most results appear within two minutes. It's been three," she said.

"It said to wait five minutes to get one hundred percent accurate results."

They stared some more. The only thing that changed was the control line, which became so dark it looked red. By five minutes the hot-looking line screamed negative.

She shrugged. "Well, it's been five minutes. I guess I'm not pregnant." She was surprised that her smile felt forced.

She expected Ethan to pop the cap off a bottle of champagne that had been sitting in their fridge since New Year's Eve. "Well, it's for the best," he said. "It'll happen when we're ready. When the time is right." He sounded as if he were trying to convince himself.

She hugged him. "You're right. Now would've been a bad time. Everything happens for a reason."

"I think we had a good plan to wait until the end of the year."

She still couldn't ignore the disappointment in his voice. "Me, too." She kissed him on the cheek. "Are you disappointed?"

"No." He shook his head. Then he opened the fridge, pulled out a Corona, and popped the cap off. "Well, maybe a little."

"We'll have our baby," she said. "When the time is right."

This should be a huge relief. They didn't have to refinance the house. She could get better insurance. They could travel. The future was free. As she stood there dreaming of Austria and Hawaii, a thought so startling it made her back stiffen charged through her mind. If she wasn't pregnant, then why wasn't she getting a period? It could only mean one thing. Something was wrong.

4

Watered Down

The doctor couldn't see her for three agonizing weeks. Apparently, the receptionist at her ob-gyn's office didn't think two months of missed periods was enough of an emergency to get her in the next day.

Instead of sitting around waiting for her appointment with Dr. Hatcher, she sought the expertise of another kind of doctor, a doctor who was available at the tip of her fingers anytime she needed him. A doctor who always had time for questions and gave Cate plenty of opportunity to consider all kinds of treatments, home remedies, and natural cures. The name of this doctor was the Internet.

The only setback of Dr. Internet was that he came with a heavy prescription of paranoia. Dr. Internet wasn't always specific, often very vague. He gave Cate plenty of freedom to self-diagnose.

According to the dozens of articles she read she could have twisted ovaries, cysts the size of eggs on her ovaries, hundreds of cysts on her ovaries, scar tissue covering her uterus and ovaries, or perhaps her twenty-nine-year-old body was just slowing down and her good eggs were dying off like pollywogs in a desert creek. By week two she was looking into in vitro fertilization and international adoptions.

"Have you lost your mind?" Ethan said when she presented him with a brochure on Chinese orphanages. "You haven't even been to the doctor!"

The week before her appointment and shortly after Ethan had forbidden her from visiting any kind of medical website or women's health message board she heard from Denise. Cate was responsible for all the scheduling for Good Time Catering and was waiting to hear from a client when the phone rang. "Can you please do me a huge favor?" She sounded desperate.

"Ummm . . . well . . ."

"Are you busy right now?"

"Right now?" The truth was that she had just settled into an episode of *A Baby Story* and a bowl of Ben & Jerry's but she couldn't think of an excuse. "Um . . . not *right* now." She regretted the words instantly and tried to retract. "I just have to be here for Ethan in two hours. He needs my help with something." It was the best she could do.

"Fine! Two hours is all I need you for."

"Okay." She couldn't keep her voice from dragging.

"Keith's kids are supposed to come to my house after school today. Another parent was going to drop them off here because Keith had to cover for someone downtown." She always referred to Keith's job as "downtown" as if he was part of the sophisticated world of law offices and jewelers. "Anyway, I completely forgot—I have to take escrow papers to one of my clients. It's mandatory that we do it today. All you have to do is come over and let the kids in. Make them a snack and they'll watch cartoons for the rest of the afternoon."

Maybe she could cut Keith Junior's tail off while he slept. "Yeah, all right, I'll do it."

Twenty minutes later she was on her way to Denise's. They'd replaced her ancient Volvo station wagon with a Toyota Prius, and even though she'd owned the car for three months it still seemed brand-new. She still got a surge of excitement every time she slid behind the wheel. It was the only car she'd ever owned that was brand-new, and it was a hybrid so days of spending a good portion of her paycheck on gasoline were over. The car was white, and she'd thought it looked like a giant egg, but with global warming she'd thought it made the most sense. If it meant that her house wouldn't be replaced with the shoreline of the Pacific Ocean then she could handle driving something that looked hard-boiled.

Ever since she'd made her appointment with Dr. Hatcher she'd felt a constant state of impatience. She felt restless at every stop sign she approached. She impatiently flipped through every single radio station. The drone of commercials filled her speakers and she turned off the stereo. She wasn't in the mood for any of her CDs. She decided to call her mother. She had wanted to ask her mother if she'd ever encountered any fertility problems.

"You're babysitting for that man?" her mother asked the moment Cate told her where she was headed.

"I couldn't think of any good excuses."

"Be careful," she cautioned. "I'm telling you he's like one of those quiet creepy people who snaps one day and holds a McDonald's hostage. I just hope you're not in his crossfire when it happens."

As far as Connie was concerned Keith holding a machine gun to a bunch of bystanders armed with Happy Meals was as imminent as rain in April.

"He's a loose cannon."

Cate couldn't help but laugh. She'd often had similar thoughts about Keith—not quite as detailed and wild. He was the quiet, scary type who made almost everyone he came in contact with feel as if he might go postal at any moment. When Connie had an assumption or an observation about someone that's what they became. Connie had been partly responsible for coining Keith Scary Dad.

It had begun when Connie had said that Keith reminded her of Cate's childhood playmate Rebecca Morton's father. Mr. Morton was a scary dad. He wasn't scary in a child molester, perverted way. The stuffed heads of deer and mountain lions mounted his wall and he carried a Dixie cup for his chewing tobacco juice almost everywhere he went. He was a man of little words and when he entered a room everyone moved out of the way.

Connie was always drawing conclusions about other people and calling them anything but the names they'd been given at birth. Mr. Morton had been called Scary Dad, and growing up in her middle-class neighborhood they'd lived on a block of drug dealers, chronic gamblers, and Satanists.

Take the German couple, the Fritzes. They had a tall fence and a lot of earthy friends slipping in and out of their yard at all hours of the day. The Fritzes didn't appear to have jobs, outside of their home at least. Cate's family had often spotted the Fritzes carting shovels and hoes from car to backyard, which Connie concluded went straight to the marijuana they were growing.

"I think those people are dealing drugs," she'd said. "They have strange people there all the time and they keep to themselves. They don't have any friends on this street. They're drug dealers."

It couldn't have been possible that they liked gardening and happened to have a lot of artsy friends. Within weeks of the Fritzes' arrival Connie was saying, "One of the drug dealers' clients parked in front of our trash cans today." Or, "I need to borrow an egg but I don't want to ask the drug dealers. Go ask the man with the gambling problem."

The man with the gambling problem was Shane Miller, a thirtysomething bachelor who'd moved to the neighborhood and purchased a different sports car every six months. He liked the horse races in the summer and had once mentioned going to Las Vegas.

Connie had drawn the following conclusion: "Nobody goes through that many cars. I think he has to sell them because of all his gambling debts. Then when he wins big he goes and buys another one. Don't talk to anyone when you're waiting for the school bus. I bet the Mob will be out here looking for him soon."

Connie's assumptions rubbed off on the whole family and Cate had grown up saying, "Mom, I think the dog ran into the gambler's yard. Someone better go get him before he goes anywhere near the Satanists."

Cate turned down Denise's street. "Mom, I think Keith will be fine. My biggest concern is that Denise is going to marry him and then he'll be my brother-in-law."

"Maybe you should call me as soon as you leave there so I know you made it out of there okay."

"I won't even see him. It's just Denise and the kids."

"I'll pray that your guardian angel is with you. Though I don't know if you even have one anymore. After the way you've been living your guardian angel has probably forgotten who you are."

"What?" She couldn't have conversations like these when she was trying to parallel park.

"Well, I'm sure your angel went off to find someone more holy to protect."

"What are you talking about?"

"You know what I mean. Never attending mass on Sunday. Living with Ethan before you were married."

"Are you still mad about that?" She drove around the block looking for a larger spot.

There was a pause, and Cate felt the energy she'd had for her fertility conversation being drained.

"No. I'm not mad," Connie said. "But who knows if God has gotten over it yet. And if things are too immoral and offensive for a guardian angel they'll just leave and go find someone pure to protect.

They can't stand to be around sin." Since her mother knew so many angels on a personal level she must know what she was talking about.

"All right, really. I gotta go. I'll call you later."

"You better say some prayers, Cate. I'm not kidding. You need that guardian angel. Watch out for that scary man!"

Cate quickly said good-bye.

Denise's front door was open. She was snapping her briefcase shut and didn't notice Cate when she entered. It was hard to ignore that most of Denise's furniture and décor didn't match. Cate thought her own living room could use a facelift, but Ethan's couch from the post-college years and Cate's old coffee table actually seemed kind of nice compared to the hideous couch upholstered in a tapestry of pastels and the black metallic entertainment center.

"Oh good. You're here!" Denise said. "Thank you so much for doing this. I can't tell you how much I appreciate it." She handed Cate a stack of pictures from Shutterfly. "You can look at these if you'd like. They're from our trip to Cozumel. There are a few from Easter in there, too. God, you looked really worked after you took that costume off. I had forgotten how worn you looked."

What was she supposed to say? *Thanks, I was hoping that I didn't look fresh and attractive. Worn and worked are really how I want to look in photos.*

"There are Fruit Roll-Ups in the pantry and they like tortellini, too. You can heat some of those up if you want. They love microwave popcorn, too."

She showed Cate a stash of videos and Cate was quickly sucked into warm memories from her childhood. She hadn't watched *Lady and the Tramp* or *Snow White and the Seven Dwarfs* in decades and was starting to think the afternoon might be kind of fun. She loved all the Disney classics, and pictured her and the two kids curled beneath an afghan with a large bowl of popcorn resting in the middle of them while they watched an old favorite.

After Denise left Cate sat down with the pictures. Denise and Scary Dad had gone to Cozumel a couple weeks before Easter and the entire Blakely family had lived in fear that Denise would come back engaged. Fortunately, she'd only come back with a horrible sunburn and Montezuma's revenge.

Apparently she'd packed and dragged her hideous hat to Mexico because she wore it with her one-piece bathing suit in nearly every photo. More alarming was Keith sprawled out on a beach towel, wearing nothing but a pair of Ray-Bans and a pale blue Speedo with black checkers covering one side of the Lycra. Cate didn't know whether to laugh hysterically or gag.

She set the pictures down.

Denise had said she could use the computer while she waited for the kids. Her office smelled faintly of a dirty litter box. Cate noticed that she'd replaced a lot of the framed photos of her cats with pictures of Keith from about fifteen years prior.

He'd had a brief stint as a professional football player. It was arena football, far less popular than the NFL. The players were smaller than the linebackers and quarterbacks who played in the Super Bowl and were paid much less, but it was still professional and the sport had a significant following. She looked at a much more svelte Keith in his uniform, streaks of black paint smeared across the tops of his cheeks. In one photo he stood amidst a group of teammates. His helmet was off and sweat had matted his hair to his forehead as he proudly held a trophy over his shoulders. Cate thought she detected a twinkle in his eye. There was something boyish and proud in his expression. He looked like a different person. He looked long and lean where he now was blubbery and thick. Even though he still made her nauseous she couldn't deny that he actually looked *kind of, sort of* cute. Kind of. She could see how in his days of glory he might have scored some arena football groupies.

Cate remembered that shortly after Denise had met Keith, Denise had described her new beau as a retired football player. Several months later they'd learned Keith was actually in the parking business and had only played arena football for a few years. Retirement had been forced after he'd injured his back.

Denise had rarely had boyfriends and the only one Cate could recall was a scrawny cell phone salesman who collected *Star Wars* figurines and read comic books at thirty-six. It had been obvious from the start of Denise's romance with Keith that Denise was proud of him. As Cate looked at the pictures of his glory days she got it. She understood Denise a little more. Not that Keith and his football playing days seemed like a catch to Cate, but she understood how Denise might see it that way. Most everyone else on the planet would've seen Keith as the chubby, bitter man that he was and Denise could only see him as someone who had tasted a moment of recognition. He was someone who'd experienced people applauding for him, cheering him. He'd had fans—something Denise had never had.

Cate looked around the office. Denise was a real estate agent and stacks of fliers with her headshot filled every corner of the room. There were signs with the same picture—the same feathered bangs she'd worn since the sixth grade—propped against the walls.

She slid into Denise's swivel chair and reached for the mouse. Instead of checking e-mail or scouring eBay for cool vintage furniture, Cate headed over to Yahoo! and typed *ovarian torsion* in the search bar. It was possible that she had the rare disorder in which her ovaries were too long and had twisted or turned so as to obstruct ovulation and thus preventing her from getting a period. The diagnosis was grim. Surgery might repair the problem, but more likely Ethan and she would be stockpiling their money for a trip to China if they wanted a child.

She was reading about the symptoms when she felt something wet and cold hit the back of her neck. "Holy shit!" she screamed as she jumped from her chair and turned to face whatever had hit her.

She looked down the barrel of a Super Soak 'Em water gun. "Freeze!" Keith Junior yelled before he sprayed the entire front side of her clothes as well as the ceiling, computer, and cat. The gun looked massive in his skinny arms.

"Keith Junior!" she screamed. "What are you doing? You're going to ruin Denise's computer!"

"Who cares? She's not my mom." He got down on one knee and aimed for Denise's cat, Bailey, who was hissing from a far corner of the room.

Cate lurched forward and pushed the gun away in the nick of time. "Give me that," she said, short of breath. "I'm serious."

"I gotcha good." She recognized the scent of a little boy fresh from an elementary school playground. Being a kindergarten teacher had made Cate used to the smell. Sweaty children weren't the same as adults. The subtle odor of youthful perspiration mixed with laundry detergent felt familiar as she wrestled the gun from his arms.

"Where's your sister?"

No sooner had she spoken the words when Ashlyn appeared in the doorway, wearing a Jack-Nicholson-with-cabin-fever expression. Wasting no time, Ashlyn didn't bother to aim. Truly crazed, she squirted water in all directions. She sprayed as though the room were ablaze and putting out the inferno was her sole mission.

"Ashlyn! Stop! Please! Please stop!" Cate screamed from behind wet bangs. She watched as the child drowned Denise's bookshelves and fax machine. She soaked her high school and college diplomas. As Cate witnessed the office become Phoenix during monsoon season she wondered, Who the hell hangs her high school diploma? Cate didn't even know where hers was.

She was just about to lurch forward and wrestle the gun from her hands when she noticed something more alarming than Denise's face on her wilting RE/MAX fliers. There, in the doorway, loomed the bald head and big butt of Scary Dad. He'd been watching them, and judging from the scowl that covered his face, what he'd seen hadn't pleased him. Ashlyn, also aware of the dark cloud that had covered the room, immediately dropped her gun.

In some ways, Cate was thrilled to see him. He could control the kids and she could go home. However, the dark look in his eyes made her feel as if she were in trouble, too. She cleared her throat and wiped a wet strand of hair away from her face.

"Hi there, Keith. You're home early. I was actually, uh . . . we were actually expecting Denise. I had no idea you were coming home."

Not a word as he looked over the room. She felt a chill run up her spine. Goose bumps popped from her arms, and she felt as though she needed to explain. However, something about Keith made her uncomfortable. Speaking seemed so frightening.

She handled him the only way she knew how when someone was extra weird. She slapped a smile on her face. Maybe if she was nice, he wouldn't kill her. "Well, it's good to see you!"

"What? The? Hell? Happened? In? Here?"

"Just having some fun with toys!" Cate said. "Can I get you a Fruit Roll-Up?"

"Cate said we could play with water guns," Keith Junior said. "Inside."

"I did not! I was just using the computer. I wasn't even expecting them to be home for another ten minutes when they came in and attacked me!"

"You lie!" Ashlyn said.

"I am not lying. I wouldn't lie about something like this. Listen, I was just doing Denise a favor," she said. "I was only trying to help you guys out. Do you really think I would let the kids destroy the house? I taught kindergarten for six years and I've never—"

She stopped. There was no point in explaining herself to him. Furthermore, she knew the kids were total brats, but what if they were lying because they were afraid of Scary Dad? What if they were afraid he would snap, too? She had a soft spot for little kids, especially ones with weird parents. "You know what? I'm sorry. I probably should've been clearer when they took out the guns that they were for outdoor use only."

The kids looked genuinely shocked. Scary scratched his head.

"I mean, I never expected things to get so out of hand." She continued only because she felt a need to fill the silence. "I should've said *outside* when I said aim."

"Yeah, you should've. Next time do you think you could behave in a responsible manner?"

There would be no next time, but she kept that to herself. She still had an urge to defend herself but she just wanted to get the hell out of there.

"Tell Denise to call me later," she said as she grabbed her purse. "And you guys have a nice evening."

The kids followed her outside. They still looked surprised.

"Bye, Cate." They waved.

"Can we come play with your dog? We always wanted a dog," Ashlyn said.

She leaned toward them and whispered, so Scary wouldn't hear, "My dog would eat you alive." They may have thought they'd gotten away with something but she had to make it clear that she wouldn't be taken advantage of. "You better not mess with me again." The last thing she saw was their stunned little expressions before she turned and walked away. It was the first time she'd ever seen them look rattled.

5

The Birth of Rumors

"He is so weird," Cate said. She was in her kitchen, tossing a salad while Ethan pulled homemade macaroni and cheese from the oven. One of the perks that came with being married to a chef was that she ate good food most of the time. Ethan viewed macaroni and cheese from the box the same way a fisherman might view eating frozen fish sticks. There was just a better way to do things as far as he was concerned and he enjoyed going the extra mile when it came to food.

Furthermore, Cate rarely cooked, which was probably a good thing. The last time she'd been left alone in the kitchen she'd accidentally left a glass casserole dish on top of a burner turned to high heat. She still marveled over the miracle that she and Grease had walked away from the accident with their vision when the 11-by-8 dish had exploded into a million tiny pieces in the kitchen. It truly was the grace of God that neither one of them had a single injury.

That's what talking on the phone and cooking causes, and Ethan had discouraged her from surprising him with dinners ever since.

"You should've seen the way he talked to me. As if I was some college student they'd hired as a nanny. *Next time do you think you could behave in a responsible manner?* As long as you promise to buy some swim trunks that cover your thighs!"

"What?" Ethan said. He took off his oven mitt and set it on top of the counter.

"Denise has pictures from their trip to Cozumel and he was wearing a Speedo."

She'd known her husband since they were children and she couldn't recall ever seeing him more disgusted. "Are you serious?"

"Dead serious. And it wasn't even like a sporty one in a solid color. It was light blue with a print on it."

He held up his hand. "Okay, enough. Please. Stop. Seriously, I can't hear about the Speedo anymore."

"He must be really nice to her when no one is around," Cate said. "What could she possibly see in that man?" Cate was still shuddering from the whole afternoon. Scary in a Speedo. Scary looming in the doorway, his mustache looking as weird as ever. The kids lying.

"White or red?" Ethan asked.

"Huh?" She was wondering if she should say something to Denise, maybe have a heart-to-heart with her about Keith. They weren't close friends but Denise didn't have any close friends. There was no one to discourage her from dating Keith. Sure, Denise was annoying but she could do better than Keith. Cate was starting to think a homeless prostitute could do better than Keith.

"Do you want white or red wine?" he asked again.

"Oh. White, please. A tall glass."

"We better make it tall," he said as he pulled glasses from the cabinet. "This might be one of the last. If you have a baby, you know you can't drink."

The remark took her by surprise. She knew the pregnancy scare and her upcoming appointment with the doctor had lit a fire beneath her, but she hadn't been sure if Ethan was ready or not. "Are you saying that you want to start trying?"

He shrugged. "I don't know. Maybe."

At this point she just wanted her period to come. Each time she thought of having a baby she felt a gnawing sense of worry in her chest. The worry was like a big zit on her forehead. She'd attempt to hide it with makeup, forget it was there, and each time she passed a mirror she'd feel self-conscious about it again. She'd try to forget about babies, but each time she heard someone mention the words *period* or *pregnancy* it would sneak up on her.

Never in her life had she wanted her period to come more. She'd even welcome PMS, and had actually been hoping for signs of violent mood swings and zits.

"Guess what?" Ethan said as they moved to the table. "I can't believe I forgot to tell you. Guess who's pregnant?"

She set down the casserole dish. "Who?"

"Sarah and Miles. She called you while you were watching the Bubiches."

"Seriously? Why didn't you tell me? I can't believe you forgot to tell me." She slid into her chair. "That's wonderful news! Oh my gosh, that's great. What did she say?"

"She was really excited and she wants you to call her."

Sarah was one of her closest friends. They'd lived together in college and had been bridesmaids in each other's weddings. The idea of Sarah having a baby was almost worth ditching a hot dinner over. Cate felt too excited to eat. "When's she due?"

"I think she said October."

"Oh wow. So she is already fairly far along. She must've wanted to keep it a secret until she knew she wasn't going to miscarry." Cate thought it was a smart move, but she wondered if she'd be able to do the same thing. She'd have to tell someone. She didn't think she could keep it from her parents or sister. And what if she did miscarry? She'd want the support of her family.

"Are they finding out what they're having?" Cate asked.

"I don't know."

She had so many questions. She wanted to know whether or not they had names picked out, if Sarah would keep working, how her pregnancy was going. She'd call her later.

They finished eating and Ethan decided to take Oscar for a walk. Cate stayed behind to call Sarah and do the dishes. She tried to call Sarah but it went straight to voice mail. Cate figured she was on the other line spreading the exciting news. While she waited to call Sarah back she attacked the dishes. She was drying the last dish when Ethan's mom, Rita, called.

"It's been so long since we've gotten together for dinner and I wanted to set a date for you guys and your parents to come over," Rita said.

They set a tentative date and Cate hoped that Rita hadn't invited Scary and his kids.

"Thanks for inviting us," Cate said. "We'll see you then."

There was a long pause. "So how is everything going?"

"Great." Cate poured more wine into her glass.

"Anything new?"

"Um, well, Oscar ate the pet sitter's Coach handbag she'd saved five months for while we were in Phoenix so we have to replace that. And we're catering a wedding in Rancho Santa Fe this weekend."

"That's what Ethan said." She was quiet. "Anything else?"

"No." She took a sip of wine.

"Well, I ran into an old friend of mine today."

"Really?" She curled up on the couch while she listened.

"Yeah, a doctor that I used to know. She was an ob-gyn but now she's specializing in infertility."

Ethan's parents were both retired doctors so it wasn't odd that they had lots of friends in the medical field, but Cate found it bizarre that Rita would bring up a fertility specialist when getting pregnant was all Cate could think about. She wanted to tell her what a strange coincidence it was, but Ethan and she had decided to keep their baby plans secret.

"Yes, very competent woman. Practicing right around the corner from you, actually. Has an office right off Juniper."

Now this was *too* bizarre. She knew Rita and Charles were dying for grandchildren, but this kind of pressure? She was hinting loudly for Cate to pay the woman a visit. How could she know? Keeping a secret with Ethan was the same as confiding in the CIA, especially when it came to his personal life.

"Oh, that's good. Well, I think Leslie's having a hard time, so maybe I'll mention it to her."

"Okay, why don't you write down the number? Her name is Dr. Rivas." She produced the phone number quickly, like she'd had the information right next to her.

After Cate took the number they said good-bye.

Ethan must've said something. It was a shock, and she really thought she knew him better. Furthermore, she felt a little annoyed. She didn't want everyone to know if they were having problems. Rita and Denise were close, so if Rita thought they were worried, then Denise knew, too. It just seemed so un-Ethan to share something so private with his parents. Ethan avoided long phone conversations the way most people avoided driving in rush-hour traffic. He wasn't a phone person so she couldn't imagine him getting into a deep, personal conversation with anyone on the phone.

She was about to try Sarah again when the front door blew open and Oscar crashed through, carrying half of a leather leash behind him. Ethan followed, sweat dripping from his temples. He held the other end of a broken leash and his shorts were ripped across the crotch, exposing his striped boxer shorts. "We're getting the damn dog a shock collar," he said.

"What happened?"

"We're getting one of those collars that comes with a remote control and shocks the hell out of them when they roam too far," he said beneath staggered breath. "That dog takes off, and I'll press a button so fast he won't know what hit him! *Ha!*"

"Ethan, stop. We're not shocking the dog."

"He broke the damn leash again. Ripped it right in half. You should've seen him. He hurled straight over the neighbors' fence like it was a speed bump and jumped into the kiddie pool in their backyard. Thank God they were inside. I climbed over the fence so fast that my shorts got caught."

"Did you walk all the way home like that?" She looked at his underwear.

"I had no choice."

Cate watched as Oscar jumped on the couch and immediately began rubbing his jowls over a throw pillow. "I'm telling you. That's it. I'm getting one of those damn collars. The next time that dog takes off I'm stopping him dead in his tracks with one push of a button." There was actually a twinkle in his eyes.

"Ethan, we are not shocking Oscar." To a stranger, her husband might appear to be an animal abuser. However, one week with Oscar and any sane person would be looking into not only shock collars but canine lobotomies as well. The dog had a tendency to bring out the worst in people. She knew Ethan would change his mind by tomorrow. "Hey, did you tell your mom about my missed periods?"

He flopped down on the couch. "No. Why would I do that?"

"It was really weird. She called to invite us to dinner and then she gave me the number for a fertility specialist."

"That is weird."

Then Cate remembered something so alarming she felt goose

bumps rise on her arms. Denise. She'd forgotten to close the computer screen when she'd been watching the Bubich kids. The water gun attack had come without warning, and she'd been reading about ovarian torsion.

This was how rumors were spread. Denise had obviously read all about ovarian torsion, then called Rita to tell her that Cate had been researching it. Up until a few days ago Cate didn't even know what ovarian torsion was, let alone whether she had it or not, and now Ethan's family thought she couldn't reproduce. Through her annoyance, she managed to laugh. "Denise. I think she told your mother I can't have children."

Cate told him about the website and how she'd forgotten to close out the computer screen. Ethan wasn't as amused. He was still in a bad mood over the dog and he looked at Cate as if she were the crazy one, and not his meddling cousin. "This is what your paranoia leads to. If you hadn't been so paranoid in the first place, none of these rumors would've started. Now my parents think we can't have kids. Way to go."

6

Baby Fever

The day before Cate's doctor appointment she met her friend Leslie for lunch. Leslie and her husband, Russ, had been trying to conceive for over a year. According to Cate's Internet research it took the average couple around seven months. She knew Leslie had spent many sleepless nights worrying about her fertility, and Cate was beginning to understand how she felt.

Cate walked to the restaurant and had brought her umbrella with her in case it rained. Spring had a way of taunting San Diegans. Warm, sunny days would appear and everyone would dig out their swim trunks and sunscreen from last summer. They'd pull the tops off their convertibles and neighborhoods would be filled with the scent of barbequing again. The next day it would rain. It was still too soon to trade in raincoats for bikinis, and this particular day was no exception. It was as if the weather couldn't decide if it wanted to rain or be sunny. Thick heavy gray clouds had been weaving in and out of the sky all morning, stopping occasionally to let the sun break through. One minute she was pulling her sweater over her shoulders and the next she was pushing the sleeves up to her elbows.

She met Leslie at Vincent's, a French restaurant on Grand Avenue in Escondido. It was delicious. Leslie was the type of friend who liked to splurge on lunches. Cate could see Leslie seated inside as she approached.

They'd been friends for ten years and Cate had gotten used to feeling slightly underdressed every time she was in her presence. Wearing khakis rather than jeans was Cate's idea of sprucing things up for a lunch date. When she arrived in khaki capris and a billowy cotton blouse and found Leslie wearing crisp black slacks with a matching jacket and a sharp lime-colored scarf around her neck, Cate felt as if she'd shown up for a wedding in workout gear.

Leslie had also always been a little ahead of her time—a couple of decades off as far as behavior went. Cate would never forget the time that Leslie, Sarah, and herself had decided to throw a Christmas party in college. While Cate and Sarah had been mixing red and green Jell-O with vodka and ordering a keg of Natural Light, Leslie had tried to call their party a cookie exchange.

She'd decorated their apartment in poinsettias and purchased Christmas china from Macy's before spending an afternoon alone with her cookie press and six dozen homemade shortbreads.

Cate and Sarah had used the grapevine to spread the word about their party while Leslie had sent out twenty-four invitations instructing guests to bring six dozen cookies of their choice to share with everyone. Two guests had brought cookies—a bag of store-bought animal crackers in Christmas colors and a half-eaten bag of broken Milanos. Everyone else gorged themselves on Jell-O shots and beer bongs before their neighbor, Nick, blew up a poinsettia while attempting to breathe fire. Leslie could never understand why no one had touched the hot cocoa she'd brewed or why her Carpenters Christmas hits CD had been thrown from the front deck like a Frisbee and replaced with the Beastie Boys' *Licensed to Ill*.

However, Leslie was one of the most loyal friends Cate had ever known. She was the type of girl who would hate your ex even if you were over him and would stand in line for two hours to have a book signed by your favorite author. She always had sound, practical advice. There had been plenty of moments when Cate had wanted to rip her hair out from Leslie's sheer anal retentiveness but she still loved her.

The restaurant was decorated in warm, dark colors. It felt upscale, yet cozy inside. Leslie stood to hug Cate.

"It's so good to see you," Cate said, catching a whiff of her perfume.

"I have news," Leslie sang as soon as they sat down.

She's pregnant. No. It couldn't be possible for two of her closest friends to announce pregnancies within weeks of each other. *She'd been promoted. That had to be it.*

"Russ and I are having a baby!"

It was possible. Cate sprang from her seat to hug her again. "Leslie! Are you serious? Oh my gosh, this is wonderful! When did you find out?"

"This morning! I took a test over the weekend and it was positive."

"And to think of all the worrying. See? Everything was just fine." She felt like she should be giving herself the same advice. "You and Sarah at the same time! And your kids will be the same age."

"I know. I'm so happy. We've been trying for over a year and I was really beginning to think something was wrong with me."

"I'm so happy for you." Honestly, she'd been a little worried for Leslie, too.

The news was inspiring. If Leslie had gotten pregnant after a year and a half of trying, then anything was possible.

Why couldn't Cate ignore the pinch of sadness she felt? She wanted badly to suppress it. As she sat across from Leslie listening to her talk about nursery colors and baby names she recognized a feeling of loneliness. Didn't every group have someone who never reached the next milestone? Among all her friends who'd graduated from high school there'd been one who never went to college. Among all their girlfriends, there would always be a single one. Now among all her friends with children, there'd be a barren one.

She'd sit around with Leslie and Sarah while they talked all about their pregnancies, then their babies, then preschool and homemade Halloween costumes, and she'd have nothing to add. She'd fill her boredom with trips to Europe and dinners for two while the rest of her girlfriends raised families.

There was something else in her feelings, too, something she wasn't well acquainted with—something she loathed. It felt like envy. When it seemed she'd be doomed to be a bridesmaid forever, she'd never once felt envious. Not once. Lonely maybe, but never jealous. These feelings had snuck up on her and she hated herself for having them, especially when Leslie had shared what was probably the most important news of her life.

It was selfish. Feeling selfish only made her feel worse. It wasn't that she wasn't happy for Leslie, because she was. She knew the way she felt had nothing to do with Leslie. It only stemmed from her own insecurities. *Wasn't that what envy was about? Yourself.* Once she recognized that she needed to get over herself it was easier to enjoy the moment.

"Are you going to find out what you're having?" She reached for her iced water.

"Yes. I can't stand it when people don't find out," Leslie said. "I want to plan. I want to decorate. I want to be prepared for this baby."

"I'm so glad you're finding out. Otherwise, I think I'd go crazy wondering for you." One of Cate's best friends, Beth, was due at the end of the summer and had opted not to find out. She'd kept all her friends and family in suspense wondering.

The waiter came and they both ordered steak. As soon as he was gone they were back to Leslie's news. "When are you due?"

"January. I mean I haven't been to the doctor yet, but according to my calculations the due date is January eighth."

"It could be a New Year's Eve baby!"

"I know." She smiled. "I kind of hope it is. I think it would be fun."

"Is it a secret? Can I tell people?"

"Sure. Russ already told everyone he works with, and I called my parents this morning."

Obviously, miscarrying wasn't a concern. She thought of Sarah, who'd waited the full three months until the risk of miscarrying was reduced before sharing the news. "Did you tell Sarah yet?" Cate asked.

"Yes! Our babies will only be a few months apart. I'm so excited!"

A smile spread across Leslie's face, and Cate couldn't help but notice that she was glowing. *Already,* she was a glowing pregnant woman. "I just have a feeling," Leslie said. "There's something to be said about a woman's intuition. I just have a feeling that I don't need to wait the full three months."

Cate felt the pinch again, only this time it was a double shot of paranoia and envy. Not only would she become neurotic with paranoia, but she the envy would drive her crazy. What was it about babies and motherhood that brought out the worst in her? Maybe it was because being a mother was her oldest dream. As a child she couldn't wait to grow up. Ever since she'd received her first dollhouse on her fourth birthday she'd imagined the family she would have one day. Now that day was here. She'd found her soul mate and she was ready. Ironically, it seemed as if her body wasn't ready.

Furthermore, Leslie was right. There was something to be said about women's intuition, and she couldn't deny her sense that something was wrong. The worst of all, and the hardest thing to admit, was that some of her fear stemmed from the fact that she would feel like a failure if she couldn't conceive. She'd not only be letting herself down but Ethan as well.

Elvis Is Alive

The truth was, she didn't know Dr. Hatcher that well. Their relationship revolved around annual checkups. During these visits he breezed into the exam room—his nurse, Tina, in tow—quickly pulled on his rubber gloves, pointed to the stirrups, and asked her what she did for a living, if she had big plans for the summer, and what she was using for birth control while examining her. Last summer their conversation had been a little more exciting because she'd been engaged when she'd seen him. He wanted to know where she was going on her honeymoon and what her fiancé did for a living. These meetings usually lasted less than five minutes and before she knew it the whole dreaded yearly visit with the gyno was over and done with.

She'd always thought it strange that he was the only person besides her husband who knew how much of her bikini line she'd shaved, yet if she passed Dr. Hatcher on the street he'd have no idea who she was or whether or not she'd gone Brazilian or Amazon rain forest. It felt strange that someone who knew the most private things about her was practically a stranger. She felt as if she should know more about him.

While she waited to see him her stomach ached and her hands felt damp. His office had always been exceptionally warm. She figured this was because most of his patients were in the nude when they saw him. Today it felt roasting. She sat on the edge of the exam table with a gigantic paper blanket covering her lower half. Her jeans and undies were folded next to her purse on the chair in the corner of the room.

The paper on the exam table stuck to her tush and she hoped she didn't have to peel it off the backs of her thighs before he did the exam. She could only imagine the embarrassment. "Give me a minute, Dr. Hatcher. I need to peel the paper from my sweaty thighs." She tried to adjust her weight and slide forward on the table so her thighs didn't get stuck in one spot for too long.

Maybe she didn't want to know if there was something wrong. Wasn't ignorance bliss? No. Ignorance was torture. If she found out the truth then at least there was something she could do about it.

The office had a subscription to *Us Weekly* and *People* magazines, and under normal circumstances she would've greedily indulged in all the latest celebrity weddings and breakups, snapping out of a tabloid trance only when the doctor entered. Today she found herself flipping through an issue of *People*, only halfheartedly glancing at the captions beneath the pictures.

It didn't help that Hollywood was experiencing a baby boom. Every other picture featured a skinny pregnant celebrity. How it was possible to be nine months along and look as if you lived on cigarettes and Diet Coke, Cate had no idea. How it was possible to emerge from the hospital after childbirth with hair as perfect as a Pantene commercial and a perfect body was also a mystery.

She set down the magazine before Dr. Hatcher entered. Tall and thin, he had neatly trimmed brown hair and wore wire-rimmed glasses. As Cate looked at him she realized she'd never once had a chubby doctor. They'd all looked as if they jogged on a regular basis and avoided fast food like the plague. Who wanted a doctor who looked like a couch potato? It seemed like a conflict of interests.

He shook her hand firmly. "Hi, uh . . ." He flipped through her chart. "Cate. How are you?"

"I'm a little worried." Her mouth felt dry when she spoke.

He raised an eyebrow. "Oh yeah? What's going on?"

She moistened her lips before speaking. "I haven't been getting my period." She explained how she'd never been regular, but two and a half months without a period wasn't normal and she'd never gone this long. She told him that they were thinking about having children, and she was worried that she wouldn't be able to conceive.

"Any chance you might be pregnant?"

"I took three tests and—"

The nurse interrupted. "I took a urine sample when she came in." Then she shook her head.

"Well, let's see what's going on. So, big plans for the summer? Any traveling?"

"No. I just switched jobs, so I'm trying to get settled."

"Oh yeah? What do you do?"

As she explained that she worked for her husband's catering business it occurred to her why he asked so many simple questions. Discussing the mundane was a comfortable distraction from being examined in the most private way by a complete stranger. When she was focusing on things that made her feel comfortable she hardly thought about the cold feeling of the stirrups on her feet or the clicking of the speculum.

However, she didn't want to discuss Good Time Catering. They could talk about that next time. In fact, she'd bring him a brochure if he wanted. She wanted to discuss the multitude of fertility problems she might have and wondered if he had the afternoon off. Before she had a chance, he was finished with the exam. Tina left and he remained seated on his stool. He never sat on the stool after the nurse left. He usually took off the moment the speculum was out and told her to keep up on yearly exams. If he'd thought everything was fine, wouldn't he have quickly rushed on to his next client? She could hardly speak or breathe or even move as she waited for him to explain.

"It's going to be very hard for you to get pregnant." He said it nonchalantly, as if brutal honesty came as natural as breathing.

She felt her heart plunge to her ankles. She gulped. "Why?"

"No period means no ovulation. You can't get pregnant unless you ovulate."

Duh. "I know." She waited for him to describe an irreparable problem. "Why?" she asked quietly, afraid of the explanation. "Why am I not getting my period?"

"Have you lost weight lately?"

The question came as a surprise. "I guess. Maybe just a couple pounds." Her weight was always fluctuating. If she was nervous or excited her appetite vanished and she found herself forgetting to eat. But as soon as she was comfortable again she'd make up for it. If she had lost a few pounds she'd gain it back and then some.

"In my opinion, I think it's because you're too thin."

"What?" She must've heard him wrong. Did he say *too thin*? She'd been a little stressed with the career change and, sure, a few pounds had naturally melted away. This couldn't be the reason Aunt Flo had abandoned her. It wasn't like she was growing a fine layer of body hair to keep warm. There were plenty of women she knew who were skinnier, Sarah included, who'd gotten pregnant on the first try. "Too thin?"

He nodded. "Yeah." Then he pulled out his prescription pad. "If you want to get pregnant soon I think we'll have to put you on fertility drugs."

Her head was spinning as she watched him whip out his pen. "You don't think I have ovarian torsion?"

He stopped writing and looked at her from beneath his glasses. "Ovarian what?"

"Ovarian . . ." As she said the words she realized how neurotic she sounded. "Uh . . . torsion. You know? The condition where your ovaries are twis—"

He shook his head. "When there isn't enough body fat, you can't store enough hormones to have a period. You've lost, uh . . ." He looked at her chart. "You've lost seven pounds since your exam a year ago."

It was true and she suddenly found herself babbling. "It's not like I did it on purpose. First I got married, and I don't know, I guess just being busy with the planning made my metabolism go a little crazy. Then I changed jobs, but it's not like I'm anorexic. I hate diets. In fact, if I go on one it's guaranteed failure. So you don't think I have ovarian cancer?"

He looked so puzzled that it was almost chilling. "Why would you think you have cancer?"

"Um, because I went on the Internet . . ."

His long sigh interrupted her. "It says that Elvis is still alive on the Internet."

"What?"

"It says that Elvis is alive on the Internet. Are you going to believe that, too?"

The sound of her own nervous chuckling made her even more uncomfortable.

"In my experience I think you just need to gain five pounds. Even losing one or two pounds will throw off a cycle. Stress will do it, too.

Women stress about getting pregnant, and then they don't get periods, and then the whole thing snowballs." He finished writing and ripped the prescription from the pad. "Here. We'll try you on this first. I want to see you back in a month. Then we'll have to give you something to ovulate."

"What's this?"

"It's Provera. It's going to make you get your period."

"Well, how long do you think it will take me to get pregnant?"

He shrugged. "I don't know. I've seen these things take a year. Maybe longer."

She took the prescription even though she wasn't thrilled with the idea of heading straight for fertility drugs when she hadn't even switched insurance or tried putting pregnancy in the hands of Mother Nature. "I haven't even tried getting pregnant yet, and we're not in a huge rush."

"If you want to wait that's fine. Just take it with you, and you can decide later. In the meantime go gain some weight. And relax. Don't worry." He patted her on the back.

In some ways, she was amazed by her body's ability to sense trouble. It was as if her body had taken a signal from her weight loss that the environment was plagued with famine, thus not a stable place for a baby to thrive. If Dr. Hatcher's theory was right, she found it even more disturbing that the media bombarded women with so much pressure to be thin. Being too thin could screw up nature's ability to reproduce.

However, a baby had prompted Gwyneth Paltrow's shotgun wedding. Kate Moss was a mother. Kate Moss. Cate was probably twenty-five pounds heavier than both, and she wondered how it was possible that those two seemed to have conceived without a hitch. The doctor's theory seemed hard to believe and as she left the office she hoped she wouldn't be seeking a second opinion. It just seemed too easy.

* * *

"He said you're too thin?" Ethan asked. His confusion was a little unsettling. She'd been surprised by the doctor's diagnosis, too, but Ethan may as well have pointed and said, *You? Too thin?* then thrown his head back, cackling. She watched as he pulled his catering shirt off, then reached for his favorite Waylon Jennings T-shirt. He wasn't exactly looking like Marcus Schenkenberg these days. Ever since they'd exchanged vows he seemed to have settled into a comfort zone where ten extra pounds existed.

"What else did he say?" He still looked puzzled, as if he was waiting for her to say that Dr. Hatcher had said to drink the blood of a monkey and stand on her head if she wanted to get pregnant.

"He said it's going to be really hard for me to get pregnant. He wrote me a prescription for a drug that's supposed to make me get my period. Then he wants to put me on fertility drugs."

He paused before pulling the T-shirt over his head. "He does? Do you want to do that?"

"No. I mean, we haven't even tried. I think we should at least try on our own. Don't you? And I remember a girl I used to work with saying that she had to go on something to ovulate and it increased her chances of multiples."

"You mean . . . like twins?"

"Yes."

"Let's try it on our own first," he said without hesitation.

"I agree. Before this whole scare we were going to wait a year to get pregnant anyway. So if it takes a year, it takes a year."

"That's a good attitude." He smiled. "So does this mean we're going to start trying?"

"If it's going to take a while, then why not?"

His face lit up. "Okay. But you have to promise me you'll stay off the Internet."

"Okay."

"Seriously, you have to quit going on there diagnosing yourself with everything."

"I promise."

His smiled. "Making a baby? That sounds like fun." He leaned in and bit her ear.

· 8 ·

The Labor of Love

Ethan didn't know what hit him. There had always been an equal initiation of sex between the two of them, but for the first month of their baby-making life Cate was after him like a cat in May.

"This is great," he'd mumble as she undressed him. "It's not even noon." They'd trip over last night's teddy and roll onto the bed, if they even made it that far. Later, he'd lay breathless next to her.

They traded watching television for becoming tangled in the sheets. She surprised him in the shower and while he was on the phone. She'd kiss his neck while he took business calls, then slowly unzip his pants, waiting while he quickly wrapped up his conversations.

Ethan woke each morning with a twinkle in his eyes. He hummed while he brushed his teeth and whistled while he walked the dog. He'd return to bed each night, falling into a deep sleep with a smile on his face.

That was the first month.

By the second month Cate noticed that each time she walked in the room he greeted her with an expression similar to Janet Leigh's right before she was attacked in *Psycho*.

"Please, can I just have one minute to myself?" Or *"Again?"* replaced his bliss.

"Yes, *again*."

It was the middle of the second month when Ethan began complaining of back and groin pain. He limped around all morning before Cate made him call the doctor. She wondered if she should've given him a break after he'd said his butt felt as if he'd walked around a theme park for three solid days.

He made an appointment for that afternoon. Cate offered to go with him, but he'd insisted on going alone. So she'd stayed, worrying about him while she tried to focus on work. She was preparing a meal plan for a retirement party when he returned home with a bottle of Vicodin and an order from the doctor to take it easy for the next few days. Translation: abstinence.

"What else did she say?" Cate was concerned.

"She said I pulled a groin muscle. And hurt my back."

She was afraid to hear the rest.

"It's from all the sex we've been having and she said we should probably lay off for a week or so."

"What did you tell her? You told her you've been having a lot of sex? And she made a diagnosis based on that?"

"I told her I can't even make it through the front door without you attacking my penis these days."

Attack. There was no attack in making a baby. She felt guilty. "I'm sorry," she said. "I guess I've just been walking a fine line between wanting to start a family and obsessing over having a baby."

"You think? She said I have to stay off my feet for a few days, and I can't lift anything heavy for at least a week."

Her husband had been injured by sex? What had she done?

For two days she waited on him hand and foot, delivering his meals in bed, renting his favorite movies, and providing unlimited massages. She felt like this was her fault, but she also couldn't help but wonder how much he was taking advantage of the situation. He'd gotten out of walking Oscar and taking out the trash. Instead, he ate ice cream straight from the tub and watched marathons of *Miami Ink* and *Deadliest Catch*.

Since he was out of the baby-making game due to injury she tried to focus on work. Midweek, she received a phone call from a woman named Taylor Kimball. In a foreign accent she explained that her daughter had recently attended a sweet sixteen they'd catered in Del Mar.

"Ve interested in you catering my daughter's sveet sixteen."

"Certainly," Cate said.

"My husband Vayne and I would like to meet vith you first. Maybe see the manyou and taste some hors d'oeuvres. Ve vant just appetizers. Not a sit-down dinner."

"Of course. We actually have an opening a week from tomorrow if that works."

"The day after tomorrow would be better."

"Well, our chef is, uh . . . injured right now, so we won't be able to meet on Friday."

"Vell, I have to double-check vith my daughter and husband. Because my daughter has hair appointment that day, but I let you know."

"You said your husband's name was Wayne?" Cate liked to take notes when she spoke with people over the phone. That way, when she met them face-to-face, the experience was more personable.

"Yes, Vayne Kimball."

"Wayne Kimball," Cate said as she jotted down the name.

No sooner had she spoken the words when Ethan came running into the office like he'd just received a pass from Joe Montana. He slid to a stop on his socks. "Are you on the phone with Wayne Kimball's wife?" he whispered.

Cate nodded. Was there something she was supposed to know? What on earth could've dragged him from bed? Yesterday she'd told him Heidi Klum was washing their neighbor's car in the nude just to see how injured his back really was and he'd only shrugged.

"Tell them we'll meet them on Friday." He whispered so forcefully that spit flew from his mouth. "Tell them!"

She wiped her cheek. "Um, actually, Ms. Kimball, we *can* meet you the day after tomorrow. I just heard that our chef is doing much better."

"Oh! You can?"

"Yes?" She looked at Ethan, making sure he wasn't having delusions from his pain medication.

He nodded vigorously.

She set a time with Mrs. Kimball, then said good-bye. "What the hell was that all about?" she asked as soon as she hung up.

"Don't you know who Wayne Kimball is? Don't you?"

"Sorry, no."

"He is only the biggest golf legend in the world. Before Tiger, there was Wayne. And he lives here in San Diego. Rancho Santa Fe, I believe. I can't believe his wife called. How did they hear about us?"

"His daughter was at that sweet sixteen we did a couple months ago. And now she's having one, and they're interested in using us."

"With this kind of clientele we can really start building our business." He threw his arms in the air with triumph. "And they're coming to my kitchen? Wayne Kimball wants to use us?"

For some reason, he still thought she was lying.

"That's right."

"This is huge! I can't wait to tell my dad." He paused for a moment. "On second thought, let's not say anything until we know for sure that they're going to use us."

"Why?"

"I don't want to jinx it, and if they don't use us, I don't want people to wonder why."

"All right. I won't say a word."

Cheese Dust

The following evening they went to Ethan's parents' house for dinner. Scary and Denise were invited and Cate's parents were coming over as well.

Cate never knew how to approach gatherings like these. On one hand, it was kind of nice to bring both families together. On the other hand, evenings like these were usually highlighted with the kind of awkward moments that resulted from putting two groups of people who would normally never spend time with one another in a room together. The only reason their families socialized was because Cate and Ethan had married.

Cate planned on strange moments like her mother asking, "Shall we all say grace?" when the Blakelys didn't believe in God, or her mother-in-law replenishing her own wineglass three times during the first course when Cate's parents abstained from all alcohol. To add to the awkwardness, Scary Dad would be there. Even Cate's father, who rarely had a negative thing to say, didn't like Keith.

Cate and Ethan were the last to arrive at Ethan's parents' house. Ashlyn and Keith Junior were with their mother for the weekend. Cate's parents and Ethan's father struggled to make conversation with Scary while Rita finished cooking and Denise was in the bathroom.

Ethan's parents' house was an old Spanish-style casa near the beach. Dark russet tiles covered the floors and a fountain trickled in the foyer. Rita and Charles traveled in their spare time, and Rita had decorated with a number of Spanish-style souvenirs she'd collected from their ventures. Brightly colored tiles covered the walls, and pottery in earth tones decorated her shelves and tables.

"Ethan, are you limping?" Connie asked as soon as they entered. Charles looked worried. "What happened?"

"I was lifting something heavy last week for an event and I hurt my back."

Rita came from the kitchen wearing her apron. "Have you seen a chiropractor?"

He nodded. Ethan and Cate had discussed what they were going to say about his groin and back injury on the car ride over.

"Ethan, you really need to be careful," Connie said. "You can really hurt yourself. And back injuries are things that are hard to recover from. If you're not careful, you may never be the same again. Before Cate was born, her father injured his back." Concerned, she turned to Cate's father. "Remember that, honey?"

He nodded. "I've never been the same since."

"He has to sleep on a special mattress," Connie said.

It was a horrifying thought, and one that Cate tried to shove from her mind as quickly as it came. However, she couldn't help but wonder what her father had been doing when he injured his back. Her mother had said it was *before* she was born. She wondered how often people injured their backs as a result of baby making and blamed it on something else. What if Ethan was never the same again? She pictured him with a cane in his thirties, covering up the lie so many times that they'd eventually convince themselves that his back injury was due to something else.

Her worries were interrupted by something almost as disturbing—the sight of Scary Dad lounging in Ethan's father's recliner.

"Hi, Keith," Cate said.

"Hey," he mumbled, avoiding eye contact with her. Ethan and Cate had discussed his inability to make eye contact with people. As far as they were concerned, it only raised his level on the creep meter.

"So Keith was just telling us that he used to play professional football," Cate's father said. Her dad always tried to connect with people, no matter how strange they were. If he was stuck in a room with someone like Scary, he'd be able to figure out the one interesting thing that Scary had to offer and make the most of it. "I was telling him that he should look into a coaching position somewhere. With a background like that, he'd be great."

Cate didn't think they should encourage it. She'd never been very good at sports, but she'd spent enough time at summer camps to know that if she'd had a coach like Scary, the team would've fallen apart. He wasn't exactly the type of guy who could lead people to victory. Her father was always trying to bring out the best in people, to focus on their strengths rather than their weaknesses and she thought it was nice of him to suggest coaching to Keith, but honestly, it was a really bad idea. She sat down on the couch next to her father, then dipped a tortilla chip in guacamole. She smelled something delicious coming from the kitchen and felt her stomach growl.

"So, Keith, how has your weekend been?" she asked.

"Watched some dumb movie," he grumbled.

"What was it?" She assumed his reply would involve any of the straight-to-video ones that Paris Hilton had starred in.

His voice was low and irritable when he mumbled, *"Life Is Beautiful."*

"Oh," she replied. *Life Is Beautiful?* Dumb? It was one of her favorite movies, but maybe subtitles weren't for everyone. "Did you watch the subtitled version or the voice-over?"

"Thavezza."

"I'm sorry. What?" She'd never gotten used to his mumbling and if Denise had been present she probably would've translated for him.

"The voice-over," he snapped.

"And you didn't like it?"

"Itwassped."

She'd seen the movie in the theater. Glued was actually the first thing that came to her mind.

"It was dumb," Keith said, now speaking quietly but clearly. "Who wants to watch this guy run around hiding his kid the whole time, and shouting that damn princess word in Italian?"

This was a real window into Keith Bubich's soul. Everyone was entitled to his or her own opinion, but a statement like that illustrated that Keith was about as deep as a puddle of mouse piss.

"I loved that movie," Connie said. "It was phenomenal, and what a story. How could you *not* like—"

Fortunately Rita interrupted. She was still wearing her apron. "All right, I think we're ready to eat. Does everyone have a drink?"

"Where's Denise?" Ethan asked.

"Oh, Cate, will you go get her?" Rita asked. "I think she might be doing her makeup."

"Sure." She had just begun to leave when Rita tapped her on the arm.

"I saw my friend again yesterday." Her voice was low.

For a moment Cate didn't know what she was talking about. Was she trying to tell Cate that she was having an affair? Then it clicked. The fertility specialist. "That's nice. How was she?"

"Great."

There was an awkward silence. "Well, I better go get Denise."

"Okay."

She felt Rita watching her as she walked away. Maybe they should just bring everything out into the open. Perhaps they should tell Ethan's parents that as far as they knew Cate could conceive. Their suspicions were beginning to make her uncomfortable.

The bathroom door was closed.

"Denise?" she called softly through the door. "It's time for dinner."

The door creaked open and Cate faced a teary-eyed Denise. The first thought that came to mind was that she was pregnant out of wedlock. Why not? Everyone else was getting pregnant. Her nose was red and her short eyelashes stuck together from tears.

The bathroom was cold and a strong odor of perfumed toilet paper filled the small space. Cate put her arms around her and she felt stiff and big. "What happened?"

"Oh, it's nothing." She blew her nose.

"Obviously it's something. You want to talk about it?"

She shook her head, then spoke anyway. "It's just some stupid fight Keith and I had. It's nothing really."

Maybe there was hope. Maybe Cate could have her little heart-to-heart with Denise after all. "Was it over the kids?"

"No." Denise shook her head. "The kids are wonderful. They've been perfect."

"They have? I mean, they have. Of course they have."

"It's just that I'm thirty-three. I'm not getting any younger, and I know Keith's been married once." She shook her head and began to sob. "But I figured he would want to marry again. I don't know . . . maybe I'm just overreacting. We should probably go back out there before everyone starts to wonder what's wrong with me."

Cate handed her a tissue. "He doesn't want to get married?"

Denise shook her head. "It's not that he doesn't want to get married. He just says he's not sure."

"I've heard that one before." It was the first time Cate and Denise had something in common. "My ex-boyfriend Paul was the same way." She wanted to tell Denise not to waste her time. What she needed to do was kick Scary to the curb, get drunk for a few nights, make out with someone who looks like Brad Pitt even it takes five beers before she can see the resemblance, then forget about the Bubiches as soon as possible. Scary Dad would never find anyone better. "We finally broke up, and it was the best thing that could've ever happened to me. Getting him out of my life only paved the way for Ethan to come in." She felt one of her mother's phrases coming to her lips. *When God closes one door, he opens a window.* Or, *Sometimes God sends us a bad one so we can really appreciate the good when it comes along.* She usually avoided saying things like these but there was some truth to them.

"It's not the same," Denise said. "Keith *loves* me. And I love him."

Cate felt their common ground cracking like a windshield struck by stone. It wasn't like Cate hadn't thought she was in love with Paul. Denise automatically assumed that her relationship with Keith was more significant that anything Cate had ever experienced.

"He just has so much fear in him," Denise said. "I think quitting football must've destroyed him. His wife left him, and he has major trust issues."

Oh Lord. This was far worse than Cate had imagined. She was making excuses for him, trying desperately to psychoanalyze his behavior so she could rationalize it. Cate had seen it a million times from her single days. Her friends did it. She'd done it. Quite frankly, it was a waste of time. A prick is a prick as far as she was concerned. There weren't any excuses that could rationalize being an asshole and treating women badly. Everyone had problems in their lives. It was how people came out of them that mattered. Normal people became better as a result of their struggles. Losers became worse. Keith was never going to change and Denise would probably have to figure this one out on her own. Anything Cate said at this point would be met with ten excuses from Denise.

If Cate told her that thirty-eight-year-old men usually had their personalities well settled in cement, Denise would say that he had a sensitive side to him and that if she could just break through that hard exterior he'd be sweet and kind all the time.

If Cate said fear was only an excuse for not wanting to commit, then Denise would say that he had committed, he just had issues and she could help him through it all. She'd rationalize and find excuses until they were both tired of the topic. The only thing Cate could do was listen and gently guide her to realizing the truth about Scary Dad.

"We should go back out there," Denise said. "I'll be fine, really. Thanks for checking on me though."

"Of course. And if you ever want to talk I'm always here."

"Thanks. But I think everything will be fine. It's just a small fight."

Small fights didn't involve locking one's self in a bathroom for an hour.

Everyone was seated at the dining-room table when they returned. Baseball was the conversation topic and Rita was carrying in steaming platters of rice and beans. She'd made cheese enchiladas.

As soon as everyone noticed Denise's blotchy face the conversation died like a kinked hose. It was obvious she'd been crying and Cate felt like something should be said to distract them from staring.

"Why don't we say grace?" Cate said.

Ethan raised his eyebrows.

"That's a great idea!" Connie exclaimed. "You go ahead and lead us, Cate."

Being raised Catholic a million prayers should've come to mind. However, as they all bowed their heads she couldn't think of one. *Bless us, O Lord, for these thy gifts . . .* She couldn't remember the rest. Was it, *and we thank Him for this food?* She could feel her mother's eyes watching her. She decided to make up her own prayer. She never did well on the spot and had always been hit with a babbling reflex, but she had to say something.

"Dear God . . . bless us for this food and bring us peace and happiness as we join together for this meal." She thought that was enough, then felt her pulse quicken as everyone kept their heads down and hands folded. They wanted more. "Um . . . God let us all have a good week and help Ethan and me get Wayne Kimball's party."

Her father's face lit up, and Ethan looked at her like she was out of her mind. She shrugged. She knew they'd agreed to keep it a secret, but she couldn't think of anything else to say.

"Wow!" her father said. "Wayne Kimball? You're doing a party for Wayne Kimball? Don't they live out in Fairbanks Ranch?"

Even her mother had unclasped her hands and raised her head to hear the details.

"Yes," Cate said. "It'll be huge if we get this."

"I believe his wife is German," Cate's father said.

"Oh yeah," Charles said. "She was a big model back in the eighties."

"Is he still married to her?" Connie said. "I can never keep up with anything these days. One minute people are married. The next they're not."

"I know." Rita laughed. "Me, too."

"Still married to her and has two kids," Denise chimed in. Cate watched her butter a roll and was glad to see that she was feeling better. "A friend of mine sold their house a couple years back. They had a bowling alley inside of it."

"I wonder what a house like that sells for," Rita pondered.

"Four million," Denise said.

"Four million?" Connie exclaimed. "That's—"

"I didn't get any feta cheese on my salad." The remark came

from Scary Dad and was so out of place that it was almost as if something had exploded on that side of the room.

They all looked at him. He munched on his bed of lettuce with his elbows on the table.

Rita spoke up. "Oh. I'm sorry, Keith. I actually didn't put cheese on anyone's salad. Some people don't like cheese and I wasn't sure if everyone would want it. I have some in the fridge. I can grab it for you. Maybe other people might like it, too. Why don't I grab it for you?"

"Okay," he mumbled as Rita hurried into the kitchen. "Could you please get me a steak knife while you're in there, too?"

An awkward silence followed Rita's departure and Cate looked at Denise. She seemed oblivious, as if her boyfriend asking for a steak knife for his salad and enchiladas was normal.

By the time Rita returned the conversation had resumed. However, Cate was too distracted by Keith and what he did with the cheese to pay attention to Wayne Kimball stories. She watched as he dumped three quarters of the mostly full carton of feta cheese on top of his salad. She should've known better, but she expected him to pass what little remained around the table. Instead, he set the rest in front of him and continued eating. She looked around to see if anyone else had witnessed Keith and his cheese. Ethan gave her a knowing smile. Then he turned to Keith.

"Uh, Keith, could you pass that feta cheese please?"

"Huh?" He looked at the carton. "Oh." Rather than picking it up and passing it to Ethan he poured some more on his salad. When he gave it to Ethan a few tiny crumbs remained.

Ethan held the container up. "Feta cheese anyone?"

Everyone shook their heads. Ethan turned the carton over and tapped the bottom of it. Cheese fell on his salad like dust. There wasn't much left. Cate watched as Keith carved his enchiladas with a steak knife. She caught her mother from the corner of her eye, staring at him as well.

If Ethan had done something like this at a family dinner, she would've been crawling under the table in shame. Denise, however, didn't seem to care. Cate realized that love is not only blind but it is deaf and mute as well.

·10·

Feeding the Beast

The Kimballs were a half hour late. Cate was starting to feel like it was going to be one of those days. She'd probably jinxed their chances of getting the job by mentioning it at dinner.

What's further, she was worried. As each day went by and her period failed to appear she became more concerned. What if Dr. Hatcher was wrong? She thought he should've at least ordered an ultrasound. She still hadn't ruled out the multitude of fertility problems she'd read about. Furthermore, she didn't recall seeing any credentials on his wall. For all she knew, he was a phony. He could be a fake doctor. She'd seen situations like this all the time on *Dateline*. The only thing that had stopped her from visiting the Medical Board of California website to check his credentials was that she'd promised Ethan she'd stay off the Internet. When she mentioned investigating Dr. Hatcher's background Ethan had told her she needed to have her head examined and that her paranoia would not only give him gray hair but would make him insane, too.

Ethan had been hobbling around the kitchen, trying his best to prepare appetizers for the tasting. She did everything she could to help, but some of the things he had to do himself. He was the chef, and he knew all the secret ingredients. It was hard to watch him limping, and she was beginning to wonder if his injury was a bad sign. Maybe this wasn't the best time to get pregnant.

The sound of tires screeching into the parking lot was a welcome distraction from her worries. They went to the kitchen window and watched as a brand-new Cadillac Escalade popped over the curb as if it were on springs. The beast still had dealer plates. It looked like a monster that trampled pedestrians and devoured clean air with its gigantic appetite for gas and fossil fuels. She caught a blur of bleach-blonde hair and big sunglasses behind the wheel.

"Good grief—" Ethan mumbled. They watched in horror as the Escalade plowed right over the Good Time Catering sign like it was a sprinkler. Cate covered her ears as the deafening sound of metal scraping over concrete filled the air.

"My sign!" Ethan yelled.

Her heart raced as the car came to a halt a mere inch from the building—the large sign trapped beneath its bumper.

"Is that them?" Cate asked. "Do you think it's the Kimballs?"

She watched as a plump bottle-blonde teenager hit the steering wheel with her palms before jumping from the car. "You told me to step on it!" she screamed.

"I said, '*Step on the brakes.*' Not the gas. *Step on the brakes!*" A sun-bronzed man with brown hair as trim and tight as a Ken doll's emerged from the passenger side of the car. The worry in his eyes looked as if it was as deep and permanent as a wrinkle.

A woman who appeared to be his wife followed from the back-seat. Also bottle blonde, she looked as if she'd probably been stunning at one point but had frozen her features with BOTOX.

"That's definitely them," Ethan said. There was a slight growl to his tone.

"We should go see if they're okay," Cate said.

"They took out my damn sign."

He'd saved for months for that sign and she could still see the pride on his face the day he'd poured the cement to install it. "Ethan, I'm sure it was an accident. We should go out there."

By the time they had made it outside Mrs. Kimball had taken over the wheel, and Wayne Kimball stood in front of the Escalade, trying to pry the mangled sign from beneath. "Hit reverse!" he called.

The air smelled of burnt plastic. A small crowd had formed from the dry cleaners next door. Several people covered their noses and Cate heard someone whisper that it was Wayne Kimball.

"Is the car scratched?" Wayne's daughter yelled.

"Yes, the car's scratched," Wayne said. "You drove over the photographer's sign." He paused to sign an autograph. Cate caught someone from the dry cleaners taking a picture of him with her cell phone.

"Dude, you are *such* an idiot." They hadn't noticed the teenaged boy who had clearly inherited his mother's turned-up nose. "You don't even have your license and you wreck the car." He laughed. "You are *such* an idiot."

"At least I didn't fail my driver's test four times," she sneered.

"No. Only twice."

"Hi there," Cate said. "You guys all right?"

Ethan immediately went to the sign.

Wayne Kimball looked for his wife. "Honey, the photographers are here."

"It's the catuhers!" she called from the driver's seat in a heavy accent. "Ve're meeting vith the catuhers!"

"Dad, what about the car?" the girl whined in the background.

"I can't drive a scratched car to the Panic! At the Disco concert to-morrow night."

"We'll get it fixed," he said.

"By tomorrow night?"

"No! We can't have it fixed by tomorrow night. You're just going to have to drive it scratched!"

"But I can't! We have backstage passes! I can't show up in a scratched car."

"Fine. You can take mine."

Wayne turned to Cate. "Wayne Kimball." His grip wasn't as firm as Cate would've imagined.

"Hi, I'm Cate. I'm with Good Time Catering. And this is my hus-band, Ethan."

They watched Ethan pick up a mangled piece of plastic.

"Sorry about the sign there," Wayne said. "My daughter's still learning to drive." He turned back to the car. "Honey, can you grab my checkbook?"

Ethan smiled and Cate thought he did a pretty good job of cover-ing his annoyance. "No problem. I got in a few fender benders when I was her age, too."

"How much does something like this cost?" Wayne asked. "A hundred? Two hundred dollars?"

"Nine hundred."

He wrote them a check for nine hundred dollars and handed it to Ethan before introducing the rest of the family—his wife, Taylor, and the kids, Hunter and Bryce. The kids were unfriendly, and the wife was as pleasant as she could be for just having been in a minor car accident.

"Well, let's head inside," Ethan suggested. "I hope you guys are hungry. We have everything prepared for the tasting."

The family followed Cate and Ethan into the building. "Is that injury sports related?" Wayne asked.

Ethan stopped limping to answer. "Actually I was lifting something."

"I know how you feel," Wayne said. "I've had horrible back pain for years now." He paused. "It started before the kids were born, so I guess it's been around sixteen years."

Cate and Ethan exchanged glances.

"I want sesame-crusted ahi wraps for appetizers," Hunter said.

"We can do that," Ethan said. "I didn't prepare those for the tasting today. But if you would like those we can put them on your menu."

"When I called I said I wanted sesame-crusted ahi wraps. Just like you guys did at Veronica Somer's sweet sixteen. I thought I made it clear."

She was lying. One, her mother had called. Cate would've remembered speaking to Veruca Salt. Two, Veronica Somer had mini tuna rolls—not sesame-crusted ahi. Cate politely corrected the mistake. "Actually, those were our mini tuna rolls. It's tuna wrapped in rice. It's similar to sesame-crusted ahi."

"I want whatever Veronica had, and I want to taste it today."

For some stupid reason Cate was expecting the parents to intervene, but they all stared at Cate. "We usually don't offer sushi at the tastings because we like to buy the fish fresh, and we can't always get sushi-grade tuna on the days of the tastings. So we won't be able to taste ahi today, but we have plenty of other good things to taste."

"That was the whole reason I wanted to hire you," she said.

"It won't be a problem to have those at your party," Ethan said. "We can absolutely do it. We just don't have sushi-grade tuna in the kitchen today."

"But—"

"Hunter, if you already tasted it, vhy you need to taste it again today?" the mother finally interrupted.

The Kimballs were maddening. Cate and Ethan had gone above and beyond what they normally offered at tastings. They uncorked champagne for the parents and let the whole family sample desserts, even though the Kimballs had specified that they only wanted appetizers for the party. By the time they left Cate hoped they weren't hired for the job. It would be hell.

"They were by far the most annoying clients I have ever met," Ethan said as soon as they were gone. "And my sign!"

"I know," Cate said. "I don't think we should take this event."

He nodded. "I'm with you."

"How are we going to get rid of them?" she asked. "Maybe we should tell them we're booked solid for the rest of the year."

"Knowing that child, that would probably make her want us even more."

Cate thought for a moment. "Well, on the other hand it might not be bad to just do it. The whole point is to get other clients," she said.

"Yeah, but if you think about it, it's just a party for a bunch of kids. I don't think we'll get too many clients."

"No. Didn't you hear when he said a hundred adults would be there, too? We should probably just bite the bullet. Especially with a baby in our plans."

Ethan shook his head. "Yeah, but I've worked with people like this before. I mean, not this bad, but just as annoying. These are the kind of people who will end up costing us. They'll complain about everything, change their minds ten million times, and at the end of the day I will end up losing money."

Cate cleaned off the plates they'd used. "I guess you're right. I just hate to lose the referrals we could get."

Ethan shrugged. "I could just give them a huge estimate," he said. "They'll have to say no, and if they say yes, then . . . well . . . at least I won't lose money."

"It's worth a shot."

Grease, the Natural-Born Killer

Cate had gotten over her awkward feelings about purchasing pregnancy tests the same way most people got over their fear of public speaking. The more she did it, the easier it became. After several weeks of trying to conceive, buying home pregnancy tests was second nature. She'd tried the generic, the expensive, a couple from the dollar store that were in Spanish. They were all the same, and they all had one thing in common. They'd all blared negative.

She'd quit telling Ethan when she was taking them. He was starting to think her new habit was getting a little expensive. Furthermore, she couldn't stand to see the disappointment in his eyes each time the results were negative.

In the beginning, taking a pregnancy test had been exciting. They'd wait with fingers crossed beneath the glow of the microwave timer while results appeared. Now she took them in private and buried them beneath mounds of tissue paper in the trash.

She was also beginning to wonder if she was overanalyzing every possible pregnancy symptom she thought she felt. Any sense of tenderness in her breasts and she whipped out a test. She couldn't even tell any more if her boobs hurt, or she'd just slept the wrong way. She found herself debating whether or not she was having early signs of morning sickness or if she just wasn't in the mood for breakfast.

As she dipped the latest test in a Dixie cup of pee she wondered if she was having cravings. She'd been obsessing over blueberry-frosted doughnuts from the best doughnut joint in the world, Peterson's Donut Corner, for three days. After what Dr. Hatcher had said she hadn't bothered depriving herself.

She had just set the timer when the sound of the doorbell startled her. Working from home had its perks, and one of them was staying in her pajamas until dinnertime. Other than UPS, they rarely had visitors. She'd always figured that applying makeup and getting dressed was a waste of time when she could be working. She shoved the test in their silverware drawer and tiptoed to the window in the spare bedroom. Very carefully, she pulled the curtain aside and peeked through a tiny slit.

Her mother stood on the porch. A large box rested at her feet. Cate watched as she rang the doorbell again. "Coming," Cate called. She ran to the front door.

"What are you doing?" Connie asked as she looked her up and down. "Are those your pajamas? I rang the doorbell twice."

Cate thought of the pregnancy test, lying next to their forks. A positive pregnancy test could be sitting inside her silverware drawer, and she had no idea. "I was just working." Cate lied.

"Do you always stay in your pajamas all day?"

"What's the point in getting dressed when I don't leave the house? It's comfortable." She led her mother into the living room.

"I bought you something," Connie said, carrying the box inside.

"It's an air purifier. They were on special at Costco. I just thought you could use one for the spare room."

"Thanks. So what does it do? Trap dust?"

"Well yes, that, too. But hopefully it will do something about all the cat dander in this house."

Cate was surprised. No one had ever complained about cat dander in her house. Hardwood floors covered the whole house. It wasn't like they had carpet that collected the fur. No one had even mentioned itchy eyes. "Do you have allergies when you come over?"

"No. But I can just tell a cat lives here."

"Does it smell?" Cate sniffed the air.

"I can just tell."

Her mother had never liked Grease. Grease had been a part of Cate's life since her early twenties and she doubted if her mother even knew his name. From the moment Cate had told Connie that she'd adopted the stray her mother had instantly brought up her friend from church, Anne Clement. This woman blamed her bad vision on a cat who'd given her some disease Cate couldn't even pronounce.

As Cate looked at the air purifier she suddenly felt self-conscious. Had people walked into her house and instantly smelled a litter box? "Now you have me worried that it smells in here. Does it smell to you?" She inhaled deeply.

She pulled the purifer from the box. "A little. But I'm more worried that the baby may not be able to handle the dander."

"Baby? What are you talking about?"

Her mother suddenly looked worried, as if she'd spilled the beans for a surprise party. "I'm just thinking ahead to when you do have one. Really, it would just be best if you found Gus a new home, but I'm trying to help you out."

"It's Grease. And who said a baby is coming anytime soon?"

"No one. Well, aren't you? Eventually, I mean." Her mother plugged the purifier into the wall, and the machine began to purr.

"I have no idea!"

"Really, Cate, the cat should go." She pulled a brochure from her purse. "I got this from Anne Clement at mass yesterday."

A picture of a harmless long-haired tabby kitten with sad eyes was featured beneath the caption "Protecting Yourself Against Toxplasmosis."

"Mom, what is this?"

"I'm serious. Read that. Cats cause blindness and they're natural-born killers, too. You can't bring a child into that kind of environment."

How had Cate gone from thanking her mother for an air purifier to talking about finding Grease a new home? She wasn't even pregnant yet. They were talking about a hypothetical situation. Furthermore, they were talking about a ten-pound indoor cat. Her mother made it sound like they lived with a rabid mountain lion.

"Mom, millions of people all over the world keep domestic house cats and children under the same roof. It's not that unusual."

"Well, people are crazy, Cate. You need to read that brochure. Or ask Dr. Rivas."

Then it clicked. "What did Rita say to you?"

Guilt returned to her face. "Nothing. What does Rita have to do with this?"

"How do you know about Dr. Rivas?"

"I don't know anything about Dr. Rivas, except that she is a friend of Rita's."

"Yeah, right. You two have been talking, and for some reason you guys think I'm trying to have a baby, don't you?" Grease sauntered into the room and jumped on top of the bookshelf with one leap. His land was unsteady and the case wobbled a tad before two hardcovers slid from the shelf and landed with a thud.

"Look at that animal, Cate. Just look at what he did." She pointed to Grease who watched them through slitted eyes. "He's going to jump in cribs. He'll smother a child."

Cate scratched him behind the ears. "Mom, he is not going to hurt a baby and how do you know I'm even having one?"

"I know you'll have one at some point, and you need to start doing something about the cat. Why don't you make him a nice home on the porch? He belongs outside, Cate."

One would've thought that Cate's sister's child was enough to cure Connie's craving for grandchildren. However, Cate's niece wasn't enough. As far as Connie was concerned, married women had children. Her mother had once shared with Cate that the only reason she'd sent her to college was to find a husband. When Cate had "finally" married at twenty-eight Connie had said she was "a late bride" and barely saved from being an old maid. Connie couldn't understand why most people in Cate's generation waited "until they were old" to marry and have children. Now that Cate was married she knew her mother would never leave her alone.

There was no point in arguing. She had tons of work to do and she knew her mother would never confess to any kind of conspiracies she'd brewed up with Rita, so Cate dropped it. "All right. Thanks for the air purifier." She walked her to the front door.

When they stepped outside Connie made a face. "You know, Cate. It wouldn't kill you to mow the lawn every once in a while."

Cate looked at the yard. She'd gotten used to passing knee-high grass, and had hardly noticed that their front yard looked like a set for *Survivor*. "We're going for the untamed look," she said. "If we mow it, it will ruin the image we're trying to achieve. After all, we do have a wild animal inside. A natural-born killer. We have to keep things consistent around here."

Connie rolled her eyes. "Really, Cate. Just get out the mower and mow the lawn. It will take you ten minutes. Ethan has a bad back. He can't do stuff like that."

Ethan was fine, but she kept that to herself. She waited until her mother's car looked like an ant on the horizon before she went back inside. She ran to the silverware drawer.

"Negative again." She sighed as she tossed the test in the trash. Grease rubbed against her calves.

"Come here, little button," she said. "You're not a natural-born killer, are you?" He purred and she held him close to her chest.

·12·

Period Party

It was hard to focus on nonbaby-related things when everywhere she turned she felt bombarded by baby stuff. Beth's shower invitation came in the mail, and Sarah had scheduled an appointment to find out if she was having a boy or a girl. All Leslie could talk about was nursery décor and stroller brands.

In her spare time she researched naturopathic fertility treatments. She stocked up on chaste berry and vitamin B_6 tablets. She bought evening primrose oil and magnesium and took them religiously.

Rather than waking to the sound of Ethan's alarm clock they rose to the light beeping of Cate's thermometer. Where novels had once resided on the bedside table, stacks of books on how to conceive had taken their place. She ate healthily, and she ate to her heart's content, gladly piling seconds on to her plate and remembering with each spoonful the joyous words Dr. Hatcher had said before she left his office. "Go gain some weight!"

Ethan often reminded her that what Dr. Hatcher had really been trying to say was that she'd lost weight, thus causing disruption in her cycles. It wasn't necessarily being too thin that had made her periods disappear.

Fifty-one days and five pounds after her doctor's appointment her period returned. It was the only time in her life she'd been happy to see it. Considering the amount of sex they'd had she figured that if all had been okay with her reproductive system she would've been well into the first trimester right now.

That afternoon, Cate stepped out of the shower to find her husband holding the phone with a troubled expression on his face. "Who is it?" Cate asked, her heart racing a little. Being greeted with worry and a phone was never a good combination.

"It's Leslie." He covered the receiver. "She's crying."

Cate reached for the phone. Her heart pounded and she didn't bother to dry off. The air felt cold against her wet body and she ignored the puddle of water gathering at her feet.

"Les, what's wrong?"

"The baby's gone."

Cate could hear her weeping.

"Oh my God, Les." She sat down on the edge of the toilet seat. "What happened?" She began to shiver and wrapped her towel around her shoulders. Ethan watched her.

"We went for my first ultrasound." She sobbed, and Cate had to listen closely to understand her words. "And there was nothing there. The doctor couldn't find a heartbeat and we just kept waiting and waiting and she finally said I had miscarried."

"Oh, Les, is she sure? I mean, maybe she just couldn't find it."

"No, she was sure." She blew her nose.

"But wouldn't you know if you'd miscarried? Did you have cramps or bleeding?"

"No, I didn't. But I have to go back so they can clean everything out. I can't imagine a worse thing to do."

What kind of words made sense at a moment like this? *Everything happens for a reason?* What was the reason? Things like this never made sense.

"I know there is nothing I can say that is going to make you feel better. And I wish there was. I wish I had some insightful, powerful words that could change it all, but I don't." Cate felt like crying, too. It was hard to listen to a friend sound so wounded. She could only imagine how she must feel.

"Now I have to tell everyone," Leslie said in between tears. "People are going to ask when the baby is due and I'll have to explain the whole wretched story over and over again."

"I'll tell everyone. I mean it. Just give me a list and I'll call everyone so you don't have to repeat it."

She was quiet for a moment. "Will you?"

"Of course. And I got my period today. After two solid months of sex and temperature taking there is nothing."

"I know how you feel," Leslie said. "It sucks." She blew her nose.

"Well, the only thing we can do now is get drunk," Cate said.

It was good to hear Leslie laugh. "No kidding."

"On the bright side, at least we can drink!"

"That is true. I'd much rather be pregnant, but at least there is a bright side."

"Well, I'll tell you what. I don't know if you just want to be alone with Russ tonight but Ethan is playing poker with the guys. Why don't you and I have a period party? Instead of commiserating we'll get drunk and eat sushi and do all kinds of things you can't do when you're pregnant."

"Oh, I don't know. I don't think I'd be much fun right now. I'm so sad."

"I don't expect you to be much fun, but it'll cheer us up a little bit. I don't want to lie around feeling sad all night while Ethan's gone. And furthermore, it won't be long before either one of us can't drink or eat raw fish again so we may as well take advantage."

"All right."

"In the meantime, make a list of everyone you want me to call."

"Okay." She paused. "Thanks, Cate. I don't know what I would do if I didn't have you. Everyone else is pregnant, and I'm so glad we have each other."

"Likewise. Of course you always have me."

Ethan shook his head after Cate told him what had happened to Leslie. He looked worried. "Shit, that's scary."

"I know. I feel so bad for her. She was trying so hard to get pregnant and I know how much she wanted a baby, and then to see her go from being so happy to so upset."

By the time they were finished talking about Leslie's horrible loss Cate's hair had dried in the shape of a lopsided, lumpy birthday cake. It was poofy yet square, and she didn't feel like fixing it.

All she could think of was poor Leslie at home with a stack of pregnancy books, a bottle of prenatal vitamins, and a broken heart.

Cate had expected to find Leslie balled up in bed with bloodshot eyes and a mountain of Kleenex on her end table. She wouldn't have blamed her. However, Leslie looked much better than Cate had expected. A few hairs were out of place and it looked like her makeup had rubbed off. For Leslie, looking this way would've been comparable to Cate picking through the trash and wearing urine-soaked clothes. However, it seemed as though having the period party had given her something to look forward to. She'd gone grocery shopping and picked up three different flavors of expensive, imported cheese and a ninety-dollar bottle of red wine.

"A time like this calls for buying the expensive stuff," Leslie said. She held up the bottle of wine for Cate to see.

"That was a good move, Les. Very good move." Cate set a four-dollar bottle of pinot grigio and the sushi she'd picked up on the counter. "I hope you're ready to pig out because I got quite a bit of stuff from Meiki's. Sushi just never fills me."

She handed Cate a list of names written on monogrammed stationery. "Here's the list." Then she began to weep.

Cate hugged her. "Why don't we open that bottle of wine? May as well go straight for the expensive stuff first while we can still taste it!"

Leslie laughed. "Good! I need to get drunk."

Russ had a dog before they'd married and Cate had been shocked that Leslie had let him keep it. "How do you keep your house so clean of dog hair?" Cate asked, admiring her fur-free couch. She would've never known a German shepherd lived there. They uncorked the wine and moved the period party to the couch.

"I vacuum every single day," she said.

Leslie had never owned a pet until she'd met Russ, and she was the type of person who had looked as if someone were holding a gun to her head each time a cat rubbed against her calves or a dog came bounding up to her. Cate could recall several instances when Grease had sat next to her on the couch. She'd stiffen, then turn to Cate. "Um, what's he doing?" she'd ask, her body rigid with fear.

"He's purring, Leslie. He won't hurt you."

She never thought Leslie and a dog would live under the same roof, but it seemed to be going okay. "Where is Howie right now?" Cate asked.

"Russ took him to the dog park."

"How is Russ doing?" Cate dipped a spicy crab roll in soy sauce. "Is he okay?"

"Oh, he's not as bothered as I am," she said. "He thinks it probably happened for a reason and that it's nature's way of saving us from having a child that would have birth defects." She shook her head. "Maybe he's right, but it still hurts. I was already so attached to that baby."

"I know," Cate said.

"He's not worried. He thinks we'll get pregnant again in no time, but I don't know, I just feel like something is wrong. I've always had this feeling that I won't be able to have children."

"I know exactly what you mean!" She wiped a drop of sauce from her chin. "I've always had that feeling, too!"

"You have? Really?"

"Yes. Ever since I was a kid."

"I wonder if lots of women feel that way. Because Sarah said the same thing." Leslie reached for a piece of tuna.

"She did?"

"Yes, I remember her saying that several times."

"See, we'll be fine."

Leslie shook her head. "I don't know, Cate. I'm not so sure. I really think there might be something wrong with me." She avoided eye contact with her. "I haven't told anyone this, but they're going to start running some tests next week."

Cate felt a knot in her stomach. "What kind of tests?"

"They want to run some blood tests to check my hormone levels."

Cate relaxed. "Oh. Well, then you'll be fine. If something is off with your hormones they can just regulate that. The birth control pill regulates hormones. And look how simple that is. I'm sure it's nothing."

"Maybe. But they're also doing an ultrasound. They want to look inside me." She looked tortured when she said the words.

Cate topped off their glasses and thought they were going through the bottle a little quickly with only rice and raw fish in their bellies. "Okay, let's not worry. Let's just have fun tonight, and worry about everything next week." She raised her glass. "To period parties!"

Leslie toasted Cate then tilted her glass back and swallowed until her wine was gone. Then she held out the glass to Cate. "More, please."

"That's the Leslie I know!" Cate hadn't seen her drink like this since college. Cate had forgotten how well Leslie could handle her liquor. Leslie could outdrink most men, and except for the occasional slurred word, one might never know she was intoxicated. She also had a remarkable ability to avoid hangovers. While everyone else had been bedridden and calling out for salty food and water, Leslie had been tying her running shoes. Leslie jogged when she was hungover. Cate had never understood how she could exercise with a hangover and had always tried to figure out her secret. Every time Cate had asked, Leslie had always shrugged and said it made her feel better—something about the release of endorphins.

"I bought clothes," Leslie said. "Yellow and green stuff. I have a teddy bear and receiving blankets. My mom bought us a baby book and I'd already started filling it in."

Cate felt her heart break. It was unbearable.

"I can't stand to see it in our spare room," Leslie said.

Cate wiped away a tear. "Maybe we should put it in a box. And just put it away for a while. I'll do it if you want."

Leslie shook her head. "Russ will do it." She reached for a napkin. "I feel like such a fool. I shouldn't have registered. I had already picked out a stroller and a car seat."

"Well, then you have a head start for the next one. And there *will be* a next one."

Cate tried to think of things she could do to cheer her up. Maybe they should take a cab to a bar and go dancing. But neither one of them had done much barhopping since their engagements and being in a club might make Leslie long to be moving on to the next phase of her life even more.

By the time they finished the sushi and wine Leslie seemed like she was in a better mood. They opened Cate's pinot grigio and dug up Leslie's old photo albums from college. They reminisced and laughed hysterically at their clothes and old boyfriends. When Russ returned from the dog park they sent him out for ice cream. He seemed happy to help. On his way out he made eye contact with Cate. "Thank you," he mouthed.

She nodded and turned back to Leslie, who was nose deep in an album and grinning at old pictures of them from a disco party.

"We don't even look disco," she said. "Sarah looks like she missed a turn to the pimp and ho party and you and I look seventies, like we got our decades mixed up."

They spent the rest of the evening in front of Leslie's computer downloading all their favorite songs and singing shamelessly. They fell asleep in front of a juicy reality television show on Leslie's bed.

The following morning Cate felt as though someone had taken a hammer to her head the night before. Through foggy eyes she looked at the empty glasses next to the bed and instantly knew why. She expected Leslie to jump from bed and tell Cate about a million errands she needed to run. However, Leslie rolled over and groaned.

"Water," she whispered. "Do you have water over there?"

Cate thought Leslie's breath might singe her bangs. Leslie was hungover? "No," Cate said. "But I'm dying." The kitchen seemed like it was another country. However, the taste in her mouth was enough motivation to get up. She threw her legs over the edge of the bed. "I'll get some." She felt dizzy when she stood up and her hands shook. She grabbed two cold bottles of water from the fridge.

Leslie was sitting up when she returned. Black mascara dipped beneath her eyes like dark half-moons. She chugged the entire bottle of water without stopping. She took a deep breath when she was finished. "I could drink four of those. Let's make Russ get us breakfast."

"Where is Russ?" Cate hoped he didn't want his half of the bed back anytime soon because the thought of going anywhere seemed dangerous. She would fail a field sobriety test if pulled over.

Leslie giggled. "He's on the futon in the spare bedroom. Doesn't it seem like hangovers have gotten worse as we've gotten older?"

"Definitely." Cate knew she'd be as useful as a dog with a lawn mower for the rest of the day.

"I wonder why."

"I don't know. We're just old now."

Leslie laughed. "We downloaded the nastiest rap song ever last night."

"*You* downloaded the nastiest rap song ever." Cate laughed, "I was perfectly happy with No Doubt."

"I can't remember whose idea it was. I just remember Russ walking in and telling us to turn it down." She laughed harder. "You were dancing on the couch, and I told him to go to bed."

"Poor Russ."

They sent Russ for breakfast burritos and stayed in bed watching *Overboard*. It was one of those movies Cate had seen a million times and never got tired of. They both knew most of the lines by heart. By the time Cate left, her hangover was bearable and Leslie seemed to be in excellent spirits. The period party had been a success.

However, Cate left with a funny feeling. She felt out of place, as if she were too old to be drinking too much and lying in bed all day as a result. It was like she'd pulled out an old pair of jeans, squeezed into them, and then regretted it later when her stomach hurt from the tight fit. She felt like it was time to get rid of the old and move on to the new. She felt ready for next chapter of her life.

·13·

A Charles Manson Fairy Tale

Seeing Denise's number on the caller ID often felt like stepping into the shower and finding a spider climbing out of the drain. It was unexpected and cause for alarm. The last time Cate had answered her call she'd ended up being attacked with water guns. Cate let it ring three times before she picked up. She was in a good mood, and ever since she'd gotten roped into babysitting the Bubich children she'd been prepared with excuses. However, nothing could've prepared her for what came next.

"Cate!"

"Yes. Hi, Denise. What's up?"

"I'm so glad you answered! I have good news."

She dumped Keith? Keith dumped her? Keith and his kids were missing and the police had no leads? "You do?"

"Yes, and I have to ask you something, too."

Those very words sent a chill so tingly up Cate's spine that she almost dropped the phone. She'd heard these words many times before.

They'd always arrived in the same exact sequence. *I have good news* followed by *I have to ask you something* could only mean one thing. "You're engaged."

"Oh my gosh! How did you know? Did Rita tell you?"

"No. Just a safe guess." She forced the following from her lips. "Congratulations! You must be thrilled. And Keith, wow, what a . . . a . . . real surprise, Denise." Denise was getting married? To Scary Dad? Scary was going to be family? And his kids? She saw her holidays flash before her eyes. Carving turkeys and opening gifts with the Bubiches. Denise may as well have invited Mike Tyson and Janice Dickinson over for every single family event for the rest of their lives. *Please don't ask me to be a bridesmaid. Please don't ask me to be a bridesmaid. Please don't ask me to be a bridesmaid.*

"I wanted to ask you if you'd be my maid of honor."

Her mouth dropped and she quickly closed it. "Of course. I'd love to." She noticed Oscar nosing through the trash and ignored him. She was too shocked to care if he turned their kitchen into Mission Beach after the Fourth of July.

Cate had basically been the last in her circle of friends to marry. She had one unmarried friend left, and Jill had made it crystal clear that she would never marry because she was a complete commitment-phobe. Cate had rejoiced the day Jill had made this announcement. As far as Cate had been concerned her days of racking up credit card debt on dresses and shoes she would only wear once were over. Getting diarrhea over toasts and sporting hairdos fit for prom queens with bad taste were things of the past. She'd never feel the concrete hair that came along with a gallon of aerosol hairspray or worry about tripping down the aisle again.

For some reason she'd never thought Denise would marry—not that it wasn't possible. She just hadn't thought much about it, and if the thought had ever crossed Cate's mind, she never imagined that she would be the maid of honor. They weren't even that close, and after the way Denise had complained about being a bridesmaid when Cate got married she figured Denise wouldn't even have bridesmaids. She thought about it for a moment. Really, who else did Denise have?

"And I hope you don't mind," Denise said. "But I've also asked Janet to be a part of the wedding. She's going to be a bridesmaid."

Denise may as well have told her she was marrying Charles Manson, and all his girlfriends would be planning the shower with Cate. Janet? She was the AntiChrist. She was Ethan's ex-girlfriend who had thrown herself at him in the days leading up to their wedding. She was a hurricane, a forest fire, a car accident. Cate couldn't think of anyone she liked less. For a moment she felt like telling Denise to go find a different maid of honor. There was no way in hell she was standing up next to Janet at the altar. Janet had hunted Ethan after he'd proposed to Cate. She'd crashed Ethan's bachelor party then tried to seduce him. However, this wasn't fourth grade, and she couldn't whine about who she'd have to stand next to. She was going to have to suck it up and deal with Janet. On the bright side, at least there was another bridesmaid. There would be someone else to help pick up the expense of throwing a shower and bachelorette party.

"Okay." A neutral attitude was the best she could do.

"I'm so excited!" Denise shouted so loud that Cate had to pull the phone away from her ear.

"How did he do it?"

"Oh my God, I didn't see it coming. Really, I had no idea."

That's what people say right before they're hit by a car, Cate thought.

"He stopped at the grocery store for me and when he walked in he set the bags on the counter and said, Look inside that one. I was expecting Chips Ahoy or maybe a good bottle of wine and there was a box! And it wasn't cookies. It was a jewelry box. I still thought it was maybe just a tennis bracelet. I couldn't believe it!"

"Did he get down on one knee?" Her other line beeped and she ignored it. Stories like these didn't come around often.

"No. He said his back was acting up again so he was just going to stand but he asked me right then and there."

Denise described the ring and said that Scary's brother, Jeff, was flying in from Alaska for the wedding. The brother and Keith Junior would be groomsmen. Beyond that, they weren't sure when or where the wedding was going to take place. The other line beeped again, and again. Even if she'd wanted to interrupt Denise she couldn't. Denise was speaking so rapidly that Cate couldn't even interject to tell her to hang on for a second. For a moment she worried that it was Ethan. They were catering a wedding for four hundred the following weekend and things had been a little stressful. However, Ethan would understand. Denise was like a sister to him and she was getting married.

"I've been waiting so long for this!" Denise said. "We are going to plan a huge wedding. It's going to be a fairy tale!"

Cate had heard these words before, straight from the mouth of the biggest bridezilla she'd ever known. *It's going to be a fairy tale* was really a forecast for women who had watched too many fairy tales and believed that every detail, every moment of the wedding planning must fulfill every fantasy they'd ever had about the big day. *It's going to be a fairy tale* was the forecast for trouble. God help them all.

"I'll let you know as soon as we set the date, but I think it will be in September of next year."

"That's good," Cate said. "That will give you about a year to plan the wedding. I'll be more than happy to help with anything you need." *Professional counseling. An intervention. Finding someone to determine whether or not you were sane when making the decision to commit your life to Scary Dad.*

They said good-bye and Cate stood by the phone for a moment, soaking it all in. Denise was getting married to Keith Bubich. Denise was ruining her life. She couldn't marry Keith. Was it possible that she could actually be in love with someone like him? No. She was settling. She wanted the ring. She wanted the party. She wanted the idea of a family, and Keith was the first willing partner she'd found. But who was Cate to judge? Denise was a grown woman. Plus, she seemed genuinely happy. If she was happy maybe that's all that mattered. Keith wasn't right for everyone, but if he made Denise happy, was it really Cate's business if she married him or not?

She remembered the missed phone calls and scrolled down the caller ID, expecting to see Ethan. Instead she saw Ethan's parents. She checked her voicemail and had no messages. She'd call them back, but first she had to check on Oscar. Lord only knew what he'd dragged from the trash.

She found Oscar sitting on their sofa as if it were a throne. He was chewing on the last pregnancy test she'd taken like it was a piece of beef jerky. Bits of plastic were scattered over the cushions. Nothing ceased to amaze her with Oscar, especially the fact that he hadn't cut his mouth. Then again it was Oscar. He'd ingested two whole lobsters—shells included, a bath-sized terry cloth towel, countless tubes of lipstick, sunglasses, half a leather Coach bag, and a number of other things that should've killed him.

No matter how much they disciplined Oscar it did no good. If they went on *The Dog Whisperer*, it would probably be the most highly rated episode ever. Not only because Oscar was the worst dog to roam the planet but also because for once Cesar Millan would meet his match. Cate was certain of this.

Before cleaning the mess she called Ethan's parents. The line was busy so she hung up. She'd try again later. As she cleaned up Oscar's mess she thought of a timeline. If she got pregnant today the baby wouldn't be due until late May, early June, which would mean the baby would be a few months old and she wouldn't have to be a pregnant bridesmaid.

She was throwing the remains of her pregnancy test in the garbage when the phone rang again.

"Hi, Rita," Cate said. "Sorry I didn't answer earlier. I was on the phone with Denise when you called."

"Then you know?"

"Yeah. Exciting. Denise is getting married." Cate knew Ethan's parents didn't like Scary, but only because she had sensed a vibe from them. They'd never sat down and discussed him at length. Rita was the kind of person who liked everyone. Even if she thought Keith was a little weird, she'd still try to find something good in him, and Cate didn't want to sound like sour grapes to her mother-in-law. Denise was like a daughter to Rita and Charles. She'd lived with them when she was in high school and had stayed in San Diego ever since.

"Cate, we have to stop this wedding."

"What?"

"Yes, I mean it. She can't marry Keith. She's doing it for all the wrong reasons. She really likes you, Cate. She really sees you as such a good friend. You have to come up with something."

"Believe me, Rita, I would love it if Denise broke up with Sca— I mean Keith. I think he's weird, too. But I can't tell her not to be with him. It'll only backfire. She'll be mad at me."

"Well, we have to think of something then. We have to think of a way to get her to break up with him."

Cate wondered how in the hell she was going to stop a wedding. She'd faced some grueling tasks as a bridesmaid—removing stains from fellow bridesmaid's gowns, removing the bride's ex-boyfriend from the church only minutes before showtime, getting sprayed by a puddle from head to toe minutes before the event. But she'd never been asked to snafu a wedding. She didn't think she'd be able to pull it off.

"Rita, if I see any kind of an opening to have a heart-to-heart with her, I will. But I think her mind is made up. There is nothing any of us can do."

14

C8 Wants to Know

There was something about baby showers that made people crazy. Not crazy in a psychotic, delusional type of way. Crazy in a loss-of-control-over-spending type of way. Crazy in a way that made them avoid practical things like a baby registry. Rather, they headed for an online shopping cart at BabyGap, or an explosive shopping spree at Gymboree. Buying a gift from someone's baby registry was the same as ordering a hamburger from Del Taco. It just didn't feel right. What felt right was spending a good two hours gushing over racks of tiny little jeans and pink dresses—little onesies and sleepers that felt softer than Cate's six-hundred-thread-count sheets.

The only thing that saved Cate from spending a king's ransom on Beth's child was that Beth had declined finding out the sex of the baby. Yellow and green unisex just wasn't as cute as denim overalls with a baseball patch on the leg or a tiny pink sweater with little daisies embroidered around the collar. Even in tiny sizes the unisex stuff seemed boring.

She'd realized some time ago that there were two different parties of people when it came to finding out the sex of the baby. It was like politics. There were the Waiters and there were the Why Waiters. As with political parties Cate respected everyone's decisions and opinions but she was with the Why Waiters.

To each his own, but the Waiters were a group she couldn't relate to. They were the kind of people who had never snooped for Christmas presents as a child—people who were appalled at the idea of peeking to the last page of a novel. These folks believed that waiting an extra four months to find out the sex of the baby made it a surprise. It had become obvious that Beth was a Waiter when she'd rubbed her belly and said, "We're not finding out. It ruins the surprise."

Far be it from Cate to judge. Beth could torture herself with suspense if she wanted to. If Beth wanted to decorate in neutrals and sit around wondering who their child was for an extra four months it was fine with her. She just didn't understand it.

Why wait? If Cate was going to carry around another life in her body, she wanted to know who it was and what they'd be wearing. Why was it any less a surprise if you found out on the ultrasound table as opposed to the delivery table? It's not as if making the decision to find out at twenty weeks suddenly made you Sylvia Browne. It was still a surprise. Why did people think it was only a surprise if the baby was carried for four more months? Maybe they only considered it a surprise if the doctor told you rather than the ultrasound technician. It didn't make sense.

Furthermore, Cate would rather be surprised when she was fresh and alert and could go do something fun after. Perhaps buy an outfit for the baby or pick out paint colors. It seemed kind of anticlimactic to find out after hours of hard labor when all one wanted was a nap and a shower. There were enough surprises associated with labor and delivery.

Cate stood in Little Threads. She looked to the right. Doll-sized dresses, tops, summer hats and sandals, little hair ribbons, and sweet pink sweaters covered the right side of the store. To her left was a wall covered in tiny Hawaiian print shirts and matching khakis, blue-and-red-striped rompers, pint-sized cargo shorts, and tiny swim trunks. Smashed in a corner, Cate thought she saw something yellow with a giraffe on it. She headed to the unisex section, a small rack that consisted of a few sleepers and onesies that were conservatively decorated with monkeys and giraffes. Who wanted their child dressed like they worked at the Wild Animal Park?

It was then and there in Little Threads that Cate finally came up with an answer as to why people chose to wait to find out the sex of the baby. The joy of shopping for baby clothes was killed. Shower guests were forced to stick to the practical gifts—the gifts that appeared on *their registry*. Why else would anyone choose to torture themselves for an extra four months, holding off on decorating and identifying with the child they carried in their womb? It seemed like there was enough to do when the baby was born, besides running around buying clothes and decorating a nursery. Didn't people want to be prepared? Either that, or they had far more patience than Cate when it came to waiting for answers.

Cate still couldn't resist the clothes and bought an adorable sundress and a Hawaiian print shirt. She'd give whichever one was appropriate to Beth after the child was born.

After she paid for the clothes she headed to Babies "R" Us and bought Beth the monitor she'd registered for. She was leaving the department store when her cell phone choked out a noise so strange that for a moment Cate thought the Babies "R" Us checker had left a security tag on her stuff.

She grabbed the phone, half expecting it to detonate in her hands. It was a text message, a line of communication she tried to avoid. She'd tried it once and had quickly decided that actually picking up the phone and calling was a faster, easier way to communicate.

Maybe there was some text-messaging method or skill that she hadn't developed, but composing one was enough to drive her mad. Who had time to type a punctuated paragraph on a keypad the size of a business card?

She looked at the message.

Denise, that's who.

Hi C8! I just wanted 2 tell u that I just had lunch with Janet and she is so excited 2 help! She wants 2 b involved with all the shower and bachelorette planning. She is going 2 text message u. I gave her your #. I hope u don't mind. Luv, D

"How do I even reply to this?" Cate mumbled as she headed through the parking lot.

It seemed like an hour had passed by the time she typed "hi denese that sounds goo" before her cell phone lost signal and went dead. She knew Denise's name was spelled wrong, but she was scared to death to edit anything because she'd tried to backspace something on her first try and ended up losing the whole thing. She put her phone away and decided to call Denise later.

When she returned home Ethan was waiting with the food for the shower. Beth's mom was throwing her shower and had hired Good Time Catering to prepare the food for the buffet she planned to serve. They loaded up the car with covered aluminum tins of food before Cate left to pick up Leslie.

She was waiting for Cate on her porch and Cate noticed that she'd lost a little weight. It was pretty courageous of her to attend the shower.

"It smells delicious in here," she said when she climbed into the passenger seat. Cate must've gotten used to the scent and hadn't noticed the smell of food.

"What did you get her?" Cate asked.

"The bathtub and washcloth set she registered for." She sighed. "I'm really not looking forward to this."

"I know. You're very brave for doing this."

"I'm just glad you're going with me. I don't know what I'd do if I didn't have you. I probably wouldn't have even been able to come."

They arrived early and carried the food up Beth's parents' driveway. Mrs. Fitzpatrick greeted them at the door. "Thanks so much for doing this, ladies." Beth was one of Cate's oldest friends and she had known her family for as long as she could remember. "You must be so excited! A grandbaby!" Cate said.

"Let me tell you," Mrs. Fitzpatrick said. "This child is going to be the most spoiled child on the planet." She squeezed Cate's arm. "I bet your mom's getting anxious, too. Are you thinking about it? When will we see a little Cate?"

Cate smiled, feeling slightly awkward. She knew Beth's mom meant well. She wasn't trying to be rude, and having a baby was exciting. People loved to talk about it. But what was she supposed to say? *We're trying but my periods are irregular so please don't ask again until I've conceived.* "I'm not sure," Cate said. "I don't know if we're ready yet." It was a lie. She'd never been more ready. But if she told them the truth, everyone would be expecting something from her. People would never quit asking.

"Plus, my mom has Emily's kid to spoil so some of the pressure is off." That was partly true. She did have Emily's kid to spoil, but the pressure was far from off. In fact, it was cranked to maximum strength.

Mrs. Fitzpatrick had done a beautiful job of decorating for the shower. She'd used "Twinkle, Twinkle, Little Star" as a theme. She rented tables that stood only a foot or so from the ground. Covered in deep blue duvets, the tables were decorated with napkins and accessories that had little gold stars all over them. Instead of eating at chairs they sat on huge, cushioned, fluffy white pillows. It felt comfortable and dreamy.

As they arranged the buffet Cate hoped that no one would make the mistake of asking Leslie how her pregnancy was going. She'd called everyone on the list, but there were a few people attending the shower who might be unaware.

Beth arrived while they were putting the final touches on the food. Cate hadn't seen her in a couple of months and was shocked by the amount she'd grown in that time. If Beth's belly got any bigger, the baby was going to fall out. Colossal came to mind. Despite this, she still looked pretty. Her face looked a little fuller but Beth was gorgeous and some extra weight couldn't change her naturally rosy cheeks or striking dark eyes.

Hugging was a challenge and Cate did her best to greet her. "How are you feeling?"

"I'm ready," she said. "A little nervous and also excited."

"So can you give your oldest and dearest friend a little hint about the names you're thinking of?"

She shook her head. "That's a secret. We're not telling anyone until the baby is born."

"You better call me the minute that child is born. I'm dying to know what you're having."

"You're on the top of the list. My mom is in charge of making phone calls."

"Let me know if there is anything I can do to help."

Guests began to pour in so Cate left Beth to greet her friends and family. She hadn't seen Sarah since she'd announced her pregnancy and Cate was shocked to see how big she'd already grown as well. She wasn't nearly as big as Beth but a bump had already started to form. "Look at you!"

She chuckled.

"How are you feeling? How is everything going?"

"Great. I really don't have any complaints. I love being pregnant. I've never felt better."

Cate thought of what a wonderful time of life it must be. Feeling the baby kick and giving in to cravings. She couldn't wait. "Are you exercising?" Cate asked.

She nodded vigorously. "Oh yeah." She took a sip from her water. "I walk every day and I have a prenatal yoga DVD."

"Good for you. You'll be in perfect shape for labor and delivery." Cate took a bruschetta from a tray.

"How's Leslie?" she whispered.

"I think she's okay."

"Poor thing. That's awful. I can't even imagine."

Fifteen minutes into the shower and half a dozen acquaintances had asked Cate when she was planning on having a child. She realized that being nosy was just a natural progression of life. When Ethan and she had been dating she was plagued with a million, "When are you guys going to get married?" Now it was, "When are you going to have a baby?"

The only friend who didn't ask was Jill. She was the only single one in the group, and proud of it. She arrived at the shower with hair dyed like a skunk. Jill was a hairdresser, and bravely experimental. Cate had always admired her style. She liked Jill's boldness and the fact that she wasn't afraid of what anyone thought.

"Enjoy these last moments of Beth," Jill whispered as they sipped on mimosas. "She'll never be the same again." Jill came from a gigantic family and had grown up with little brothers and sisters for most of her life. "She won't take phone calls after eight or have more than one glass of wine with dinner. Loud music will bother her, and God forbid . . . Well, never mind, I won't let that happen."

"Let what happen?" Leslie asked, a twinkle in her eye. Cate sensed she was enjoying the conversation. Who could blame her? She needed to hear about the pitfalls of motherhood.

"Shortly after the birth she'll decide she's tired of little hands tugging on that long gorgeous hair and she'll ask me for the mom shag. That's when I'll have to tell her to get a new hairdresser."

"You think she'll do that?" Cate said. "Not Beth. She'd never want the mom do."

"Everyone does at some point." She lowered her voice. "And don't you think she's already changed a little? I mean what the hell is with all this withholding information? Keeping the name a secret is just some weird power trip. She's already become a controlling mother. She'll be grounding people in no time."

The first game they played should've been called Shitting Candy Bars. A line of diapers had been arranged over a buffet. Chocolate was melted inside each one like skid marks across toilet paper. The object of the game was to guess what flavor candy bar rested like a giant turd inside each diaper. As Cate waited in line she watched as each guest ran a Popsicle stick over the splatters of chocolate pooh and then slid the sample over their tongues.

Most of the samples tasted the same. It was hard to determine if she was eating a Heath bar or Score while trying to forget that what she was putting in her mouth had been staged to look like diarrhea.

The next game she thought she had a shot at winning. A matching game, each guest was given a sheet of paper divided into two categories. In random order were the names of twenty celebrities. On the other side of the paper was a list of bizarre names that could only belong to the children of celebrities. Match Gwyneth with Apple and Moses. Demi with Rumer, Tallulah, and Scout.

Leslie won with flying colors. She scored 100 percent. The gift was an Henri Bendel scented candle. They were the best candles in the world, and if anyone deserved a little slice of delight, it was

Leslie. As Cate watched her take the prize she could see sadness lingering in her eyes. She passed the vanilla-scented candle around for everyone to smell. As soon as the focus was taken away from her and toward the candle she leaned in toward Cate.

"Figures I would win," she whispered. "My doctor's office is filled with tabloids. I've probably been to the doctor more often than anyone here."

Cate squeezed her hand, knowing full well that candles and parties weren't going to make her feel better.

Beth stood. "Before we begin opening gifts I just want to thank my mom for hosting the shower and thank everyone for coming. This is really the happiest time of my life. It's such a miracle."

Jill leaned in toward Cate and Leslie and whispered, "Wait until she poops on the delivery table."

Leslie laughed. "What do you mean?" she whispered.

"Everyone goes when they're pushing. Trust me, that won't be the happiest moment of her life."

15

The Start of Something

The sun had barely risen when the phone rang. Phone calls at this hour were always cause for alarm, especially since the last one they'd received had been from Ethan's brother in a jail cell. He'd used his one free phone call to explain that he'd gotten a DUI. Cate would never forget the flat tone in his voice when he asked for a ride home. She didn't tell him this, but it was probably for the best. Getting arrested had probably saved his life.

The number on the caller ID was one she didn't recognize, and she imagined that it led straight to a phone booth in a jail cell.

Thankfully the excitement in Beth's mother's voice quickly replaced her fears. "Hi, Cate! Joan Fitzpatrick here. And I have news! Little Levi Isaac has arrived! He is here! Born at three o'clock this morning."

"Oh! That's wonderful!"

The phone had awakened Ethan and he looked puzzled. Cate

covered the mouthpiece with her hand. "Beth had the baby. A boy," she whispered.

"He is eight pounds, eleven ounces," Mrs. Fitzpatrick continued. "A big, healthy boy and he's *beautiful.*"

"I'm so happy to hear that! How are they doing?"

"Well, they're fine. The baby was delivered via Caesarean section, so Beth hasn't been able to get up or eat, but they're both safe and healthy. She wants you to call her later in her hospital room. But for now I'm making all the phone calls from her call list. It says here that she wants you to call the other girls as well."

"Oh, of course. I'll tell everyone."

"Let me give you her room number so you can call her later."

As Cate reached for a pen on the nightstand the other line beeped. Hopefully, this caller had good news, too. She glanced at the caller ID. *Wayne Kimball.* She quickly took down Beth's number and said good-bye.

"It's Wayne Kimball," she mouthed to Ethan before answering.

Actually it was his wife. "Yes, hello? Hi. This is Taylor Kimball. Is this Kim vith the catering business?"

"This is Cate."

"Oh yes, of course. Vat did I say? Kim?"

"Yes. It's okay though."

"Ve vant to go ahead and set the date."

"Great!" She'd practically forgotten about them and had assumed they'd found someone else to cater their daughter's party after Ethan had submitted a high bid. Cate didn't know whether or not to rejoice, or whether she should be afraid—very afraid.

"Yes, Hunter vreally vants you and you have the best price, too."

"Really? I mean, that's wonderful, Taylor." She glanced at the clock. Couldn't this have waited a few more hours? It was six-thirty in the morning. They'd been awakened by Beth's mom, but Taylor

Kimball didn't know that. For all she knew they were still sound asleep. Then it dawned on her—how did she get this phone number? They had a business line. Clients didn't have this number.

"Um, did you call the office?" Cate tried to be as polite as possible as she probed into figuring out how they'd gotten the home number.

"Seven times. I finally look your husband's name up in the phone book."

Cate felt as though they were plunging headfirst into a tornado. These people would never let them rest. Any guilt she felt about over-bidding the party was gone. They were going to earn every penny.

What could she say? *Don't call us here.* The Kimballs were paying ten thousand dollars for snacks. "Okay. Well, the next step is setting up a meeting to plan a menu. In the meantime, I will fax you a list of things to choose from so you have an idea of what you want before we meet."

"Don't we get another tasting?"

They'd already had one tasting. "We usually only do one tasting but I'm sure we can arrange for another."

"Ve vant to taste it all. How vill ve know if ve like it?"

"I'll fax you a list of items and pick seven or eight things you want to taste." It was generous. Most people got one tasting *after* they put down a deposit. They'd already had one tasting.

"Humpf."

"What does she want?" Ethan whispered.

"If you see anything beyond the seven or eight things you want, let us know and we'll let you taste those, too," Cate said. "In the meantime, I'll fax you the menu and the contract."

Cate spent another twenty minutes discussing the logistics of the contract. Mrs. Kimball couldn't understand the point in having a contract, or why she needed to put down a deposit. There was no way Cate was bending the rules with the contract or the deposit. These people couldn't be trusted.

After she hung up she felt drained.

"I can't believe they went for it," Ethan said.

"She said we were the best price, too."

He nodded. "I bet everyone else realized what a pain in the ass they were and overbid them, too."

Cate could hardly wait to see Beth and quickly faxed a contract to the Kimballs so she could run to the mall to purchase something for them. She already had a little Hawaiian shirt for Levi, but she thought Beth and Isaac deserved something, too. She ended up buying Levi the most adorable pair of cowboy boots she'd ever seen in her life. It would be a few months before he fit into the boots, and considering he'd probably outgrow them in a matter of minutes they seemed a tad expensive, but Cate couldn't resist. If she couldn't buy baby clothes for her own baby, then she was going to spoil everyone else's.

She bought Beth and Isaac slippers. They'd be spending a lot of time at home, and they should have comfortable, cozy feet. She was so excited for them. She wanted to be there, to share a moment in such a special occasion.

She reached Isaac that afternoon in their hospital room. "Congratulations!" Cate said as soon as he answered.

"Thanks." He sounded tired.

"How are you guys holding up?"

"We're pretty beat. Beth was in labor for eighteen hours so she's trying to sleep."

"Okay, well just let me know when you guys are ready for visitors," Cate said. "It sounds like you really need your rest, and if it's easier I can wait until you guys get home. I'll bring you dinner."

"That would probably be better."

Cate kept the conversation short so he could rest, too. After she hung up she felt a little disappointed that she'd have to wait a few more days to see the baby. It seemed so out of character for Beth,

too. She'd always been the type of person who loved to be sur-
rounded by friends. But Cate understood. She'd just given birth and
probably wasn't in the mood to socialize.

After she hung up she heard the sound of the fax machine from
the office. It had to be Taylor Kimball's contract and a copy of her
credit card for the deposit. Cate went to the machine to finish the pa-
perwork. She wanted to have their commitment in writing as soon as
possible. She picked up the copy of the credit card and almost began
laughing out loud. The name on the credit card read Hilda Kimball.
Hilda must not have fit in well with her country club lifestyle. Taylor
was much more glamorous.

There was a note in loopy cursive on top of the contract.

> Kate,
>
> I gave Hunter your cell phone number.
>
> She wants to talk to you about the cake.
>
> Taylor

There were so many things wrong with the note that she didn't
know where to begin. They didn't make cakes, and how had they
gotten her cell phone number? She must've meant home phone number. These people were freaking her out. It was creepy.

Her cell phone released the obnoxious choking sound that could
only result from a text message. What did Denise want now?

She picked up the phone and read the following:

> dear kayte, i would like 2 talk 2 u about my cake. i have lots of
> ideas and i want to make it in the shape of myself. i want it to
> look like me. just like veronica somer's had.

Cate called Ethan. "For some reason she's under the impression that we're making her cake."

"What? I never told her we make cakes. Give her the number to that baker in La Jolla that we like. Tell her that we don't make cakes. And tell her to call the office if she wants to get ahold of you."

Cate wrote back.

Dear Hunter, We want to make your sweet sixteen as special as possible, and so I'm giving you the phone number to our favorite baker. They specialize in cakes and will do a beautiful job designing just the right cake for you. 222-9998. If you have any other questions you can reach me on my office line. Thank you, Cate

The sun was setting by the time she finished composing it. As she pressed send something told her that the message had been a waste of time, because Cate had a feeling they wouldn't hear the end of it.

16

Snooping

She was forcing herself to wait until two weeks had passed. For once in her life she was going to exercise self-discipline. She had one test left and she was saving it for a good cause. She wasn't wasting another fifteen dollars on pregnancy tests.

As long as her thermometer was accurate she'd definitely ovulated. According to her fertility calendar, her period or a positive pregnancy test should follow fourteen days later. As each day had passed by she talked herself out of taking a test. All the books had advised to wait until fourteen days to whip out the stick. After fourteen days the hormone levels were high enough to detect a pregnancy.

On the tenth day she asked herself what was really the harm in taking one? It wasn't like she was hurting anybody. She wasn't cheating on a diet. There wouldn't be any negative consequences. Maybe some shattered hope, but she was starting to get used to having her hope destroyed in the form of a Dixie cup filled with pee. As long as she could handle it what was the big problem with taking one little measly test? The suspense was torturing her.

She pulled her last test from the packet and went through the drill. She waited. Three minutes passed. Nothing. She gave it five minutes. Still nothing. She was well acquainted with the blank space where a positive result should've appeared. The disappointment now felt like a sting rather than an aching blow that throbbed every time she saw someone pushing a stroller. Just as she was about to toss the test in the trash she thought she saw a line. A contact lens in a swimming pool may have been more noticeable, but she was still convinced she'd seen something. She looked closer. She moved into a room with better lighting. She turned on lamps. She stood beneath windows. She squinted. If held at a sharp ninety-degree angle, under direct sunlight next to the west-facing window she could see *something*.

She raced to the computer and went to a website devoted entirely to pregnancy tests. Before she let her excitement soar too high she learned that there was such a thing as evaporation lines. Apparently they were evil little lines that fell in the .01 percentage of accuracy on pregnancy tests. After all, no test claimed to be 100 percent accurate. The website, as gross as it may sound, actually had pictures of the wicked little threads that were never mentioned on the instructions of any pregnancy test she'd ever seen. These lines tended to be more on the gray side, almost translucent. She held her test up and compared. The more she looked at her test the more she wondered if there was any line. Was she going crazy? Was she starting to become so obsessed with pregnancy tests that she was seeing positive results?

This was why she should've waited until she missed her period. This was why every website, book, pamphlet, and piece of literature devoted to conception strongly advised women to wait until they missed their periods to test. Otherwise, it made them delusional. If she'd waited, she wouldn't be standing beneath her windowsill with a magnifying glass and a lightbulb whose wattage could cause skin cancer.

She'd never been one to wait. As a child, she'd snooped for Christmas presents in her mom's closet. She'd known about her first Cabbage Patch doll, Pearl Matilda, whose name was promptly changed to Carissa Connie, months before Christmas Day. In fact she'd actually held Pearl/Carissa in her arms long before she'd acted out the surprised hug for her parents. If her friends watched *Survivor* before she had a chance to watch her recorded episode, she made them tell her who got voted off even if they said, "Are you sure you really want to know?"

She hated suspense. Who wanted to wait for answers when life was so short? She had to live for the moment and living for the moment didn't always have the best results. She had no idea if she was looking at a positive test result or an evaporation line. If she'd just waited an extra four days like a normal person, there would be no doubt. No frantic online searches. No examination of digital photos featuring other women's urine-stained tests. However, the fact that there was a website devoted to this stuff gave her some comfort. There were millions of other women out there who were just like her.

She concluded that her result was an evaporation line. She threw the test in the trash and went back to work. Within a few hours the evaporation line was a faded memory.

They catered a wedding that night. A pair of boring youths who, in Cate's opinion, looked too young for marriage and had no idea what they were missing out on by depriving all their guests of alcohol. Frankly, the wedding was a total flop. The only person who ever graced the dance floor was the bride. She tried hard to summon the rest of her pals to snap along with her to Beyoncé. They all reluctantly stood on the sidelines, content to let her look like an idiot.

Cate had been in enough weddings to know that a few drinks always invited a white guy with damp rings around his armpits and a loose tie from the shadows. Some form of this fella had graced almost every wedding Cate had attended. He could usually be found attempting to moonwalk and performing the helicopter before a crowd of 200. There was usually the middle-aged woman fresh from a divorce who had forgotten that her tolerance level had lessened since her days of binge drinking in college. She took over the dance floor like Liza Minelli after eight Red Bulls. And of course there was the multitude of group dances such as the "Electric Slide" and the "Conga Line" that brought down the roof. The guests at this wedding seemed content to watch an empty dance floor and listen to toasts that could make a crack addict yawn.

Cate and Ethan were exhausted from sheer boredom when they returned home. Catering a wedding was hard work, but a nonalcoholic one was like watching a slow movie at two in the morning. They slipped into cool sheets before mumbling tired I-love-you's. Just before Cate was about to drift off she remembered her pregnancy test from earlier that day. There still was a slight chance that it wasn't an evaporation line. She'd only drawn that conclusion so she wouldn't go insane trying to analyze it. She realized she'd been so convinced that the test was negative she hadn't even bothered mentioning it to her husband.

"Ethan?" she whispered.

"Huh?" His voice sounded thick and heavy with sleep.

"Never mind." She decided it was best not to bother him. He was tired and bringing him into her world of Internet-based conclusions and jumping the gun with pregnancy tests would only annoy him.

He rolled over and she listened to his breathing become ragged.

The following morning they spooned in front of a *Miami Ink* rerun. It wasn't until she got up to brush her teeth and use the bathroom that she glimpsed the test in the trash and remembered. She knew it was totally against the pregnancy test rules, but she pulled the stick from a pile of crumpled Kleenex. The line was darker—much darker. Still, she knew this could happen when tests dried out and that was why the instructions implicitly said not to read a test after five minutes. So far she'd broken almost every rule, so why not continue? Furthermore, none of the other ten million tests she'd taken had done this. She'd dug them out of the trash, too.

She ran back to the bedroom and spilled the whole story to Ethan.

She expected him to shake his head and tell her what a nut she was for reading so much stuff on the Internet and digging through the trash like a homeless person in search of sandwich scraps.

"Well, go take another test. What are you waiting for?" he said.

"I don't have any more."

He looked disappointed. Then he glanced at his clock. "I have to leave for the game in an hour," he said.

She'd almost forgotten about his plans to go to the Padres game. She had plans to see Beth that afternoon. Ethan had made them a turkey sausage lasagna, and she planned to deliver it and see the baby.

"We can make it to the store and back and take a test by then," she said.

They went to the store together and Cate grabbed three different brands of tests.

"What are you doing?" Ethan asked.

"Just to be safe," she said.

The first test she took was a generic brand. They set the timer. They waited. A negative result was supposed to show up in the form of a subtraction sign and would appear no matter what. A positive result came in a mathematical sign for addition and would appear only if she was pregnant. The negative line appeared, fast and dark. She wasn't sure how many seconds passed before the faint form of a plus sign appeared. However, it crept up so quickly it seemed as though it was racing to fill up space.

She screamed. Then she grabbed the test and held it out for Ethan to see, as if he'd missed everything that had occurred within the last twenty seconds. "It's positive! This is positive! Do you know what this means? Oh my God, Ethan, it's positive. We're having a baby!"

"Are you sure?"

"Yes, I'm sure!" She held the test with one hand and pointed to it with the other. "Look at it! The positive sign is so dark, it's practically black."

He scratched his chin. "I think you should take another."

She laughed. "Ethan! Don't you see it? Look at it!"

"Yes, I see it. But what about those evaporation lines you were telling me about?"

She should've never introduced him to Dr. Internet. He was confused. "Ethan, trust me, this is no evaporation line. This is the real thing! This is *positive*!" She jumped up and down then threw her arms around his neck and kissed his cheeks. "Oh my gosh, Ethan! It's positive!"

He didn't budge. He looked as if he'd just walked into a dark room and flipped the lights on to find fifty of his friends wearing party hats and screaming, "Surprise!" It wasn't like he looked frighteningly startled. It looked like pleasant disbelief, as if he needed about twenty minutes to let the joy soak in.

"I still think you should take another."

The addition sign was now darker than the subtraction.

She shrugged. "All right."

Just to please him she took two more. Several minutes later they had the three tests lined up, each one screaming positive like a trio of sirens.

He rubbed his chin again. "Maybe you should take one tomorrow."

"Ethan! I'm pregnant! Three tests have confirmed it. There is no way all of these are wrong." She began to twirl around the room. "Oh my gosh! I'm so happy. When should we tell our parents? I mean, I know we should wait, but I can't keep it from my parents or my sister. Should we tell them today or should we tell them in a special way? I don't want to do anything too corny, but I don't know if I can just come right out and say it either. And I don't think I can keep it a secret from my sister, or Beth. Plus, I'll need their advice on pregnancy stuff. Oh my God, can you believe this? We're going to be—"

"I don't think we should tell anyone yet." He was still wearing the startled expression. It was a face she'd seen dozens of times on episodes of *Take Home Chef* when the unsuspecting spouse walked into his kitchen to find a camera crew and a hunky Australian chef teaching his wife how to make a gourmet meal. He opened the fridge, and she watched as he pulled out sliced turkey breast and a loaf of bread.

"What are you doing?" she asked.

"I'm going to make a sandwich," he said. "You want one?"

The man was clearly in denial. Was he upset that they were having a baby? Did he want to wait longer? Was he only going along with the plan to conceive so he could get unlimited sex all day long? Why didn't he say something if he wanted to wait?

"What's wrong?"

"I don't know if we should get our hopes up. And I don't want you to be upset if something goes wrong. I'm just wondering if we should wait before we get too excited."

This made her feel a little better. His denial was just a defense mechanism in case anything went wrong. She watched him spread mayonnaise over the bread. If it weren't for the shell-shocked look in his eyes, she might think Ethan had been absent all morning. He went about making his sandwich, then eating it as if nothing had happened, as if he hadn't just learned that he was going to be a father. She pulled out the calendar and immediately calculated their due date.

"So if my calculations are correct we're due on June twenty-sixth. An early summer baby, and that would make him or her a Cancer. It's the perfect time of year to have a baby. That way I don't have to be pregnant during an August heat wave." She flipped to December. "And I'll be finished with the first trimester in December. So that's when we can start telling people. But don't you think we should tell our parents—"

The sound of a horn beeping interrupted her. "That's Sean," Ethan said. He stood up and grabbed his Padres baseball cap and his wallet from the counter. Then he leaned over and kissed her on the forehead. "I'll call you on my way home."

"Okay." She already felt like a glowing pregnant woman and couldn't control her smile. "I love you."

"I love you, too." He smiled back, then ran out the door. As she watched him go she wondered when it would hit him.

17

Armed with Soap

The fact that Levi had just been born was the only thing that would keep Cate from sharing the news with Beth. Most of the attention would be focused on him and Cate would be able to control herself.

She was dying to tell someone. It had taken all her willpower not to pick up the phone and call her family. She could hardly wait to get advice from her sister. Her parents would be ecstatic.

Cate wasn't sure what she expected when she arrived at Beth's. She knew they'd be tired, but she figured there would still be a flicker of excitement in their eyes, a look of pride as they handed over their bundle of joy. They lived in a town house about twenty minutes from Cate's and parking was always a nightmare. She drove around for several minutes before she finally found a place. Their neighborhood was a ten-minute drive from the beach and the area seemed much cooler than Escondido. Fog had already begun to roll in and she thought of what a welcome sight damp air would be in the inland valleys. The last months of summer were always the hottest in San Diego and Cate's area was no exception.

She carried the gifts, the lasagna, and a grocery bag full of other goodies. Several steps away from the car she wondered if it was safe to be carrying loads of stuff. Her load wasn't all that heavy, so she continued; but she'd have to find out what the limit was.

Cate rang the doorbell and waited. The only sound that came from inside was the muffled bark of their dog, Poco. She waited until her arms began to ache before she set the stuff down and rang again. It seemed like several minutes before Beth's husband, Isaac, greeted her. He had a severe case of bed head, yet looked as if he hadn't slept in days. It was a strange combination. "Hey, Cate," he said quietly. "I forgot to tell you not to ring the doorbell."

"I'm sorry." She felt embarrassed.

"The dog wakes the baby."

"Oh my gosh, I'm so sorry." She felt like the inconsiderate, stupid intruder.

He handed her a bottle of antibacterial hand sanitizer. "You better put this on."

"Oh yeah, sure. Of course." She took the tube of gel. The scent of alcohol was strong as she squeezed sanitizer onto her palm. "You don't want to get any germs near the baby. I understand."

"And can you take off your shoes, too?" he said. "We've made a new rule. No shoes in the house."

"Of course." She slipped out of her leopard ballet flats.

Jill was right. Already, they'd changed. She could see Leslie meeting her at the front door with a tube of antibacterial hand lotion, but Beth and Isaac? The same friends who had thrown a New Year's Eve party two years ago complete with belly dancers and a fountain that spit vodka. They'd bypassed a traditional wedding and had married on Halloween. All the guests had come in costume. She knew they didn't mean to be rude, but the way Isaac treated her made her feel like a grimy intruder.

"Beth will be out in a minute," he whispered. "With the baby. They're waking up."

"I can come another time," she said. "I really don't want to bother you. I understand if you're tired."

"It's okay. You can stay."

He said it as if he were doing Cate a favor.

She looked around the house. The blinds were drawn and there was no sign of their Doberman or the cat. "Where are Poco and Ginger?"

"We've put them in the laundry room. Beth doesn't want them around the baby."

"Are they jealous?" Cate asked.

"No. They've been fine. Beth is just afraid the baby might get allergies or something."

"Oh." Beth and Isaac had not only changed, but they'd turned into people she didn't like. A month ago they adored the animals. Beth had said they were turning into a family of five with the baby on the way. Those pets were like her other children. She felt sorry for Poco and Ginger. It wasn't their fault that their parents had turned into weirdos. She heard a long, sad meow from behind a closed door. She couldn't imagine locking Grease in another room. Oscar, maybe. Grease was her baby. He'd been with her since college.

"I'll go get Beth," Isaac said.

"Well, don't wake her up. Really, I'll come back."

"No, she's not sleeping. It's fine."

While Cate waited she noticed a stack of books on the coffee table. *Discipline Starts in the Crib—Getting Your Baby on a Routine, Secrets of a Baby Schedule—How to Make Life Easier for You and Baby.* She couldn't see the rest.

Beth finally emerged, holding the baby in her arms. She was in pajamas, and she also looked as if she hadn't slept in days.

"Oh my gosh," Cate said. She went to her friend and looked at the tiny little addition to their family. "He is precious. Absolutely precious." She turned to Isaac. "He looks a lot like you."

"That's what we've heard." Pride lit up his eyes.

Cate couldn't believe how tiny he was. He looked so new and fragile. At the same time, she couldn't believe that something his size had been inside Beth. "I won't stay long. I know you guys are really tired and busy," Cate said. "But let me show you what I brought."

She hadn't expected them to do cartwheels when she pulled out Ethan's lasagna, but she did expect more than a nod. "Thanks," Beth mumbled before she went to the couch.

Suddenly Cate felt afraid. What if she became this way? Beth and Isaac were the last people she would expect to turn anal. If someone had told them that bringing a child into the world was going to turn them into people who treated their friends like strangers, they wouldn't have believed it.

Cate put the lasagna in the oven for them and then joined Beth on the couch. She listened to a grisly tale of labor and delivery and all Cate could do was brace herself and thank God for epidurals.

The alarming sound of a text message came from her phone. The way Isaac and Beth looked at her when the phone choked up the text message was similar to an expression she'd given a teenager who'd cut her off on the highway a couple days ago. She felt as if she were sitting in church and her cell phone had started ringing right in the middle of the priest's homily.

"I hope he doesn't wake," Beth said. "We're trying to get on a schedule."

"Oh gosh, I'm so sorry. I'll turn my phone off." She told them about Denise and Hunter and how much she hated receiving text messages. However, it seemed as though Beth wasn't listening. She was staring dreamily at the bundle in her arms. "So then I ran Denise over with a tractor and left her for dead. I haven't heard from the police yet, so I must've gotten away with it," Cate said, testing her.

"Oh, that's good," Beth said.

Test failed.

She wanted to hold the baby but she didn't want to interrupt *the schedule*, so she didn't ask. For some reason she sensed that Beth was never going to offer to pass over her newborn into bacteria hands. So she stayed for a few more minutes, and when she stood to leave they both walked her to the door.

She knew the moment she saw Ethan that it had hit him. She recognized the twinkle in his eyes instantly, because she'd seen the same spark in her own eyes every time she'd glanced at herself in the mirror. He kissed her on the cheek.

"Hi, Mama," he said. They smiled at one another the way only two people who shared a wonderful secret could smile. "I told Sean."

"You did? I thought we weren't going to tell anyone!"

"I had to. I just couldn't keep it in. It hit me at the game, while we were standing in line, actually. I saw this man with a little boy buying him cotton candy and I realized that will be me"—he rubbed her belly—"I mean *us* soon. Sean was really happy for us. He said to tell you congratulations."

"I hope he doesn't say anything."

"He won't. He swore up and down he wouldn't."

The phone rang and Ethan handed it to her. "It's Leslie."

In a way she was glad that they'd chosen to keep it a secret. She wasn't ready to tell Leslie. The wounds from her miscarriage still seemed fresh and Cate didn't want to rub it in. For some reason she felt guilty when she took the phone. "Hey, Les, what's up?"

"Not much. What are you and Ethan up to this evening?"

"Nothing really. Just the usual. I think there's a good *Dateline* on later."

"I got my period," she groaned. "You up for a period party tonight?"

Cate felt a combination of guilt and panic. Guilty that she was going to have to lie and panicked that she had no idea what she was going to say. Keeping a secret meant that she simply wouldn't mention her pregnancy to friends. It didn't mean she'd be lying and she hadn't expected to be put in this position. There was a fleeting second when she felt as though she should tell Leslie the truth. She didn't know if she'd be able to keep it from her friends for three months. However, she didn't want to be the one to pour salt on such fresh wounds.

"A period party? Tonight?" Cate stalled.

"Yeah, I know it's last minute, but Russ is working on his thesis and I can kick him out, or we can go to the Silver Fox like old times. Take a cab home."

"I really wish I could but I have to get up early tomorrow morning. We have a huge event to plan." It was sort of true. "I'm sorry."

"All right." She sounded a little disappointed.

"I'm really sorry, Les." She realized that she should quit apologizing. She sounded guilty. Deep down, she knew she wasn't really apologizing for missing the period party. She was apologizing because her conscience was beating her up for lying. Cate knew she was going to have to tell her sooner or later. In the meantime, she was going to have to think of a very delicate way to break it to her. How was she going to tell her? There wasn't going to be an easy way.

· 18 ·

A Conflict of Interests

Cate felt her stomach turn sour from nerves. Perhaps it was because Denise was calling and not text messaging. As tedious as the text messages were, Cate was starting to see the benefits. She didn't actually have to speak to the person.

Aside from Leslie, Denise was the only person Cate dreaded telling about the pregnancy. She worried that Denise would believe that they were stealing her thunder. Cate had begun to realize there was no point in talking with Denise unless she was talking about the wedding. It was all Denise thought about, talked about, and probably dreamed about when she slept. A rational person would be happy for Cate and Ethan. However, this was bridezilla. As far as Denise was concerned Cate and Ethan's child might be seen as interference.

"Hey, Denise."

"Hi! How is your day going?"

"Good. Really good." It was nerve-wracking to have such a huge secret, and to pretend as if things were business as usual.

"Guess what?"

"What?"

"We've set a date. Finally. It was hard because we had to coordinate with Keith's ex-wife, Tammy, and the kids' schedules but we finally have one. And I just wanted to tell you and Ethan so you didn't book a catering event or make plans."

"Great. We'll put it on the calendar."

"It's going to be June twenty-sixth."

If Cate had been eating, she would've choked. What were the odds that Denise would set her wedding date the same day as Cate's due date?

"Hello? Are you there?" Denise said.

"Yes! Just looking at the calendar." The calendar had slipped from Cate's fingers when Denise had announced the date.

"So does that work for you?"

It worked if the baby was a month overdue. However, Cate couldn't tell her now. "I'll have to double-check with Ethan." It was true. She had to talk to Ethan to figure out how they were going to break it to Denise that her wedding was going to have to change if she wanted them to attend.

"Well, it would be great if you could let me know as soon as possible. We've gone to a lot of trouble to set this date. I mean, it hasn't been easy, so if you could just let me know as soon as you find out, that would be great. If it doesn't work for you guys, then we'll have to wait until October to get married because the kids have to spend the summer with their grandparents in Arkansas and neither one of us really want to wait that long. We're kind of eager to get the ball rolling here."

Cate absolutely abhorred lying, and she felt like blurting out right then and there that it wasn't going to work. If Denise was already laying guilt trips about the date, what would it be like when she found out that she'd have to move the date because they were expecting a child—Rita and Charles's first grandchild. However, she couldn't say anything. She promised to talk to Ethan and get back to her as soon as she possibly could.

"I was thinking about stopping by this afternoon," Denise said. "I have some pictures of bridesmaid dresses I want to show you, and I haven't seen either one of you in a while."

"Okay." After Cate hung up she ran to the other room. She found Ethan on the phone with one of the Kimballs. She could tell by the expression on his face. Every time he spoke with the Kimballs a little wrinkle formed in between his eyebrows. Working with them had made her understand how it was possible to get wrinkles and gray hair as a result of stress.

"So apricot cream cheese frosting," he said. "And vanilla cream cake."

She listened to the rest of the conversation.

"Are we making the cake for them?" she asked as soon as he hung up.

"They won't take no for an answer. They're threatening to get a lawyer."

"Let them! What nerve. We're not bakers."

He shook his head. "I don't want to get caught up in a bunch of legal crap. This is why I knew I needed to overbid this. I'm going to have to order it from a baker myself. I'm going to subcontract it."

"How much is a cake like that going to cost?"

"At least a thousand. Thank God I overbid this."

"We have a problem on our hands," she said.

When she saw the alarm register in his eyes she realized that she probably shouldn't say things like that while pregnant.

"What? What is it?" he asked.

Cate told him about the wedding date and how Denise was coming over later to look at bridesmaid stuff. "We have to tell her soon, and I don't think she's going to take it lightly."

"I thought she was getting married next fall."

"They changed their minds."

"Well, don't say anything to her yet. My parents get back from Spain on Friday and we have to tell them first."

"I agree."

They spent the rest of the afternoon trying to find a baker who made apricot cream cheese frosting and could replicate Hunter in the shape of the cake. It took three hours of digging through the phone book before they found a bakery downtown who could fulfill their request for two thousand dollars.

Cate knew it was a bad sign when Denise arrived carrying a briefcase. Ethan had run to the grocery store, and Cate wished he'd stayed to help her deal with Denise. She watched as Denise set the cache on the kitchen table. "This is my wedding briefcase," she said. "I've realized that planning a wedding is really a full-time job."

Cate had heard this before. Sure, it was a full-time job if you were obsessed. Cate picked out some flowers, found a hotel she liked for the reception, and ordered a cake. The rest of the details had been fun, something to do in her spare time. However, she was well aware that a great deal of women were as serious about planning a wedding as they were about impressing their boss, and in some ways this was the biggest promotion they would ever get in their lives.

"So how are you?" Denise asked.

"Pretty good. Just busy with wo—"

"I am so stressed with the wedding. Keith's ex-wife has made it nearly impossible for us to set a date and the napkins I want have to be special ordered from Vienna. So let me show you the dresses I like." She pulled out a pile of magazine clippings from a large binder labeled Keith and Denise's Wedding. Covered in wedding-themed clippings collected from magazines, Keith's head had been cut and pasted to the top of a headless groom with strong square shoulders beneath an expensive tuxedo. Denise had pasted her own head to the top of a bride with delicate collarbones and an eighteen-inch waist.

The first bridesmaid dress was made of the kind of clingy silk that accentuated every bad feature. Unless Denise wanted her bridesmaids to look like their asses were made of Jell-O and had thighs like chicken drumsticks, the dress wasn't going to work. Cate knew this because she had tried on a similar style dress when she'd hunted for wedding gowns. It was hard to act excited when Cate would be nine months pregnant and counting. She did her best to fake it.

For a moment she was tempted to be honest with Denise. She had an overwhelming urge to come clean about the baby. Denise had a binder with an entire section reserved specifically for lighting. Other sections included napkins and shoes. Changing the date was obviously going to be an issue, and the sooner they told her the better.

She was trying to think of ways she could stall Denise when she pulled a manila file from her briefcase and slid it toward Cate casually as if she slid a napkin across the table to Cate.

"This is for you," she said.

"Oh." Had she made photocopies of the dresses for Cate? "Well, you really don't know until you try the dresses on," Cate said. "Maybe next month we can go look at some stuff in person." As she took the envelope she realized it wasn't pictures of overpriced dresses inside. The envelope had been labeled Shower Ideas.

"I was just surfing the web the other day," Denise said. "And I thought I'd do some research for you. Just some ideas."

She was speechless as she opened the folder. Cate had thrown a few showers in her day and the brides had *never* been involved in the planning. It probably would've been okay if they'd wanted to get involved but everyone she'd known had just been grateful that someone hosted a shower for them.

She opened the folder and immediately realized that Denise

hadn't been *just* surfing the web for a *little while*. There was a stack of printouts as big as a novel. Cate skimmed the first one. "How to Throw a Modern Shower." The subtopics included "Throw a Shower on the Harbor! Rent a cruise ship and host a party" and "A Day at the Races! Rent a box and let your guests bet while they shower your bride." As if spending money on a shower gift wasn't enough. They needed to gamble on top of it. Or maybe the idea was designed to help bridesmaids win back the money they threw away on the wedding.

"Okay," Cate said as she read on. She could feel Denise eyeing her the whole time. Did Denise think she was Oprah? Who did she think was going to pay for all this? "Well, I'll keep this all in mind," Cate said, wishing Denise's heavy gaze wasn't weighing over her face.

She was relieved to see Oscar. Something dangled from his mouth and she couldn't have cared less. Whatever he'd destroyed was a welcome distraction from Denise's packet of shower tips. "What does he have now?" she asked. "I better go take it before he chokes."

"That's okay," Denise said. "You can keep reading. I'll get it."

"No, really, I better—" She was about to take a step forward when he ran toward them. His ears flopped over his head and spit flew from his jowls as he approached. "Oscar, stop!" Cate screamed, and not because he was running. She could see the tip of a pregnancy test sticking from his mouth. She commanded him to go lie down. Instead, he headed straight for Denise. He dropped the test at her feet. Cate lunged for it. As she reached for the test she watched in horror and Denise bent down and swiped it up.

"What's thi . . . oh . . . oh! *Oh!*" She watched the realization register over her face. "It's . . . oh my . . . are you? You're pregnant?"

"We were going to tell you. We were just waiting to tell Rita and Charles. We thought they should be the first to know."

"Oh my God. You are? Well, that's exciting." A stiff smile crossed her lips.

"Yes, we found out a couple weeks ago."

"When are you due?"

She'd never wished for an earthquake, but as she stood there she wished they'd have one. Anything to save her from answering. "Um . . . well, that's the thing. I want you to know that this won't interfere with your wedding. I still plan to be there for you a hundred percent. I want to be in it, and I'm going to throw the shower. We can go to the races or whatever you want."

"So when are you due?"

"June twenty-sixth." The words were almost a whisper.

"Are you serious?" She hadn't expected Denise to cry. Her bottom lip quivered and a lone tear trickled down her cheek. She looked so vulnerable and Cate didn't know how to feel. Was she supposed to feel guilty? She was about to put her arm around Denise's shoulders when Denise's expression suddenly went from wounded child to starving pit bull. "No one is going to give a shit about my wedding!"

Cate took a step back. "That's not true, Denise. This really won't interfere and I promise—"

"I can't fucking believe this." She shoved her binder inside her briefcase. "Never mind. Just forget everything." She grabbed the case and headed for the front door.

"Denise, wait! Please let me explain. There was nothing we could do. We thought you were getting married in September. We didn't plan—"

"Oh yes! Yes, there was something you could do!"

What was that supposed to mean? Cate didn't even want to know.

"I have been waiting for this day my whole life! And I'm older. I really should've been first to get married and have children, and you! You just had to go ahead and have a baby the same time as my wedding."

Cate kept her voice low. Someone had to remain rational. "Denise, please. I'm sure something can be worked out."

"Yeah, right!" she snickered. "What are you going to do? Change your due date? Of course, I'm the one that has to change everything. I'm the one who always gets put on the back burner! Do you know how hard it was to get this date? Try telling Keith to change it. His only brother is flying in from Alaska. Alaska! And you want us to change it now. All because you had to go and get pregnant."

"But, Denise. We didn't do this on purpose. You told us you were getting married next fall. We had no idea you would get married in June."

"Well, just forget it. You don't have to be in the wedding."

"But I want to be in the—"

"No, you don't. All you want is to have your baby." And with that she walked out the front door and slammed it behind her.

Cate looked at the test on the floor, the dog panting over it, oblivious to the mess he'd just made. Cate had expected some huffing and puffing on Denise's behalf when she found out that Cate was pregnant. She'd expected a guilt trip. She'd never expected Denise to act like a twelve-year-old whose idea for a Halloween costume had been stolen. She knew it would be an inconvenience to change the date, but they were bringing a child into the world. Shouldn't congratulations have been in order? Cate knew one thing for certain, she didn't feel the least bit guilty. Not even a shred. She was having a baby, and contrary to whatever Denise seemed to think they hadn't done it to ruin her wedding.

Spreading the Word

They decided to tell the rest of Ethan's family that evening. They called his parents in Spain and shared the news with them on speakerphone.

"We're going to be grandparents?" Rita yelled. "Screw Spain! I want to come home. I want to see you guys. I can't wait to get my hands on my grandbaby!"

"Mom, the baby is not due until June," Ethan said. "We don't have it yet."

"Oh yeah, well, I can't wait until June!"

They told her about Denise, to which she replied, "Oh, don't worry about it. I'm hoping the wedding gets called off anyway."

"I don't think that's going to happen," Cate said.

"Don't worry about it. I don't want to talk about Denise. I want to hear about the pregnancy. Have you gotten sick yet?"

Cate shook her head. "No. I feel great."

"Good. That's good. Maybe you'll have a really easy pregnancy."

It was early, but Cate hadn't felt a thing. In fact, she was starting to worry that she may not be pregnant at all. It didn't help her nerves that her doctor's appointment wasn't for another month. She thought that Dr. Hatcher would've asked to see her as soon as possible. However, his receptionist explained that as long as everything was going okay they didn't see patients until they were at least six weeks along.

On the other hand, she felt relieved and a little privileged that she was having such an easy pregnancy. She'd be a glowing mother to be who ate heartily, but stayed in shape by doing prenatal yoga and walking regularly.

They called Chuck next. Ethan's older brother was an aspiring screenwriter/actor in Los Angeles, which really meant he was a waiter. He went through girlfriends as often as he auditioned for parts in low-budget films. He drank like a fish and still lived with roommates.

They put him on speakerphone, too. They stood over the kitchen table, the phone between the two of them as if they were communicating with a miniature person. "What time is it?" He sounded groggy when he answered the phone.

"Two."

"In the morning?" he asked. "Are you drunk?"

"No." Ethan looked at Cate. "It's two in the afternoon."

"Shit. Really? Hold on."

They heard the sound of a muffled female voice in the background before he returned. "I've gotta give this little actress a ride home in a minute. She just went into the bathroom. You would not believe the night I had last night. This chick is—"

"You're on speaker," Ethan warned.

Cate sort of wished he'd let him continue. She was curious about Chuck's evening the same way people drove past a car accident and couldn't resist looking.

"Oh, Cate's there? Hey, sister! How are you?"

"Really good."

"So we have exciting news," Ethan said.

"Oh yeah? What's up?"

"We're having a baby. Cate's pregnant."

"Holy shit." He exhaled loud. "Whew! I didn't see that one coming. Did you guys?"

Ethan laughed. "Of course."

"No shit. I'm going to be an uncle? Have you told Mom and Dad yet?"

"We called them in Spain. Oh, and just so you know we'd really like to keep it private until we're out of the first trimester, so please don't say anything to anyone."

"No worries. My lips are sealed."

They wrapped up the call with Chuck and called Cate's family next. As soon as the tears of joy and congratulations subsided Connie asked Cate if she had found good homes for Grease and Oscar yet. "Mom, you don't get pets and then find them new homes when you have kids. I took a lifelong commitment when I got these animals."

"Cate, that cat is a nat—"

"Okay, well, the other line is beeping. Gotta run! And remember, don't tell anyone!" She quickly said good-bye. Denise had been enough trouble for one day, and she couldn't handle any more wild ideas about her cat.

Ethan tried several times to call Denise. Each time he was greeted by her voice mail.

"I'm not going to worry about it," he said, as he climbed into bed.

Cate hated the idea of going to bed without resolving conflict and wished she could adopt Ethan's easygoing attitude. The last time Cate had been in a situation where she wasn't on speaking terms with someone was when her mother had threatened to boycott her wedding because Cate had moved in with Ethan. It was a horrible feeling and mending the fences had constantly consumed Cate's thoughts.

It felt so strange to think of Denise storming from her house, and then cutting off communication with them. They needed to talk. Cate wondered how long she would hold a grudge.

The answer came much sooner than Cate had expected. They were watching the tail end of Leno when Denise left a message on Ethan's cell phone. He played it on speakerphone, so Cate could hear.

Her tone was cold and flat. "Hi, Ethan. Cate, too, if you're listening. Ethan, I got your messages and I agree. We need to resolve this. So I've come up with an idea." Her voice perked up a little and Cate leaned into listen.

"Thank God she's changed the date," Cate whispered before the message continued.

"I've heard of lots of women scheduling Caesareans these days. People do it so they can make sure they have family in town for the birth, or child care arranged for older siblings. I know forty weeks is considered full term, but thirty-six is actually one hundred percent safe to deliver, too. Safely, you could have the baby May twenty-sixth."

Cate's mouth dropped. When she looked at Ethan his forehead was wrinkled.

"Call me back and let me know what you think." Beep.

"I'd like to tell her what I think," Cate said. "She's nuts."

Ethan nodded. "It's true. She's totally cracked."

"What do we do?" Cate asked.

"We tell her we're not scheduling a C-section, and she can take a flying leap."

"I'll let you do that."

· 20 ·

Mourning Sickness

Cate felt her first real pregnancy symptom when she went to the Cake Bowl to order Hunter Kimball's cake and thought she would puke. For the first time in her life, the idea of putting dessert in her mouth made her stomach turn. Ordering the cake was a grueling task. She spent most of the errand trying not to inhale the scent of fresh-baked goods. She knew the bakery employees had good intentions, but each time they offered her a sample she felt as though she would gag. The Cake Bowl required a deposit for half the cake. Cate used the Kimballs' deposit for Good Time Catering and signed a contract with the baker. The whole task seemed as though it took hours, and leaving was a relief.

As she drove home she wondered how she was going to cater events when the sight of food made her feel carsick.

By the time she got home all she wanted to do was lie down. The nausea seemed worse when she was standing or moving. She crawled into bed and stayed there for the rest of the day.

The funny thing was, the nausea never went away. It consumed her morning, noon, and night.

Her entire life she'd been exposed to stereotypes of women waking first thing in the morning and retching in the toilet while still dressed in their pajamas. Later, after these fictional characters were dressed in regular attire they indulged in hot fudge sundaes and chili fries. The mere thought of a chili fry or a sundae made her feel sick.

Whoever had created these "morning" sickness stereotypes must've never been pregnant. Either that, or at some point in history words had been misspelled. Perhaps at one point it had really been spelled mourning sickness. Perhaps women had been mourning the loss of their appetites when the term had been created because morning was just a small sliver of time in her sickness.

Within days pretty much anything edible sounded gross, poultry especially. The thought of anything served on a plate that had previously had feathers was disgusting. Ham followed, and she found herself flipping stations when advertisements for any variety of meat were advertised.

An overwhelming feeling of queasiness began to rule her existence. She only had an appetite for quesadillas, mustard, and chicken nuggets made of soy. She'd craved some strange things during PMS. Ahi, thai peanut salads, and Parmesan cheese were just a few, but the craving for meatless nuggets was truly the most bizarre thing she'd ever craved in her life. She'd never forget the expression on Ethan's face when she asked him to pick them up at the supermarket.

"You want meatless chicken nuggets?" he'd asked. "Have you ever even had those?"

"Once. In college," she'd said. Her freshman roommate, a vegetarian, had shared them with Cate in front of MTV's *Singled Out*. "Try the health-food store. I'm sure they have them there."

"Are they good?" he asked.

"Honestly, I can't remember but I know that I've never wanted anything more."

She lived on meatless nuggets dipped in mustard. That was the other thing—mustard. She fantasized about mustard—Dijon, plain old yellow mustard, Dijonnaise. How she found chocolate éclairs disgusting and French's yellow mustard a delicacy was baffling.

In spite of the discomfort, she was slightly relieved that she was showing signs of pregnancy. It meant the baby was growing, and her body was changing.

She was five days into her nugget-and-mustard fast when her mother showed up. Cate looked over Connie's shoulder to make sure she hadn't brought a representative from the Toxoplasmosis Society with her. She was alone, and this time bearing gifts.

"Look what I got." She held up a tiny pink jacket with little brown buttons.

"It's precious," Cate gushed. She took the jacket from her mother and held it out to admire. "But what if it's a boy?"

"It's not a boy." She pulled out little black patent Mary Janes. "Have you gotten sick yet?" her mother asked.

"Yes. In fact, I'm glad you're here. What did you do for this?"

"It's starting," her mother had said with a singsong tone in her voice. "You've started the sickness."

"How long will this last?" Cate asked.

"Mine lasted until I was about fourteen weeks along. Then it magically disappeared." She reflected for a moment. "And it was awful. I had to stay in bed all day and it was during the worst heat wave San Diego had ever seen. And we didn't have air-conditioning. I was just miserable."

"What? Fourteen weeks? That's nine weeks away. I thought this was only a symptom of the first trimester. Fourteen weeks goes into the second. And why didn't you ever tell me about this? You never told me you were bedridden." The thought of two extra weeks of sickness was startling.

Connie shrugged. "I don't know. Because I forgot about it. Once you have the baby you forget how horrible pregnancy is. And you'd never have kids if I told you how uncomfortable pregnancy was anyway."

"What do you mean? What else is uncomfortable?"

"I was pretty much uncomfortable the entire time I was pregnant," she reflected.

Great.

By the following week Cate's nausea had changed. She felt poisoned and was nostalgic for meatless nuggets and mustard.

Every cell in her body felt nauseated. Any form of food was disgusting. It really should've been called pregnancy poisoning because she felt as if she'd eaten rotten seafood. On the third day of vomiting she called Dr. Hatcher.

"Give me something," she said behind a green complexion and sour breath. "Whatever you have." She felt like a heroin addict going through withdrawal, desperate for something to take the pain away.

He asked to see her that afternoon.

The thought of driving herself to the doctor seemed as doable as ice-skating while eating barbequed spare ribs. Ethan cancelled all his appointments and helped her into the passenger seat of the car. She wore the same loose velour sweatpants she'd been living in for two days and an old T-shirt. No makeup was going to cover the dark circles beneath her eyes or her pea-colored skin, so she didn't bother with foundation or blush.

Her hair had been loosely put in a rubber band taken from a bouquet of flowers Ethan had bought her the day before. The rubber band had been the only thing he could find when he'd pulled her hair back while she'd puked in the kitchen sink earlier that day. She ignored the long wisps of hair that dangled down the back of her neck and over her cheeks. She looked like she'd just rolled out of the back of a wagon after three months of hard travel on the plains.

They drove to the doctor's office and all Cate could think about was getting her hands on whatever he had to offer. Misery had taken on a new meaning. She had never felt worse.

"Well, at least we get to see the doctor a couple weeks earlier than planned," Ethan said.

"That's true."

"I talked to Miles before we left," he said. Miles was Sarah's husband and he'd become good friends with Ethan. "And he said we might get an ultrasound today since it's our first appointment."

She perked up a little. "Really?"

She was only six weeks along and didn't know if the doctor would be able to see anything so early. However, the thought of seeing the baby lifted her spirits.

That was, until she barfed on Ethan's shoes as he helped her out of the car.

"No worries," he said. "I can get a new pair." He found a gardening hose attached to the wall outside the office.

She felt like a trapped cat when they entered the building. She looked for every possible escape route in case she needed to make a run for it. The waiting room was crowded with healthy-looking women—gals who flipped through tabloids covered in sparkly celebrity faces while humming along to the soft-hits station that blasted from the speakers. The music in the office seemed so loud.

All she could do was pray she didn't throw up. She was haunted with images of spraying puke across Angelina Jolie's rosy complexion while "Jesus, Take the Wheel" filled the room.

By the time she was called into the exam room there was nothing left to throw up, which was a relief. The nurse had asked her to undress from the waist down and she could only imagine what it would've been like to throw up while having some kind of gynecological exam. What could be worse?

She wondered if she was the only one who thought it felt like Palm Springs in August in the exam room. She looked at Ethan. Sweat beads covered his forehead and his face looked pink.

"It's roasting in here," he said.

"I know. I think they crank up the heat so it's not cold when you're half naked."

They were interrupted when Dr. Hatcher walked in. "So . . . Cate, you're pregnant?"

"Either that or I'm the first person to ever experience the world's worst hangover without drinking."

"Not feeling so well?"

She nodded.

He set her chart down and slid onto a stool. "How far along are you?"

"Six weeks."

"Ah yes. That's about the time that it all begins."

"No one told me I was going to be sick all day long," she said. "No one tells you this."

"No. Because then you wouldn't have children."

"So calling it morning sickness is just a big lie to make sure the human species continues?"

He laughed. "Could be. Let's take a look here."

She'd always thought ultrasounds were conducted over the stomach with a small object that looked like a computer mouse. She was surprised when he pulled a long wand from a machine next to the examination table and put what appeared to be a giant condom over it. What the doctor held looked like something he might toss to a teammate if he were running in an Olympic relay race. As she watched him grease his baton with enough K-Y jelly to polish a small car she realized where he was going to put the wand. It was a little awkward, and if she hadn't felt like she was going to start dry heaving, she probably would've felt more self-conscious.

Remarkably the procedure was pain-free. She was too curious as to what the doctor was looking at to really care that he was moving a large telescope-like object in places that were meant for childbirth and husbands.

"There it is," Dr. Hatcher said. "Right there." He pointed to a flickering dot the size of a caper on the screen. "That is the heart beating."

"Are you serious?" Cate gasped. "That's the baby? Oh my gosh, Ethan, look." She glanced up at her husband. In that moment she forgot that she felt as though she'd eaten sushi from a garbage can the night before. The only other time she'd seen her husband look the same way was the day they were married. The moment she'd stepped onto the aisle on their wedding day every feature on his face seemed warm with light. He looked young and he looked in love.

Though their child looked no bigger than a tiny firefly flickering about in the darkness, it was still their child. She reached for Ethan's hand and he kissed it.

She caught Dr. Hatcher from the corner of her eye. Even he looked aglow as he gazed at the screen. She'd always wondered what had led men into the gynecological profession. Why would a normal man want to look at vaginas of all shapes and sizes all day? Old ones, large ones, hairy ones. Cate was fastidious about grooming before she went to the gynecologist, but she imagined there had to be some women who weren't. What kind of man would want to deal with that? They couldn't be perverts because what sexual pleasure could be experienced by looking at genital warts? Furthermore, they could just go buy *Penthouse* if that's what they were after.

As she looked at her baby's heart beat for the first time she realized why a male might choose the profession. He witnessed the best moments of people's lives. There was a lot of happiness in Dr. Hatcher's career.

She could've stared at that little heartbeat all day. Dr. Hatcher freeze-framed the image, then printed a small picture of their child. It was the first photo she had of her baby.

"The baby looks great," he said after the ultrasound was over. "Measuring six weeks and two days. Good heartbeat. Everything looks good. Now let's talk about you."

"What do you think the chances of a miscarriage are?" Ethan asked.

Dr. Hatcher shook his head. "Not with her being this sick. Very unlikely. The nausea and vomiting are a good sign. It means the proper hormones are being produced. Things are moving along as they should be."

He handed her the prescription. "Try this," he said. "I only want you to take half a tablet. They'll knock you out if you take a whole one." He slipped his pen into the pocket on his lab coat.

"If this doesn't work, call me. I want to see you again in two weeks."

Cate stared at the ultrasound picture the entire way to the pharmacy. It was the only way she could distract herself from the nausea. "I think it looks like a girl."

Ethan laughed. "It looks like a freckle. How can you even tell?"

"I don't know. That just looks like a girl to me." She couldn't explain it. "What would you want to name a girl?"

"Maturda."

"Seriously."

"Hagartha."

"Ethan."

"Hagartha Blakely."

She ignored him. They still had plenty of time to pick names. For now, she just wanted to look at her little firefly.

* * *

Cate noticed the stargazer lilies as soon as she climbed from the car. It was a huge arrangement and her first thought was that they had come from Ethan's parents. Rita and Charles had returned from Europe, and all they could talk about was the pregnancy and the grandchild.

Ethan picked up the bouquet and carried it inside. She followed him to the kitchen and watched as he pulled out the card.

He read it out loud. "Wishing you guys the best. Can't wait to meet the baby! Let's look toward the future. Save the date for May thirtieth. Denise."

It was an apology, and probably the best Denise could do. After the message Ethan had left explaining that they wouldn't be scheduling a C-section, they thought they would never hear from her again.

"That was nice of her," Cate said. "I'm glad she changed the date." Cate was just about to look for the phone when she caught a whiff of the flowers. The odor was heavily sweet and acrid. What all the books said about a heightened sense of smell during pregnancy was true. She'd felt like a bloodhound ever since she'd conceived. Odors that she normally liked were too strong to stand, and she'd asked Ethan to throw away a couple of her favorite candles. Cate hoped that pregnancy also hadn't brought forth a sixth sense in her. Even though Denise had changed the date, she still sensed trouble.

The Secret of Evolution

The prescription only made things worse. On top of barfing for most of the day she felt exhausted. She took it for two days, then quit. She called Dr. Hatcher.

"Honestly," he said, "there isn't much more we can do. The concern now is dehydration. If you get any worse, we may have to discuss hospitalization."

She was too sick to be shocked.

"Ask him if this is normal," Ethan whispered in the background.

"Dr. Hatcher, I'm worried that this isn't normal. It seems so excessive. I've never heard of anyone being this sick."

"It's a little worse than what we typically see, but I have patients who are worse than you. Several."

He had to be joking. Why didn't anyone tell her this? Her mother had waited to share the sordid details of her pregnancy sickness until after Cate had produced a grandchild.

Dr. Hatcher offered to prescribe a medicine used to treat cancer patients battling nausea during chemotherapy. Insurance wouldn't cover the medication and the pills came with a whopping price tag of sixty dollars a pop. With the Kimball event coming up she had to help Ethan.

Desperate, they forked over the money for two days' worth of medication. It was after trying this drug that she realized two things. One, people who had cancer kicked ass. As she lay in bed, unable to function, she found a new appreciation for those who were gravely ill. She'd always felt sympathy toward those who suffered, but her views were different now. It wasn't just sympathy, it was credit. It was recognition. Forget the Oscars. She was over the Grammys. Anyone who was battling an illness that brought along unbearable, long-lasting symptoms deserved an award. It took a warrior to get through something more than the flu or a cold.

Two, the only medical cure scientists had come up with for "morning" sickness was sleep. There was nothing else, and all the medical community had to offer were pills that rendered women unconscious through the sheer misery of it all.

As each day passed things only became worse. She preferred food poisoning. She couldn't function and she lay in bed listening to the sound of daytime television in the background. Reading was out of the question, as it only intensified the nausea.

Each morning she woke and wanted nothing more than to feel better. She would've even traded in one symptom for another. She'd take the vomiting if she could just get rid of the nausea. She wanted to work. She wanted to run horrible errands like going to the DMV, or having blood drawn. If it meant that she would feel better, she'd gladly accept waiting in line for hours, or sitting in traffic. Not much was worse than having your health swept out from beneath you.

Due to her condition, Ethan had to pick up all of her responsibilities. This doubled his workload, making his presence scarce while she was left to wither away next to a wastebasket. While he worked all day she lay alone, watching *The Price Is Right* and hoping she could keep a tiny amount of rice and water down before the showcase showdown. She'd lost track of how many times she'd watched the full hour of the game show only to end up in the bathroom during the most critical moment.

After two weeks of hell they decided to hire a temp to take Cate's place for a few weeks. The decision came after Cate received one of Hunter's most annoying text messages yet. She'd made it to the showcase showdown only to be interrupted by her cell phone choking.

> hi Kayte i changed my mind. i don't want that cake anymore. i want one of a star. i want it to be silver with pink trim. Stars are my favrite symbol and cince my parents wont let me get a tattoo I want my cake to be a star. hunter ☺

Cate fantasized about replies.

> Hunter, you may have all the money in the world, but you will never be happy. Go find someone else to order your cake. You idiot. And it's spelled CATE!

She called the bakery to see if the change was even possible. "Sure, we can make a star," the baker said.

"Great." It was a relief. Now she only wished they would be able to coordinate over the phone. There was no way she was setting foot in any establishment whose primary tool was an oven.

"However, you won't get your deposit back for the other cake." The words fell on her like cold water.

"Why not? Can't we just consider it an exchange?"

"Nooo." Her voice was long. "They didn't explain that to you when you signed the contract? We don't give deposits back under any circumstances."

Cate gagged. "Excuse me, I'll have to call you back."

"Sure, no problem. And stop by anytime to order the other cake."

"Okay. See ya." Cate dropped the phone and barfed in a glass next to her bed.

There was no way she could return to the bakery. She couldn't go to the grocery store, or even make it to the car without vomiting. They contacted the temp agency and waited for the helper to arrive.

Cate had expected a recent college grad who hadn't quite retired from the partying lifestyle to move into a full-time career. Someone who still wanted flexibility and valued freedom, but was capable of handling part-time work. She hadn't expected her to be drop-dead gorgeous. Fresh from college, she had the smooth, wrinkle-free skin and bright eyes of a supermodel. When she smiled her naturally rosy cheeks lifted to perfect little apples. Soft, naturally straight blonde hair that hadn't been fried by straightening irons or hair dryers folded over her shoulders. Her thin body looked as if it were meant for a runway, not Good Time Catering.

Cate had answered the door with dried barf in her hair and the same sweatpants she'd been wearing for two days.

"I must have the wrong address," the girl said.

"Are you Kayla?"

"Yeah?" Her rosy little apples perked up.

"You're at the right place." *I'm the troll you're going to be working for,* she felt like saying. "I'm Cate. Nice to meet you. Ethan should be home any minute."

"Oh." She seemed puzzled.

"They didn't tell you that we have a home office and another office?"

"No. They did." Cautiously, she stepped inside. She looked around, then sneezed.

"Bless you," Cate said. "I usually don't answer the door in my pajamas, but I haven't been feeling very well." Cate explained her pregnancy and the sickness.

Kayla nodded politely, but Cate sensed she couldn't relate whatsoever. "Well, anyway. C'mon in. Ethan will get you started with everything when he gets back."

He'd run to the store in a quest for motion sickness wristbands. He'd read about them on the Internet and thought they might be worth trying. Cate had received a ton of advice that involved homeopathic remedies. With each suggestion she'd been hopeful. She'd lay in bed while Ethan went on a quest for whatever remedy they were trying. She'd tried it all—ginger ale, ginger tea, ginger candies, ginger capsules, vitamin B_6, green apples, soda crackers, chewing gum, lollipops for pregnant women. However, this nausea monster was far too strong for some crackers and tea. Taking home remedies was like going to battle against a dragon armed with a BB gun. She wasn't getting her hopes up about the wristbands.

Kayla sneezed again. As Cate sat in the living room, scaring the temp out of ever having children, she realized what a dump their house had become. Perhaps it was the way Kayla clutched her purse that made her notice. She also seemed careful not to touch anything. Looking at this young, healthy girl made Cate realize that they'd been living in squalor. Ethan's responsibilities had doubled since Cate had been sick. Dusting, vacuuming, and doing the dishes had taken a back seat to making a living.

Airy clumps of dog and cat fur rested in nearly every corner of the room. Cate imagined there was enough fur on their floors to stuff a pillow. She could probably write a poem with her fingertip over the layer of dust that settled on the coffee table. She noticed Grease's small paw prints in there as well. Mail had piled up near the front door and the plants looked limp.

Seeing Ethan walk through the front door was a breath of fresh air. He looked normal. If it weren't for his freshly shaven face and clean jeans, Kayla probably would've left.

Cate was glad to see him. She didn't know how long she was going to be able to suppress the need to vomit in front of Kayla. She put the wristbands on and told them to call her if they needed anything. All she wanted to do was lie down.

She spent the rest of the day trying to sleep. Daytime television was as interesting as reading the obituaries. Most of her time was spent staring at things she couldn't wait to change. The first thing she wanted to do was remove the cobweb that hung from the right corner of their bedroom ceiling. A couple of months ago, she would've never imagined she'd have fantasies that involved a stepladder and a broom. However, her hours were consumed with staring at the same things every day. If she closed her eyes she could picture every detail of the cobweb—the way it brushed up against the wall when a breeze came through the windows, and how it hung like loose threads in the early morning sunlight.

Being miserably sick had given her plenty of time to notice details and she wondered how the cobweb and the dust covering the light-bulbs on their chandelier had managed to escape her attention before.

As soon as she had her health back she was destroying the cobweb and attacking the chandelier. Next, she was touching up the walls in their bedroom. There were several marks in the paint and she knew each one like the back of her hand. She decided that she hated their furniture. She didn't know if it was because she'd looked at it for too long or if she really didn't like it anymore. At any rate, she was replacing her dresser and the mirror that hung above their television as soon as possible.

Kayla stayed until seven o'clock that night. As soon as Ethan said good-bye to her he came to check on Cate. One of the only things that helped her relax and brought a minor temporary relief to her nausea was massage. He rubbed her shoulders.

"Kayla's working out great," he said. "She's really smart, and she's good with people. She spoke with Taylor Kimball today and practically had the woman eating out of her palm."

Cate was impressed. How had they found this little jewel? "Good."

·22·

A Showdown

Cate thought she actually might make it through the show-case showdown. She was cheering for the grandmother who'd been flirting with the host. Her competition was an obnoxious frat boy who wore a plastic lei and tennis shoes with no socks.

Grease was curled up next to her. He'd become a regular fixture on her bed since the pregnancy sickness had started. He was content to cuddle up next to her warm body every minute of the day. He'd also begun hissing at people on a regular basis, especially if they were carrying anything large. Ethan would carry the vacuum out of the laundry room and Grease would confront him as if he were the neighborhood tomcat trying to steal his food. Her mother arrived with a rocking horse and Grease hissed like a dragon when Connie came near Cate. It had only supported Connie's case. She'd heard of dogs sensing pregnancies and she wondered if it was true with cats, too. At any rate, she was glad for his company.

Oscar was completely oblivious to the pregnancy and now spent his days away from her. Keeping him out of the bedroom was saving her life. His gas would be her ticket to the hospital. The dog had always been plagued with the foulest flatulence she'd ever been exposed to, but with the nausea his gas was intolerable.

The phone rang and Cate debated answering. This was important. She rarely made it to the showcase showdown and the *The Price Is Right* was one of the only daytime television shows she enjoyed. Soap operas were mind-numbing. She could no longer watch any baby-related shows. *A Baby Story*—gone. *Bringing Home Baby*—history. *Special Deliveries*—impossible. It was like adding salt to open wounds and for some reason seeing other pregnant women exercising and cooking food made her want to cry. She glanced at the caller ID. It was Denise. Cate was getting used to an incessant line of communication with Denise. She was just relieved it wasn't a text message.

"How are you, Cate?"

"*So* sick. I haven't eaten anything but rice in three days and I've never felt this nauseated in my life. How are you?"

The moment the words left her lips she regretted it. Ever since Denise had become engaged there was no quick answer to that question. Cate braced herself for an earful. "I am so stressed. I finally found the dress I want and it's in San Francisco. So I have to buy a plane ticket to try it on. The dress is four thousand dollars but I figure it's worth it. You only get married once, right?"

In her case, she'd be better off renting a dress.

"Then I've called three photographers and they're all booked that day and I can't get in to see a florist for another month. The band I want costs twenty-five thousand dollars."

Cate had realized that unless she talked about Denise's wedding there was no point in talking to her at all. Denise never discussed anything but her wedding. As far as the pregnancy went, it seemed as if Denise had forgotten that Cate and Ethan were expecting. She never brought it up.

Cate gagged. "Excuse—" She gagged again, and Denise continued.

"And we went to our tasting yesterday at the Hotel Del and let me tell you they treated us like royalty. We tasted the chicken, the filet mignon, two different salads. One had little slices of prosciutto on it, or maybe it was bacon. I'm not sure. But they have the best croutons."

Cate dropped the phone. She couldn't help it. She ran to the bathroom, desperately trying to block out the thought of bacon and salads before it was too late. The toilet was so close, yet seemed so far. She was just rounding the hallway corner when she felt it coming up. There was nothing she could do to hold it in. She raised her hands to catch it and ran face-first into Kayla.

"Oh sorry. I didn't hear you," the temp said. She felt it coming up. She tried to dodge her, but there was no room. She was horrified as vomit cascaded all over Kayla's leather pumps.

Ethan ran from the office. "Oh shit," he said as he looked at Kayla's soiled Marc Jacobs shoes. "I'll get a towel."

"I am so sorry," Cate said.

"No worries." She tried to be polite, but beneath her easygoing façade Cate sensed horror. All the color had drained from her face and she looked like she was going to faint. To make matters worse, Oscar had been in the office with them. Far be it from him to miss any kind of commotion. It was as if the dog had a radar for filth. As soon as he caught a whiff of the mess he began licking Kayla's shoes.

"Oscar, stop," Cate yelled. *Welcome to your new job,* Cate wanted to say. *And you thought you'd be filing and answering phones. Isn't working for someone who is the color of split pea soup and barfs on your shoes more interesting?* As she tried to stop Oscar she felt her stomach turn again. She ran to the bathroom and slammed the door behind her. She made it to the toilet this time. She sat next to the bowl for a moment, feeling weak and listening to Ethan and Kayla's muffled voices on the other side of the door. She heard Ethan say something about replacing her shoes and then she heard Kayla laugh and say they were her roommate's and not to worry about it.

Cate rinsed out her mouth and washed her face.

"You all right?" Ethan knocked on the door.

She felt like crying. She wanted to be like them—living a normal, nausea-free life. She was sick of lying in bed all day. She was embarrassed for puking on Kayla's shoes. She was hormonal. "I'm fine." She held back tears.

"Let me know if you need anything. Okay? I cleaned everything up."

"Thanks," she said quickly. She wanted to apologize to Kayla, but was afraid she'd start blubbering. Her head began to ache from holding back tears, and she took a deep breath.

She listened until their footsteps disappeared down the hall.

After they were gone, she trudged back to her dungeon. As soon as she walked in the room she noticed the phone on the floor. "Shit," she mumbled.

Denise would be angry. Frankly, Cate didn't care. She picked up the phone, prepared to get a dial tone. Instead, Denise's voice came through like a little echo over a mountain.

"So anyway there is so much to do still. I have to make programs and . . ."

Cate had to pull the phone away to hide her laughter. She couldn't help it. She wasn't sure exactly how long she'd been gone, but it had to be close to ten minutes. Denise hadn't even noticed.

"And I was wondering when you wanted to go look at bridesmaid's dresses," Denise said.

Cate closed her eyes tightly, trying to keep from laughing. "Oh, uh, well . . ." She did everything she could to suppress it. The more she tried to control her laughter the worse it became. It was too strong. It came gushing out in thick, heavy, belly-aching laughs. "I'm sorry," she gasped in between peels of laughter. "I'm really sorry. I would love to look at—"

"What's so funny?" Her tone was frosty.

"It's nothing, really." She took a deep breath, and tried to compose herself. "It was . . . the . . . Oscar. You wouldn't believe what he just did."

She expected Denise to ask what he did, but she was silent.

Cate cleared her throat. "I don't know when I'm going to feel better but I can look at anything you like online."

Going out in public was out of the question. Aside from a couple of trips to the doctor's office and an excursion to Target that involved two janitors and a security guard she hadn't left the house.

Denise wasn't shy about hiding her frustration. Her sigh came through the phone like a gale during Santa Ana season. "Well, I need to take care of this soon."

"Denise, I don't even go outside to get the mail. Yesterday I woke to blood in my mouth from vomiting so many times. I burst a blood vessel in my esophagus from throwing up."

"Just because the doctor told you that you were going to be sick until twelve weeks doesn't mean that you have to be sick!"

"What?"

"I'm just saying, maybe you could try harder. Try to talk yourself out of it. Janet's sister had a baby and she wasn't sick for one day. Because of mind over matter."

Cate was speechless. Did Denise honestly think that Cate *wanted* to be rotting away in bed, throwing up so many times that blood vessels in her esophagus broke? Did she think that Cate wanted to look like Ellen Burstyn toward the end of *Requiem for a Dream*?

Cate wanted to scream with frustration. How could someone be so stupid? She wanted nothing more than to feel better. It took all her willpower to remain civilized. "Denise?" she said between gritted teeth.

"Yes?"

"Send me a list of websites you want me to look at and we can pick out a dress online. I believe David's Bridal has maternity and Janet can find something in a matching color." Her tone was controlled.

"Janet has already done some research and she wants you to look at some stuff."

Of course Janet was the perfect bridesmaid.

It was all she could do to keep from hanging up. "You have my e-mail address. Please forward."

·23·

Crush

Each morning she woke to the sound of Kayla at the front door. Ethan had decided it was best for them to work from the home office while Cate was sick because he wanted to be close by in case she needed anything. He checked on her several times a day, bringing toast and water with him. She looked forward to these visits. She was lonely, and he had no idea how much a few minutes of his time meant to her.

Connie came over as often as she could to help. She always brought well-meaning things like ginger candy and ginger ale. The truth was that Cate thought she'd never be able to eat or smell anything ginger related for the rest of her life. She'd thrown it up so many times that she was convinced there was a ginger-colored scar on her stomach. Other items on the list of Foods Seen in the Toilet too Much to Ever Touch Again included soda crackers, yogurt, ham (she'd had a rare moment of hunger and made the grave mistake of splitting a sand-wich with Ethan), and lettuce.

Her aversion to lettuce was probably the biggest blow. Salads were as much a part of her life as taking a shower. She couldn't imagine cutting them out of her life, and at the same time, couldn't fathom the thought of putting anything green and leafy on her plate again.

She lay in bed, listening to Ethan and Kayla laugh and chat in the other room. It would've seemed that hearing them would make her envious. However, she actually appreciated the sound of voices.

Several days after Kayla's arrival Ethan brought Cate the phone. Grease hissed at him. "Grease, what's your problem?" Ethan tried to rub his ears, and Grease hissed at him again.

"Sorry." Cate shrugged. "He only likes me."

"It's Beth," Ethan said.

Hearing the words had been enough for Cate to sit up. It was a voice from the outside world. She missed Beth. "Hey, how is everything going, Mommy?"

Beth's voice was low. "Good. Levi is sleeping right now, so I had to steal a moment to call you. I feel so bad that we haven't talked in a while. I'm attached to this little guy twenty-four-seven. Sometimes Isaac comes home from work and I'm still in my pajamas and I haven't eaten anything all day."

"Don't worry," Cate said, thinking how similar their lives had become. Maybe severe morning sickness was nature's way of preparing women for motherhood. "I totally understand."

"I'm trying so hard to get Levi on a schedule and it's almost impossible."

"He's, what? Six weeks?"

"Seven."

Had it been that long?

"Don't worry. Just enjoy it."

She sighed. "I know. I am. But I don't want him to develop bad habits. Anyway, how are you?"

"I'm sick."

"With what? The flu?"

"Yeah, stomach flu." Cate thought the words had sounded natural.

"Are you pregnant?"

The question had taken her so off guard that she allowed a long pause to precede her response, giving Beth plenty of time to draw conclusions.

"You are! You are so pregnant! Oh my God!"

"Beth, you can't tell anyone. Promise. Please, don't say anything."

"I promise. Oh my God! This is so exciting. When did you find out? Do your parents know? How far along are you? I want to hear everything."

It felt therapeutic to share the details with someone. As they chatted she wondered why she hadn't done it sooner. Cate didn't expect Beth to have a miracle cure for morning sickness but at least she understood what Cate was going through. Ethan sympathized, but he had no idea. Kayla was practically a stranger, and pregnancy was as foreign as forks were to dogs. Though Connie claimed her sickness with Emily was horrific, she seemed to have forgotten just how bad it was.

Commiserating with Beth was wonderful. "Honestly, nothing helped my nausea," Beth said. "I wasn't as bad as you, but mine lasted until I was twelve weeks along. Then it magically disappeared." She still seemed bothered by the memory. "I'm sorry you're going through that. The nausea is the worst. Just remember that it's only temporary. And think of it on the bright side—while some pregnant women are already packing on the pounds in the first trimester, you're keeping your figure."

"I've lost five pounds. And my boobs are getting bigger. Now that you mention it, being pregnant has been the best thing that's ever happened to my body. I've lost weight and moved up a cup size!"

They laughed but Cate would've gladly taken connecting thighs and a big butt over her new friendship with the toilet bowl.

"I wouldn't buy a lot of bras now," Beth advised. "Because you'll outgrow them each trimester. By the end of the ninth month you're going to feel like Britney Spears. As soon as you're ready I can go to Babies "R" Us with you and help you register. I can tell you everything you'll need."

After she hung up with Beth she realized how much she needed her friends. Even if Beth had changed, she still missed her. She decided to call Sarah next. She answered after several rings. "I just walked in from the gym," she said.

"The gym?" In some ways it was a relief to hear this. It must mean that pregnancy would get better. However, she couldn't understand where Sarah got the energy. Every cell in Cate's body felt depleted of fuel.

"Yeah, I want to be in the best shape possible for delivery."

She was truly a wonder.

"How are you?" Sarah asked. "Are you feeling better?"

She didn't feel like beating around the bush. "No. Actually, I'm pregnant."

"I knew it!" Sarah said. "No one has the flu this long. I *knew* it!"

Cate gave her a moment to share the excitement before they got into the details of morning sickness.

"Luckily, I never had that. I was never sick." Sarah spoke as if she'd gone to Hawaii and had escaped rain on her vacation. If she only knew the torment Cate faced each and every minute.

She wondered how it was possible for two pregnant women to have such different experiences. She kind of preferred talking to Beth, who had a more miserable outlook. She couldn't help it. "I guess each woman is just completely different," Cate said. "You can't compare pregnancies."

"Have you told Leslie yet?" she asked.

"No. I'll tell her soon. I just, I don't know . . ."

"I know. I understand. I never know what to say when I talk to her, because I don't want her to feel like I'm rubbing it in if I talk about the pregnancy, but then I don't want it to seem like I'm avoiding talking about it either."

Cate looked at the cobweb in the corner of her room. It seemed to get bigger as each day went by. "I think about how I would be if I was in Leslie's shoes, and sure it would hurt if all you guys were pregnant, but I'd be happy for you. And I think it would be worse if everyone kept it from me. I'd just want people to be honest and treat me like anyone else. The weirder I make it by hiding it from her, the weirder she's going to feel."

"I agree, but Leslie's different. 'Member the time in college when we threw her a birthday party and then two days later when it was her actual birthday she was stunned that we didn't celebrate again?"

"How could I forget? She didn't speak to us for a week."

She understood what Sarah was saying, but that was nearly ten years ago. Leslie was still high maintenance but she'd matured. After she hung up with Sarah she decided that she would go ahead and tell Leslie. However, she couldn't pick up the phone. Instead of calling her she procrastinated. She thought about what color she wanted to paint the walls after she felt better.

When she returned the phone to the office, Cate caught a glimpse of herself in a mirror. The circles under her eyes could cast shadows, and her complexion would make Nicole Kidman look tanned.

She smelled food as she headed down the hall and knew Ethan had made lunch for them. It smelled like chicken curry salad. Occasionally she was teased with a rare moment when things sounded good to her. These moments came and went quickly and if she got sucked into the trap of trying to eat something other than bread or rice, she'd pay dearly.

If they only knew how lucky they were. Picking up a fork and putting whatever they desired in their mouths was a luxury. She heard the sound of Kayla's laughter as she headed down the hallway.

She heard Ethan's voice. "That was great!" he said.

"Oh, it was no big deal."

"No, you're awesome."

"You were really the one who told me what to say," she said. "I wouldn't have known what to do without you."

The room fell silent when they noticed Cate in the doorway. "Hi, honey," Ethan said. "Do you need anything? Toast? Water?"

"No." She looked at Kayla. "Sorry again for throwing up on you." She shook her head. "Don't worry about it."

"You should've just seen what Kayla did," Ethan said. "She got Hunter Kimball to keep the cake as it was. We didn't lose the deposit!"

Cate turned to Kayla to thank her. Kayla's eyes were on Ethan. The girl always had a naturally rosy glow to her cheeks, but there was something else there. Something in her eyes—something Cate had seen before. She looked shy and girlish. Maybe Cate was suffering from hormonal delusions, but if she wasn't mistaken, it looked as though Kayla had a crush on her husband.

·24·

Snow White Has
the Coolest Boss Ever

"I think someone has a crush on you," Cate said. Grease was curled up next to her arm.

Ethan was reading *Newsweek*. His parents had ordered him a subscription for his birthday and each time one came in the mail he spent the evening glued to the latest stories.

"Who?" He wore a blank expression when he looked up from the magazine.

Cate smiled. "You know what I mean. It's so obvious."

"No, I don't know what you mean." He looked her square in the eye. "What are you talking about?"

"Kayla."

He rolled his eyes then set the magazine on his nightstand. "Cate, turn off the light. Let's go to bed."

"You honestly don't know what I'm talking about?"

"No, I don't. I do, however, know that she just saved a thousand-dollar deposit."

Cate rolled onto her elbow to face him. "I think she likes you. The way she looks at you and laughs at everything you say."

He shook his head. "She just broke up with a very serious boyfriend."

"You know this? You guys talk about this?" It was worse than Cate had imagined. They were confiding in each other.

"He called her once while we were working and she told me about him."

"She did? What did she say?"

He shrugged. "I don't know. Just that she broke up with him and she wasn't sure if it was the right thing to do, but she felt like they were growing apart."

"Did you give her advice?"

"I just told her she'd figure it out. That it would work out and not to worry about it. Then she told me what a great guy he was."

"What do you say about me?"

He thought for a moment. "Nothing."

"Nothing?"

He shook his head. "Why would we talk about you? We're working."

"Well, if you talk about her love life, why don't you talk about yours?"

"Cate, she knows you. She knows we're married and you're sick because you're having my child. Quit being weird."

Maybe she was being weird. However, she wanted to tell him that what was weird was having the worst case of pregnancy sickness she'd ever heard of and having her husband right down the hall discussing breakups with Mischa Barton's long-lost twin. She couldn't help it if she was a little suspicious. It wasn't everyday that her husband had a heart-to-heart with a younger, beautiful woman while she bore a shocking resemblance to Linda Blair in *The Exorcist*.

She wasn't worried about Ethan. He didn't have it in him to

cheat. However, he'd always been a little bit clueless when it came to women. He had no idea how cute he was, and he had no idea when someone was hitting on him. He'd proven this nearly a year ago when Janet had tried everything but drugging and seducing him in order to get him back. It was as if the man had been blind.

She dropped the subject about Kayla because she felt a bad spell of nausea coming on and she didn't want to blow her chances of getting a massage out of him.

He dug his palms into her shoulders and she felt her body relaxing. These few minutes of massage had become her drug of choice, and she savored every moment. "Have you told Leslie yet?" he asked.

She felt her back growing stiff again. "I'm doing it tomorrow." She was dreading it, but she'd made the decision that she had to get it over with.

The following morning Cate slept in. Days like these were scarce as she usually woke early so she could sprint to the bathroom in time. However, on this day, she woke to the sound of Grease hissing. When she opened her eyes Kayla stood over the side of her bed with the phone. She stepped back when she noticed the cat. The rosy glow that Cate had begun to associate with Kayla had vanished and a paler, wan-looking girl stood next to the bed. Cate wanted to tell her that there was nothing to be afraid of and that she could come closer, but held back. Something about talking to Kayla that way stirred memories of the witch in *Snow White and the Seven Dwarfs*.

"It's okay," Cate said instead. "He won't hurt you." Cate could only imagine what she said to her roommates each day after work. "My boss is totally hot and so cool. He makes me lunch, and we have the best conversations. But he's married to this really weird cat lady."

"Sorry to bother you," she said, keeping one eye on Grease. "Ethan went to the bank and your friend is on the phone crying. I didn't want to wake you, but she sounds really upset."

Her first thought was that it was Denise. Who else would hunt her down on the business line first thing in the morning? If it was Denise, Cate planned to turn Kayla around and send her from the room with the phone. Ever since their last conversation she'd decided it was probably best to avoid Denise for the duration of her pregnancy sickness. "Who is it?"

"Leslie," she whispered.

Cate sat up. "Thanks," she said to Kayla as she took the phone. "Hello?"

"Cate?"

"Les, what's wrong?"

"We saw the doctor this morning to discuss all my test results and the prognosis isn't very good."

"What did she say?"

She stopped crying to explain. "She said it's going to be impossible for me to get pregnant on my own. My ovaries and uterus are covered in scar tissue. It explains all my horrible cramps and all the heavy periods. I have endometriosis." She explained that it would be extremely difficult for conception to occur with the state of her reproductive system. "It would take a miracle," she said.

Cate felt her heart sink. "People get pregnant all the time with worse things. There is so much that can be done now. I've read on the Internet about women getting pregnant with severe endometriosis."

She blew her nose. "I know, but it's going to be hard and expensive. I don't even know if we can afford to do it. She told us we can try in vitro but it's not always successful and each time you try it the cost is about twenty thousand dollars."

Cate felt horrible. She definitely couldn't tell her now. When would there ever be a good time to tell her? "What about refinancing the house?"

"That's what Russ wants to do."

Cate felt a wave of nausea coming on. *Please, not now. Please, not now.* She did everything in her power to keep from vomiting, but she didn't know how long she could hold it. "Leslie, I think Ethan's calling me."

"Who answered the phone?"

"Oh, we hired a temp because of this event we have coming up. It's just too much work for both of us so we needed some extra help."

Luckily, Leslie didn't seem too interested. "Thank God you were home," she said. "I don't know who else I would've called. Sarah is so wrapped up in her pregnancy, and I just can't talk to anyone who's pregnant right now. She wouldn't be able to relate. And I don't want to tell my family yet."

"I'm glad I can be here for you." She felt the bile rising again, and knew it was rude to leave her hanging at a time when she needed a friend, but she had no choice. "Ethan's calling for me again. I better see what he wants."

"All right."

"I'll call you later! Bye!" She bolted to the bathroom and felt her heart skip a beat when she nearly crashed into the closed bathroom door. There was no time for knocking. She twisted the handle, but it was locked.

"Just a minute," Kayla called quietly.

Then Cate heard something eerily familiar. Something that under normal circumstances probably would've made her toes curl. She heard gagging. Then the sound of a waterfall hitting the toilet bowl followed by the mandatory flush.

She knew it was horrible but the first thing that came to mind was that she couldn't wait to tell Ethan that Kayla was bulimic. This was accompanied, of course, with an empathetic desire to find help for her. Then Cate realized that if Kayla were bulimic, she wouldn't have made Cate wait outside while she threw up. She would've tried to hide it.

Cate ran to the kitchen sink and threw up. While she was splashing water on her face, Kayla appeared in the kitchen. She was green.

"Sorry, Cate," she mumbled. "I probably shouldn't tell you this . . ."

She's pregnant?

"But I'm *so* hungover." She put her hands over her belly. "I feel like I'm going to die."

Thankfully, she spared them both the details of what she'd been drinking the night before. Cate didn't think she'd be able to stomach hearing about it.

"How do you do this every day?" Kayla asked. "You must be so strong. I can't imagine throwing up like this every day."

"Every single day. All day." Cate just had to be clear. She was enjoying this—someone who finally understood.

"I have so much respect for you."

"Really?" She suddenly loved Kayla. Though they were at completely different places in their lives, polar opposites actually, she hadn't felt closer to anyone in a long time. However, she also couldn't imagine drinking to the point of puking ever again in her life. If she had a choice, she'd never be nauseated again. It made her feel like an old lady thinking about how foolish it was to drink until you felt sick. "Listen," Cate said. "Why don't you go home? Take the rest of the day off."

"Won't Ethan be mad? I don't want to disappoint him."

"Ethan will be fine. Really. He's been in your shoes before. Trust me. Go home and put your feet up."

She walked Kayla to the front door and inhaled the familiar odor of sour breath.

"You're the coolest boss ever," she said before leaving.

"Thanks!" Who knew? And here, Cate was beginning to think that Kayla was starting to believe that her boss had a talking mirror and a secret stash of poisoned apples.

Later that afternoon Cate felt up to checking her e-mail. She'd never had fifty messages before and felt kind of popular as she looked at her full inbox. Most of them were silly forwards from her friends.

There was one e-mail, however, that meant business. It was from Janet and the subject box read, "BRIDESMAID DRESS." Cate opened the file and found a link to an expensive wedding designer's website. At this point she didn't care about the cost. She was open to whatever Denise and Janet wanted as long as there was peace.

What popped onto her screen would've looked good on a hooker. The material was a sheer, nearly see-through clingy silk. If the V-neck plunged any lower, the model's nipples and belly button would've been exposed. This had to be a joke. They didn't really expect Cate to wear this dress when she was eight months along.

She went back to her inbox where she found several more e-mails from Janet and Denise.

C8, What do you think? I went ahead and bought it. Denise gave me the green light. Janet

She bought it? So then it obviously didn't matter what Cate thought. If Denise wanted them to match, then they expected Cate to wear the dress.

C8, Janet bought the dress. I think it will fit you if you buy a size twenty-four. I called the designer. They said they could make it that big. Luv, Denise

They weren't kidding. This was real. They really wanted Cate to cover her pregnant body in enough material to make a handkerchief. Cate replied.

Hi Denise, Are we looking at the same dress? #145675. The one with the low V-neck? Cate

It was the best she could do for now. She signed out of her e-mail account. As far as she was concerned Janet could wait.

Jon Bon Jovi
Has Morning Sickness

The day of the sweet sixteen Cate barfed on the front porch. She was outside waving to Ethan and Kayla when she caught a whiff of fertilizer and her stomach turned as quickly and unexpectedly as an avalanche. Making it to the bathroom was impossible, so she barfed right next to one of their wooden rocking chairs.

"I'll clean it up when I get home, honey!" Ethan called from the driver's side window. He was in a hurry and she didn't expect him to get out of the car. Pale, she lifted her head. Their neighbor across the street was watering his lawn and paused to watch her. She couldn't blame him for staring. She'd become a recluse ever since the sickness had started and he was probably shocked to see that she was alive, and also surprised that she was barfing like a teenager after a night with a bottle of Strawberry Hill.

She used the same hand she'd wiped her face with to wave to her neighbor. For a moment she felt tempted to explain herself. If left to draw his own conclusions, he'd probably believe she was a drug addict. Not to mention, her husband had just driven off with a younger, prettier woman who came to the house on a regular basis. However, she had no desire to shout, "Oh, hey, Mr. Dempsey! I'm pregnant! The girl you just saw—she's a temp for our business. I'm too sick to help my husband! Heard this all *magically* disappears after the first trimester though!" She hadn't even told some of her closest friends. She wasn't about to announce it to the whole neighborhood.

Kayla had met Ethan at the house and they'd left together for the kitchen where the rest of the staff would be waiting to load up the van. Even though she knew the entire staff was in for a night of torture at the hands of Hilda and Hunter Kimball, Cate couldn't help but feel a slight pang of envy. She'd rather be taking orders from a sixteen-year-old than feeling poisoned by hormones.

Leslie called while she was outside. She wanted to call her back, but couldn't. She couldn't decide which was worse—telling a lie or adding salt to open wounds. Both options seemed cruel. The last thing she wanted to do was cause Leslie more pain.

She mustered up the energy to shower. By the time she was finished she felt as if she had competed in a triathlon. Beauty had taken the backseat these days and she crawled back into bed with a wet head. She wouldn't be surprised if her blow dryer was rusty by the time the pregnancy sickness was gone. She flipped on the television and noticed that a couple of her favorite eighties movies were on. Not even the sight of *Some Kind of Wonderful* or *Sixteen Candles* seemed exciting. She turned off the television and took a nap. She woke to the loud sound of Grease purring next to her face. She scratched him behind the ears. She lay next to him, listening to his deep purr and thinking how lucky she was to have him. If it wasn't for Grease, she would spend most of her nausea alone.

She could always tell when someone was on her porch by watching Grease. His ears would perk and his eyes would slant before the doorbell even rang. This time he growled.

Someone was here? There was no time to run to the bathroom for her toothbrush before the doorbell rang. She didn't have to look in the mirror to know she looked bad. She could feel her hair, large and poofy, on top of her head. It felt as if she was wearing a wig made for the lead singer of Poison. She'd had this hairdo many times when she'd air-dried her hair and she called it her headbanger hair. She wasn't wearing any makeup, and couldn't remember the last time she'd seen sunlight.

If it was anyone she wanted to see, they would've called before showing up. They had a problem with Jehovah's Witnesses in the area and she was in no mood to deal with them.

Their front door was a French door, and covered by a lace curtain. Her bedroom door was open and she could see the front door from her bed. Through the curtain, she made out the shape of one large figure and two small ones. Dear God, it was Denise and the Bubich children. The only reason she knew was because she caught a glimpse of Keith Junior's profile and immediately recognized the tail. It had grown. She definitely wasn't answering. Just to be safe, she decided she'd better close her bedroom door. She didn't want to risk any chances of them seeing her. She tiptoed to her bedroom door and was within spitting distance when she heard Denise say, "Jump up on the windowsill there and see if you can see anyone inside. I can't imagine she would've gone anywhere."

She was ducking when Keith Junior's face popped up in the front window like a werewolf. "There she is," he said. "She's ducking."

"Shit," Cate mumbled before she went to the door. She did her best to be friendly. "What a surprise!"

The kids didn't wait for an invitation to come inside. Denise and her briefcase followed them. The only thing worse would be if Denise had brought Scary Dad with her.

"Denise said we could play with your cat," Keith Junior said.

The last Cate had seen of Grease he was hissing. Then he'd darted off. If he was smart, he was hiding beneath the bed. Cate envied him. "You probably won't see Grease the entire time you're here. Sorry." She remembered what she'd told them about Oscar the last time she'd seen him. "You can play with the dog though. He's out back."

"That's okay," they said.

"Your hair looks pretty like that," Denise said. She really meant it.

"Are you pregnant?" Ashlyn asked. "Denise said you're having a baby."

"Yes, and I'm very sick." She thought it was enough of a signal for them to keep the visit short. However, Denise sat down on the couch.

"You don't look like you're having a baby," Keith Junior said.

"That's because it's too early."

"Exactly how far along are you now?" Denise asked, popping open the buckles on her briefcase.

"Fourteen weeks."

"And you're still not feeling better?"

Cate shook her head. "Not at all."

"That's so weird. I've never even heard of anyone being this sick. I told you about Janet's sister. She was never sick. By the way, Janet said you never wrote back about the dress. She spent a long time looking for just the right dress."

"I must've been looking at the wrong one," Cate said. "Because the dress I saw was a little small for pregnancy."

"You were looking at the right one. We just thought you could order it in a bigger size."

Cate felt a tap on her leg, and looked down at Keith Junior. "Cate, where's the cat?"

"I don't know. Probably hiding."

"Ethan said you were by yourself so I thought I would bring you some fresh bread from the Farmer's Market."

It was a nice gesture and Cate felt guilty for snapping at her.

"I want a piece. I want a piece. I want a piece," Ashlyn said.

"Go show Cate what else we brought her."

Keith Junior ran to the porch and returned with a bouquet of flowers.

"Thank you," Cate said.

"Can I put them in a vase?" Ashlyn asked.

"Sure," Cate said. "Let me show you where the vases are."

She found a vase they'd received as a wedding gift. Perhaps it was because she felt like she was going to throw up and wanted them to leave as soon as possible, but she wasn't in the mood to look for one that could be trusted with the kids. The moment the vase left her hands she regretted it. Keith Junior took the vase and ran. Ashlyn chased after him. "She said we could both do it. Come back!"

She watched as Ashlyn grabbed one end of the vase and Keith Junior pulled on the other. "Here." Cate held out her hands. "You guys better give me the vase," she said.

"Give it back to Cate," Denise called.

Instead of giving it back they continued their game of tug-of-war. The glass slipped from their fingers like butter. She watched as the vase hit the floor and shattered.

Next time they came to the door, she was pretending like pregnancy had made her deaf. She wasn't answering.

"Get out of the kitchen!" Denise screamed. "Do not step on the glass! Get out of there now!" It was the first time Cate had seen Denise raise her voice with her future stepchildren. The ferocity in her tone made Cate flinch. Denise's face was bright red and a vein spidered down the side of her forehead. Cate figured this probably wasn't the best time to tell her that this is what she had to look forward to if she married Keith. The kids ran into the living room.

"I'll clean it up," Denise said. "Where's the broom?"

Cate led her to the broom.

While Denise swept, Cate caught a glimpse of Keith Junior watching from the other room. When he noticed Cate looking at him he stuck a finger down his throat and pretended to gag. "Hey, Cate, want some fish guts?"

"Be quiet!" Denise snapped. "I told you not to do that."

Listening to Denise lose her temper made Cate a little uncomfortable. Before they left Denise pulled a sheet of paper from her binder. Somehow Cate knew this wouldn't be a wedding-free visit. "This is my guest list for the shower," she said.

"Oh. Okay." Cate took the list.

"I know the shower is not for months. But I thought you might want to get started on the invitations while you're lying around all day."

Just what Cate wanted! How did she know? "Er . . . uh . . . well, I probably won't get to this for a while. But okay." Cate glanced at the list. "Who's Evelyn Horton?"

"That's my great-aunt in Vermont."

"Do you think she'll come? How old is she?"

"Ninety-two. She won't come."

Denise may as well have said, "Here is my list of people I want to hit up for gifts." Did she want Cate to make shower invitations or simply send a fluorescent list of places where Denise had registered? Included on the list were a number of other relatives dotted all over the country that Cate had never even met. Cate set the list next to the mountain of junk mail beside the front door. She couldn't even think of bridal showers.

Under normal circumstances Cate would've stayed awake until Ethan returned. She was dying to hear about the party and the Kimballs. However, she couldn't keep her eyes open. She drifted off to sleep and was awakened several hours later by noise in the kitchen.

She climbed from bed and found Ethan in the kitchen unloading a crate of champagne into their refrigerator. He looked up from the fridge and raised his eyebrows. "Hi, Jon Bon Jovi."

She'd forgotten about her hair. She laughed. "I look like a head-banger. Don't I?"

"You look cute."

"Where's Kayla?" Cate asked.

"She met someone at the party and went out for drinks with him after."

"Please tell me it wasn't a high schooler."

"No. Some relative of the Kimballs."

"How was the party?"

He smiled. "It actually went really well. The Kimballs were so happy that they gave us all this extra champagne. This is good stuff, too. And they want to use us for their son's graduation party next year. I told him it was right around your due date so we probably couldn't." He held up a bottle for her to see. "They said we should pop this open to celebrate after the baby arrives." Looking at it just made her feel even more deprived. June seemed like it was eons away.

"I threw in a few extra bottles for Kayla when I paid her. She did a good job."

"She's not coming back?"

"No, I don't really need her anymore."

Strangely, Cate felt a little sad. She'd gotten used to seeing Kayla's bright face every morning. She'd brought life into the house.

Ethan stood up. "All the big events are behind us now." He walked over to her and placed his hand on her belly. "But we still have so much to look forward to."

She hoped he was right.

Part Two

It Seems Like Forever

·26·

Who's in the Dark?

The end of the first trimester should've felt like a milestone. However, there had been no "magical disappearance" of the sickness. The only thing she felt was trapped. Each morning she woke, hoping it would be gone. She was beginning to forget what life was like before pregnancy. What it felt like to experience hunger pains and go on long walks.

The only triumph in passing the first trimester was that they were out of the danger zone. Chances of miscarrying now were slim. It was finally safe to spread the word. She no longer had to pretend she had a very stubborn stomach flu. She had to tell Leslie before someone else did.

She dialed her number. Feeling nervous only added to her nausea.

"Hey, Les."

"Hi, stranger. What's going on?" She sounded happy, the best she'd sounded in a while. For a moment she wondered if she should wait until another day.

"Well, actually I'm calling to explain why I've been such a stranger. I've been really sick. And I haven't been able to function and it's been because I'm . . . well . . . Ethan and I are having a baby."

She gasped. "Oh my God! Are you serious? You are? That's great!" The happiness in her voice sounded genuine. Cate felt like an asshole. All the fear had been Cate's problem, because Leslie was fine.

"How long have you known?" Leslie asked.

The question only made her feel worse. "Well, it was Ethan. He didn't want to tell anyone. So I promised I would keep it a secret. I'm actually heading into the second trimester. I'm still so sick though."

"I'm so glad you're past the first trimester. And I've heard that mag—"

"Magically disappears. Yes, I've heard that, too. A million times. And let me tell you, there has been no magic in this house."

"Well, it will get better," she said. She was quiet for a moment. Cate was just starting to welcome the relief that came with getting something off her chest when she heard Leslie sniffing through the phone.

"Leslie? Are you okay?"

"I totally don't want to cry, and not wanting to cry is only making it worse."

"I'm sorry, Les. I don't know what . . ."

"It's okay. You don't have to say anything. It's me. It's not you. Feeling this way is my problem, not yours." She blew her nose. "I don't want you to think I'm not happy for you. You know I'm happy for you, right?"

"Of course. I totally understand how you feel. I have to admit . . . the day you told me you were pregnant I felt a little sad."

"You did?" She stopped crying for a moment.

"Yeah, I was still happy for you, but I was worried about getting pregnant and hearing Sarah's news and then yours just made me feel lonely. I was a little jealous, too. I know what it feels like to be alone when it seems like everyone else is doing what you want to do."

"I'm glad to hear you say that. I can hardly talk to Sarah. Every time the baby comes up she changes the subject like she's avoiding me. I don't want people to avoid me."

Cate felt terrible. She should've confided in her from day one, but it seemed as though there had never been a good time.

"You're going to have a baby, too, Leslie. However you choose to do it, I'll support you one hundred percent. I'm there for you all the way."

"Thanks. I'm not sure what we're going to do yet."

They chatted for a bit about the options Leslie had. There was surrogacy, but Leslie didn't like the idea of Russ's sperm being injected into another woman. Frankly, Cate couldn't blame her. There was in vitro, which was expensive and came with no guarantees. There was adoption, which she hadn't quite fully embraced yet. They still really wanted a child of their own.

"I have a good feeling," Cate said. "I have a feeling that everything will work out just how you want it to."

After she said good-bye, she felt as if a weight had been lifted.

She called her mother next. "I just wanted to tell you that you can start telling all your friends now. We're out of the danger zone, and I know you're dying to spread the word."

"Oh, I already told everyone anyway."

"You told everyone?"

Connie laughed as if the joke were on Cate. "Oh yeah, everyone in the family knows. All my friends at church, too."

"How long have they known?"

Connie counted. "Seven . . . maybe . . . eight. For about two months."

"Well, now I know never to tell you anything again."

This whole time Cate had thought everyone had been in the dark about her pregnancy when really the only person who'd been in the dark had been her.

·27·

One Is All It Takes

She knew she was feeling much better when she climbed onto a chair, broom in hand, and swept away the ugly cobweb she'd stared at every day for over two months. She couldn't remember the last time she'd done anything more satisfying. Afterward she felt like conquering the world. She was ready to have her life back. She wanted to drive, and clean, and pet her dog.

However, she learned quickly that life wasn't ready for her. The grocery store and restaurants were still entirely off limits, but she could go to the post office! It was after throwing up in the Pier 1 Imports parking lot that she realized one errand a day was about all she could manage.

By seventeen weeks, daytime was almost back to normal but nighttime was still a disaster. She'd gone back to work and had started eating regular food again. Many aversions were still strong. Meat disgusted her and the idea of anything spicy was enough to send her to the bathroom. She felt as though pregnancy had made her a vegetarian. As soon as the clock chimed seven each evening Cate turned into a pregnancy-poisoned pumpkin all over again. She'd found it was best if she went to bed with the sun.

She realized that there were things that might trigger a gagging reflex for the rest of her life. For instance, she didn't think she would ever be able to hear *The Price Is Right* theme song for as long as she lived. Even the mere mention of a showdown or winning "a brand-new car!" could send her running for the nearest toilet. Meatless nuggets—ruined. A historic novel that had been sitting on her bedside table would be used as kindling wood if she had her way. Each time she looked at its cover she felt her stomach turn. Nausea was a force to be reckoned with and she never wanted to suffer its ugly wrath again.

Coming out of the sickness had also made her realize that whomever she was carrying in her womb would be an only child. She'd never imagined that she'd want just one. She'd always thought it selfish to deprive a child of siblings, but she couldn't imagine being sick again.

She presented Ethan with this news while they were picking out a Christmas tree.

"It will be fun to bring our kids here, won't it?" he said, as he propped a full Douglas fir up. It was a warm December day and he'd pushed his long sleeves up to his elbows.

"You mean our *kid*."

He looked puzzled, and she wondered if this wasn't the best time to break it to him. They were having a good day. She was still pale and thin, but she was thankful for the ability to smell clean, fresh pine without barfing.

"We can't have just one," Ethan said.

"I don't think I can go through this again."

It was an awkward time for physical appearances and she caught strangers looking at her belly curiously, wondering if she was pregnant or just desperately needed to suck in. Her thin legs and arms were offset by a thick middle. It wasn't a flattering look for anyone.

Ethan looked wounded, and she wished she hadn't said anything. Her recovery had been exciting for him as well. She'd gotten so used to seeing him worried and concerned about her that she'd forgotten what he looked like when he was happy. It felt good to see him smiling and joking again. Sharing her decision with him had thrown a wet towel over his good mood. "That's so sad," he said. "Think about when we go on road trips and our child will be sitting in the backseat all by himself."

"Himself? What if it's a girl?"

"Well, then we're definitely having two."

"Ethan, I couldn't even take care of myself. How will I take care of a child if I'm sick again?"

They were interrupted by the choking of her cell phone.

C8—Let me know if there is anything I can do 2 help with the shower. I would LUV 2 help. Janet

Cate turned off her phone. Janet could wait. Furthermore, Cate felt that if Janet really wanted to help she would've called.

"Will you at least think about it?" he asked. A family with two little boys walked past them. The father carried a large tree over his shoulder.

She shook her head. "I can't go through that again."

She'd always thought the main reason people had only one child was because they were selfish. And maybe it was a little selfish of her not to want more. But who could blame her for not wanting to spend another three months in bed? She now understood why a lot of people chose to only have one. Perhaps it was morning sickness, or postpartum depression, or placenta previa that had put them on bed rest. It didn't matter. There was no right or wrong. She understood now.

They picked out a tree that was probably too big for their tiny house. The little ones looked so scrawny and there was something magnificent about a large, full tree. They drove home with it hanging out the back of Ethan's Ford Explorer.

They had to move some furniture to make room for the tree. While Ethan trimmed some loose branches off the bottom she called Janet back. She was greeted by Janet's voice mail.

"Hi, Janet. Got your message. I'm glad you want to help. I have lots of ideas for games and everything so give me a call back whenever you have a chance. Thanks."

She watched Ethan string lights. The scent of pine had filled their house. Janet sent her another text message and Cate was starting to get annoyed. It was becoming clear that Janet was avoiding talking to her, which could only mean one thing. She didn't really want to help. People who helped called.

C8—I'm really interested in your ideas, but I have to tell you that money is tight right now. And I think we should go budget. I can make a cake and we can just have cheese and crackers.

The message was annoying for several reasons. Everyone knew Janet had money. A year ago, she'd collected on an insurance policy and had bought a new BMW and a house. Janet just didn't want to spend her money on Denise's shower. Denise wasn't Cate's favorite and Cate was so sick of the wedding she could scream, but they had to give Denise a little more than cheese and crackers on her shower day. She wrote back.

Janet—Thanks for offering to help. For now I think I have everything under control, but I'll let you know if there is anything you can do. Cate

That ought to make her happy.

Sometimes it was better to do things alone. One person was

enough to organize the shower and if Janet and her cheapskate ideas got involved it would only make things harder.

It didn't take long to decorate their tree. It was their second Christmas as a married couple and they only had a few ornaments. They made up for the lack of ornaments by using extra lights. They stood back to admire their work. It looked pretty.

"Now imagine one poor little child decorating by himself."

She hung an ornament. "Our child will have us."

"You won't even consider having another one? At least say you won't *completely* rule it out."

"All right. I won't completely rule it out, but don't get your hopes up. I've pretty much made up my mind."

It's Beginning to Feel a Lot Like Hormones

Ethan started Christmas morning with a Bloody Mary. Cate watched him sing "It's the Most Wonderful Time of the Year" as he stirred his cocktail. She began to wonder if the reason he wanted a second child was so he would have a designated driver for the good portion of a year again.

Before pregnancy, they'd faced each social event with a looming, burning question. Who was driving? Neither one of them had ever been eager to take hold of the keys and resign to a night of iced water while the other sipped wine with their friends.

As far as they were concerned, alcohol was completely off-limits for whoever had possession of the keys. Even one drink was forbidden. One glass of wine or a margarita wasn't worth putting one's self and others at risk—not to mention the legal fees or jail time that came along with getting a DUI. They didn't have to learn the hard way that drinking and driving ruined lives, and for most of their relationship they'd paid for cabs or flipped coins over who would be behind the wheel.

Now that Cate was pregnant, it seemed as though Ethan had taken advantage of every moment to ride in the passenger seat. "Oh, we're going to the mall. Lemme just have a beer first," he'd say.

In the past, invitations had been left on the kitchen counter for weeks while both of them created excuses as to why the other should drive before convincing themselves the party would be a waste of time. This holiday season Ethan had promptly RSVPed to every bash that came their way. She'd never known her husband was such a social butterfly, and an alcoholic.

Cate had lost track of how many holiday gatherings they'd returned from in which she'd driven home, listening to her husband snoring in an alcohol-induced nap.

Apparently, Christmas day was no exception. They were going to her parents' for brunch. As she dressed she watched him suck down his cocktail with enthusiasm, pausing only to sing Christmas carols.

The idea of labor and delivery brought on a lot of worries, and while Cate had listened to Sarah agonize about the umbilical cord getting caught around the baby's neck during delivery or not making it to the hospital on time, Cate worried she wouldn't have a ride to the hospital. What if she had to call a cab? Or worse, her parents. She'd spent a few sleepless nights with a conversation playing through her head.

"Um, Mom and Dad. I need a ride to the hospital. I'm in labor."

"Oh my gosh! How exciting! We'll be right over! Where's Ethan?"

"Passed out."

She hated to kill his fun, but she was going to have to break the bad news to him that alcohol would be off-limits once they hit the third trimester. She wasn't heading to the hospital in a Yellow cab.

She wasn't big enough for maternity clothes but had moved up a couple of sizes in regular clothes. She wore a pair of black pants and a black sweater with a red velvet blazer. Her outfit would've been boring if it weren't for the jacket. The sleeves were gathered around the shoulders and the collar was sharp. She couldn't button the jacket and as she looked in the mirror she realized that from the side or the back she didn't look pregnant.

After they were dressed they loaded the car with gifts. Her mother had thought it would be a nice idea to share Christmas with the Blakelys, so Ethan's family would be there, which meant that Denise and the Bubiches were also going to be a part of the holiday as well. She'd spent a long time thinking of what to get the Bubiches for Christmas. Ethan had suggested straitjackets. Cate thought a vacation to the Middle East might be worthwhile. The truth was she had no idea what would make them happy. Instead of going on a wild-goose chase for just the right toys she bought the whole family passes to the Wild Animal Park.

They were about to get into the Prius when Ethan paused. "Shoot, I forgot something."

"Your flask?" she called as he ran to the front door.

"Real funny." He disappeared inside.

Cate headed to the driver's side door. As she unlocked the doors she heard a car approaching. It was slowing down when Cate looked over her shoulder. Hanging from the window of an El Camino was the tattooed elbow of a twentyish man with a black eye. Because of the cost of homes in San Diego, Cate and Ethan could only afford a neighborhood that catered to people of all walks of life. It wasn't out of the ordinary to come face-to-face with a creepy man on Christmas morning or hear the occasional gunshot. He looked at Cate.

"Merry Christmas!" He smiled, revealing a chipped tooth.

"Merry Christmas!" She smiled back. He was a friendly fella after all.

"You're hot," he said. "Are you a model?"

She thought she smelled alcohol on his breath. Under normal circumstances she would've ignored him, slipped into her car, and locked the doors. These weren't normal circumstances. Hormones had seized control of her better judgment. She pulled open her jacket. "No, I'm pregnant. Do you realize that you're talking to a mother? Would you want someone hitting on your mother on Christmas morning? And if I wasn't pregnant, do you really think I would be interested in a man with a black eye on Christmas day? Do you?"

He looked startled. "You're crazy," he mumbled before his tires spun and he sped away.

"I'm not crazy! I'm pregnant! Never underestimate the power of hormones!" she yelled. She'd realized that telling people off and making demands had come easily in her second trimester.

In the past confronting a slimy pervert would've made her hands shake. Adrenaline would've coursed through her veins, and it would've taken her several minutes to compose herself after a confrontation. As she watched the El Camino screech around the corner, she straightened her jacket and felt confident. She wasn't fazed in the least and sort of hoped the guy came back because she had a few more things she wanted to get off her chest.

Ethan trotted from the house, holding his Scrabble board. "It's not Christmas unless you play Scrabble," he said as she jumped into the passenger seat. "Ready?" he called.

She climbed into the car. "Oh yes."

She was ready to face the family.

Keith Junior's hands were covered in red-and-green dye when they arrived. As soon as she noticed the nearly empty dish of M&M's she realized why. The kids were dressed in cheap-looking Christmas sweaters. Ashlyn's had a yellow snowman on the front of it and Keith Junior's featured a *101 Dalmatians* Christmas scene.

The sweaters had the faded look of clothes that had been washed too many times, and Cate wondered if Scary was dressing them in the same sweaters around Valentine's Day and Easter. On both children, the sleeves barely reached their wrists. Cate felt sorry for them. No one had combed Ashlyn's hair and she had a ratty ball of blonde bed head on the back of her scalp. Keith Junior's jeans had holes. Cate felt the sudden onset of tears.

This was the other side of hormones. Irrational crying. She'd never been one to cry in movies or release sentimental tears of joy. Lately, tears had come as easily as conversation. She'd bawled through most of *Marley & Me* and turned emotional every time she looked at her wedding photos.

As she watched the kids she felt sorry for them. It wasn't their fault that their father was weird and Denise was about to become their stepmother. Though bratty, they were just little kids, and someone needed to comb Ashlyn's hair.

She disappeared into her parents' bedroom where she found a box of Kleenex. She inhaled the familiar scents of Christmas day. Even from her parents' room she could smell cinnamon candles burning. Her parents didn't drink coffee, but her mother always kept a pot on during holidays. The scent of her dad's egg dish and fresh bread filled the house. She stayed in there for several minutes before her mother walked in.

"What's wrong?" she asked. She wore a red-and-green plaid shirt and black slacks.

"I don't know. I just feel so sorry for Keith Junior and Ashlyn. They need new clothes and their parents are idiots."

Her mother patted her on the back. "Feeling a little hormonal?"

Cate nodded. "They just don't have a very good start in life, and I hate to see little kids have a bad start in life."

Connie shook her head. "Don't feel sorry for them, Cate," her mother, the optimist, offered. "They're going to turn out just like

Scary Dad anyway. It might seem sad now, but trust me, they'll be id-iots, too. And you won't be able to stand them in ten years."

It was a terrible outlook.

"C'mon." Connie tugged on her arm. "It's Christmas. Let's go have fun."

She followed her mother back to the living room. Cate knew the hormonal tears had passed when they returned to the other room and she felt an urge to strangle Scary Dad. Just the sight of him in-cited feelings of irritation. He didn't even have to open his mouth to get on her nerves. His presence was enough.

Thankfully, her sister, Emily, distracted her from him. She'd seen Emily, her daughter, and her husband at mass the night before. After mass was over they went their separate ways so Emily could spend the evening with her husband's side of the family.

Maybe Cate was biased, but she thought her three-year-old niece was the cutest child on the planet. She was dressed in a velveteen bur-gundy gown with a bow as big as a small pillow tied around her waist. Her black patent shoes sparkled and she clutched a figurine of Dora the Explorer.

"Just a couple more weeks until you find out what you're having," Emily said as she looked at Cate's belly. "Any intuition?" she asked.

Cate rubbed her stomach. "I don't know. I've had dreams that it's a boy, but sometimes I think it's a girl so I really have no idea."

"Just make sure you drink something sugary or eat a piece of candy before you go to the ultrasound. It will make the baby active and then you'll definitely see what you're having. You don't want the baby to be sleeping in some obscure position. And if that doesn't work, drink an ice-cold bottle of water before you go—and I mean ice cold. Practically frozen. When the cold water gets into that baby's system it will wake it right up."

If they weren't able to find out what they were having, she would go insane.

Denise made her way toward them and Cate felt like throwing her into the Christmas tree. She wasn't in the mood for her. "Hi, Emily," Denise said.

"Hi, Denise." Her sister did a good job of pretending to like Denise. Ever since Cate's wedding, Emily couldn't stand Denise.

"So you went with Bradley's family last night?" Denise asked.

"Yep," Emily said. "That's what happens when you get married. You have to split the holidays."

"So make sure you like your fiancé's family," Cate said. It was a hint and Cate hoped that Denise took it.

"I feel so lucky," Denise said.

"You like Keith's parents?" Emily asked.

"Keith doesn't speak to his father and his mother became a Jehovah's Witness a couple years ago. *I never* have to divide the holidays."

Cate almost spit out her cider.

Was she telling them they were stuck with Scary Dad? Was she saying that every future holiday would be shadowed with his huge ass and mustache? She may as well have said that Christmas, Easter, and Thanksgiving had been cancelled for eternity because having Scary Dad around would ruin every single holiday.

She was starting to believe it might be possible for Denise to have a wedding-free conversation when Denise turned to Cate and said, "Janet said she's been trying to help with the shower. She said she's been text messaging you." The tone was accusatory, as if she were blaming Cate for something.

"She sent me one text message and I called her back. Haven't heard from her since."

"She really wants to help," Denise said. "She told me she'll do whatever it takes to help. And she said you haven't responded to her idea for a dress either. I think that dress would look good on you. Beth was pregnant at your wedding and she still looked good in a bridesmaid dress. I think if you ordered a few sizes bigger than you normally wear, you'd look fine."

Cate felt something come loose inside of her. She was tired of playing the nice bridesmaid, and it was about time Denise found out how she felt. While Anne Murray sang "Silent Night" in the background Cate got a few things off her chest. "Denise, Beth was four weeks pregnant at my wedding. Anything would've looked good on her. If you want people to pay to attention to *you* on your wedding day, which I suspect is what you're after, then I suggest I wear something different. Because if I walk down the aisle wearing that dress no one is going to be looking at you. They're all going to be laughing at me." She caught a glimpse of Emily before she continued. Her sister looked delighted. "I don't know, maybe you want me to look like an idiot. Maybe that's what you're after. Ha. Ha. Everyone will laugh at Cate. But in the best interests of your wedding, I suggest I wear something else."

The startled expression on Denise's face didn't stop Cate from continuing. It felt good to tell her how she felt and she wished she'd done it sooner. "So I'm not wearing that dress. I'll be more than happy to match with Janet. I'll even have my dress made. But I'm not walking down the aisle looking like a pregnant hooker. And let me tell you about Janet. She's about as helpful as a drunk bum with a—"

Ethan touched her elbow. "Cate, can I talk to you for a minute?"

"What?" she snapped.

He led her by the elbow to her parents' bedroom. "What's wrong with you?" he asked.

"I've had it," she growled. "Denise is driving me crazy. My hormones are out of control and I can't take any of her crap anymore."

"Well, try to control yourself. And stay away from Scary, will ya? He might murder us in our sleep."

He had a point.

She sat down on the edge of the bed. Something fluttered through her stomach like a pollywog. "Oh my gosh," she said. "I just felt the baby move. I'm not kidding."

He put his hand on her tummy.

"I don't think it's big enough for you to feel," she said. "It just felt like a little fish in there or something. It was so real, so amazing." At that moment she realized that everything she'd felt—all the hormonal changes and the nausea and vomiting—had been worth it.

·29·

It's a Cat?

The night before the big ultrasound Cate dreamt she gave birth to a cat, a full-grown feline who bore a striking resemblance to Grease. In her dream, it was perfectly normal that she'd given birth to an animal.

Even her mother looked glowingly at her grandcat swaddled in receiving blankets. "It's a cat," she gushed. "He's beautiful."

"Our baby," Ethan said as he took their bundle of joy and kissed him between the ears.

The only person who seemed to be alarmed by the birth was herself. More than anything, she was pissed off that she'd gone through three solid months of nausea only to deliver something that would never graduate from college. On the car ride home from the hospital they had to stop for a litter box. It was a frustrating, alarming dream and when she opened her eyes she'd never felt more relieved.

She was dying to know. Over ninety days of feeling poisoned and living with her head in the toilet—she deserved to find out more about who was in there. She would handcuff herself to the ultrasound machine and swallow the keys if that's what it took to find out. There was no way she was waiting until delivery for an answer.

Perhaps it was the cat nightmare but she woke up before the alarm went off. She stirred restlessly in bed for a few minutes, hoping that Ethan would wake up. After she listened to him snore for several minutes she kissed his forehead.

"Today we find out if we're having a son or a daughter." She ran her fingers through his hair.

"I know," he said. "What time is it?"

"Time to get up."

She was ready to leave fifteen minutes early and she killed the time by eating half a box of See's Candies that Ethan's grandmother had given them for Christmas washed down with an icy carton of apple juice. By the time they left she had a headache, was shivering, and thought she would puke from the consumption of sugar first thing in the morning.

It looked as though they were the first people to enter the waiting room, and she sat next to Ethan fidgeting and praying that she wouldn't barf on the carpet. The longer they waited the more nervous she felt and the worse her nausea became.

Suddenly, she didn't care whether they found out if they were having a son or a daughter. She just wanted the baby to be healthy. They'd be looking at the spine and the lungs, and the brain. What if something was wrong? When they finally called her in her heart was racing and her palms were slick from sweat. She felt like she had to go to the bathroom, and she wished she hadn't eaten so much sugar. She was wired.

The ultrasound technician was an older woman, which brought some relief. She seemed like she'd been doing it for a while. Cate had heard horror stories of people learning the sex of the baby then decorating in the according colors only to discover upon delivery that the baby was the opposite of what they'd been anticipating. She wanted experience here.

She introduced herself as Vicky. "Before I get started, do you guys want to know the sex of the baby?" she asked.

They both said yes before Vicky applied a layer of warm gel over Cate's belly. She rubbed the mouse-like object over her stomach and Cate immediately saw the shape of their child. The baby had grown so much since the last ultrasound in the first trimester. They could see a little turned-up nose and lips. Cate knew it was early but something about the forehead reminded her of Ethan. Looking at their baby made her relax. She felt so much love for a person she barely knew. She couldn't explain the attachment she felt as she looked at the little feet floating inside her. She could stare at the baby all day.

"Wow," Vicky said. "The baby is really active."

Ethan squeezed her hand, and they shared a knowing smile.

One by one, Vicky examined the major internal organs. She scrolled over Cate's stomach as if she were doing inventory.

"Now I'm looking at the spine," she said.

"Is it normal?" Cate asked.

"Look's good." Vicky focused on the screen.

To Cate, the images on the screen looked like a big blur of black-and-gray shapes. She couldn't tell if she was looking at a leg or the kidneys. Instead of focusing on the screen, Cate watched Vicky's face. She looked for any sign in Vicky's expression that might indicate that something was wrong. Most of the time, Vicky just looked like she was concentrating.

"Now we'll look at the four chambers of the heart."

"Is it normal?" Cate asked.

Vicky nodded. "Everything looks normal. Measuring exactly where it should be. Now I'm going to measure the legs."

"Are they normal?"

"Average size for this stage."

She measured several other things, each time sharing the information with Cate and Ethan.

Cate wondered if Vicky was getting tired of Cate asking if everything was normal. However, Cate didn't really care if she was annoyed. This was the most important thing Cate had ever been a part of. "Now I'm looking at the vagina," Vicky said.

Cate was about to ask if it was normal when it clicked. She'd said *vagina*.

"It looks like you guys are having a little girl," Vicky said.

Cate let it sink in for a moment. They were having a daughter. She couldn't control the tears that filled her eyes. She was carrying a little girl inside her. This little person she'd been wondering about for the past twenty weeks now had a characteristic she could identify. She turned to Ethan.

He looked like a deer caught in headlights. This look had only gotten worse as the pregnancy continued. It was the same expression she'd seen on his face the day they found out she was pregnant, only now it was a tad more magnified.

"This baby is busy," Vicky said. "She's just moving all over the place."

"How sure are you that it's a girl?" Ethan asked before biting a nail.

"Ninety-nine point nine," she said.

He spit the nail on the floor, and Cate wondered what the hell had come over him. "So it's safe to tell everyone?" he asked.

"Oh yeah. It's definitely safe. You're having a girl."

As soon as the ultrasound was over Cate hugged him. "We're having a healthy baby girl."

He stopped biting his nails to kiss her on the cheek. They walked through the waiting room holding hands. Cate glowed. Nothing could ruin her day at this point. She heard the sound of a text message coming through and she ignored it. She was full of energy. It was the most she'd felt her entire pregnancy. She was having a daughter and she felt like shouting it out to the world. She felt charged.

As soon as they were outside Cate looked at him. "What's wrong with you?"

"I'm going to have to buy a rifle," he mumbled. Cate laughed, and when Ethan didn't join her she realized he was genuine. He was already worried. If she wasn't mistaken she thought she noticed a gray hair at his temple, too. "Ethan—"

"She's going to date someday."

"Why do men always worry about that? My parents had nothing to worry about. I wasn't having sex in high school."

"That's because your mother is a nun."

She rolled her eyes. "Don't you think we're going to raise a child with values and intelligence? Give yourself a little more credit, Ethan. And boys could be just as much trouble, too. Really, you think if we had a boy, we wouldn't be worried about him?"

"I guess that's true." He ran his fingers through his hair. "Wow! We're having a daughter. *I* am having a daughter. We're going to be parents!"

Where had he been?

"It's just really starting to sink in," he said. "It seems so real now. I'm having a daughter."

For her, the reality had sunk in the day she'd peed on a stick. Her daughter had been with her every second since she'd gotten the positive pregnancy test. She couldn't ignore her growing belly or the tsunami that had invaded her digestive system.

He rubbed his hand over her belly. "Hello, little girl. Hello in there."

It made her happy to see him excited. He no longer looked like a deer caught in headlights. He wore the expression of a man who owned a winning lotto ticket. He was proud.

"Now comes the hard part," she said.

"What's that?"

"Picking out a name."

·30·

Claiming Names

For the past couple of years she'd thought she'd known. She'd had it all figured out. Her daughter was going to be Edie. The middle name was up for grabs but she thought it should be a family one. Perhaps Rita or Constance. Maybe they'd use one from her family this time and one from his next time—or vice versa.

She'd never expected Ethan to look as if he'd just walked into a Dumpster filled with fish guts when she'd suggested it. "I am not naming my daughter Edie."

It was the evening of the ultrasound, and she felt her idea being crushed like a pinot grape after harvest. How could he not like Edie? "What did you have in mind?"

"I like Maggie." He propped a pillow behind his back.

"Maggie was your dog growing up!"

"I know. And she was a great dog. What better name is there?"

"We are *not* naming our daughter after your dog."

"Why not? It's a good name and we're not naming her Edie."

"What's wrong with Edie? It's a good, solid name. Unique but not weird. There won't be three other Edies in her class. I *love* Edie!"

He made the face again. "It's not going to be Edie."

She knew he was the father, but she was annoyed. Did he really need to have a say in this? What did he know? She was the one who'd barfed for three months solid and felt schizophrenic from hormones. This should be up to her.

The following afternoon Ethan came home with a baby name book that was thicker than a Bible. It boasted having over 50,000 names. Seeing this renewed her faith that they could come up with something. Certainly they had to be able to find something they could agree on with over 50,000 names to choose from. However, they were only into the As when they realized the book really should be called *A Couple Hundred Decent Names—48,801 Ridiculous Made-Up Ones.*

Somehow the author had gotten away with calling most of her ludicrous ideas names. Sifting through all of them gave Cate a headache.

The bed was becoming their unofficial spot for name discussions. Before they went to sleep they conferred about what they would call their daughter. Cate held the book and read names out loud. "If the origin is American," she said. "I think it really means that it's just made up. Conlee? Maitlin? Landy?"

"Those are names?" Ethan asked. "Let me see that." He took the book. "Larby? That's a name? It sounds like fishing bait." He laughed. "I'm not using night crawlers today. I'm using Larby."

She chuckled. "I know. It's like Barbie and Darby weren't original enough so they made up Larby."

She watched wrinkles spread over his forehead. "Jaylo is in here. Jay-lo. Who would name their kid Jaylo? It's a nickname. And it belongs to Jennifer Lopez. They may as well put the E Master in here, too. My friends have called me that, so I guess that means it qualifies as a name."

She laughed. "I think the author needed to fill up pages so she could beat out the competition of other baby-name books."

Annoyed, he looked at the cover. "I should've gotten the pocket-sized one."

Their plan was to go through one letter of the alphabet every night and begin a list of the names they liked.

Shortly after their quest for the perfect name began Cate realized there was a way to torture Denise. She figured this out the day they met at the fabric store to pick out material for Cate's dress. Denise showed up equipped with her briefcase and a swatch of yellow fabric the size of a Wheat Thin. The binder had doubled in size and each time Cate looked at it she felt a sense of dread.

They were on a quest for material to match Janet's dress. Ever since the Christmas confrontation Denise had gone out of her way to accommodate Cate. She was offering to pay for Cate's dress and buy shoes to match. In a strange way this only annoyed Cate even more. She felt used. Denise was only being nice because she was scared. She was afraid if she pissed Cate off she'd have no one to throw her a shower and plan her bachelorette party.

They walked through mazes of fabric bolts, looking for the same shade of pale yellow. They were in the silks when Denise brought up the baby. For a moment Cate made the foolish assumption that Denise was actually interested in something other than her wedding.

"So have you picked out a name?" she asked. It was a harmless question and one that Cate had been asked at least once a day since she'd announced her pregnancy.

Before Cate had a chance to answer Denise spoke, "I decided that if I have a daughter I'm naming her Abigail. I love that name, and always thought it would be so cute for a girl. Abigail Rose. Abbey for short."

"That's pretty," Cate said.

Women had been picking out names for their children since dolls had been invented, and Denise was no exception.

"What do you think of this?" Denise held up a bolt of yellow silk.

Cate ran her fingers over the cloth. With lining underneath it wouldn't be as clingy as Janet's. "It matches Janet's pretty well. I think it'll work."

They bought three yards.

It wasn't until they were at the tailor's when Cate realized what Denise was up to. The seamstress, Kat, was a Russian woman with tinted glasses and a perm. She had three children of her own, and shared the details of each one of their births as she took Cate's measurements.

As Kat wrapped measuring tape around Cate's belly she asked if Cate had names picked out. Denise's head shot from the inside of her binder as she perked up and listened to Cate's reply.

"We like Julia. Grace. Madeline."

"Those are all beautiful. Good, classic names."

She watched Denise's shoulders soften, as if she were relieved. "If I have a daughter, I'm naming her Abigail," she chimed in.

This time the remark didn't sound like the fantasy of a woman who someday wanted children. It felt as though Denise were driving a stake into the name with her clan sign over the top of it. Denise was claiming the name. She was scared to death that Cate and Ethan were going to select the name she'd chosen for her hypothetical child. Fear showed in her eyes like a bad sunburn.

As Cate stood in her underwear she couldn't help but think about the torment she could inflict on Denise. Denise was going to lose sleep until Cate and Ethan's daughter was born and any name but Abigail was printed on the birth certificate. She knew it was evil and probably immature but she fantasized about conversations with Denise.

"So, Denise, we decided on a name."

"Really?" she'd say, dropping whatever she was doing. Sweat would drip from her forehead and she may even shake a little. "What is it?" she'd ask cautiously.

"Actually, I hope you're not mad. But we really like Abigail. We've made up our minds. It's Abigail. Abigail Rose actually. And by the way I'm scheduling a C-section for the day of your wedding!"

Or perhaps she should tell Denise they were seriously considering Abigail even if they weren't. They could play this one up for several months, torturing her. They'd keep the real name a secret until the day the baby was born of course. Denise would have a full head of gray hair for her wedding. However, the only person Cate would really be torturing was herself. Denise already thought the pregnancy was Cate's plan to ruin her wedding. If they chose her beloved Abigail she'd make Cate's life a living hell. Furthermore, Cate really didn't have the energy to get caught up in Denise's childish games.

Over the next few days Cate realized that Denise wasn't the only one who was worried. Emily had asked what names they were considering with the same tone of caution in her voice. She sounded afraid of Cate's answer. As soon as Cate was finished going through the list Emily had informed her that their next daughter would be Brianna.

Leslie called the same evening and declared the right to Olivia. "That's going to be my daughter's name," she said before Cate had a chance to share the names they were considering. "What are you guys thinking of?"

"We like Julia—"

"She'll be a Julie," Leslie interrupted. "Do you want her to be called Julie? Because that's what people will end up calling her."

If Cate wasn't mistaken she recalled a conversation before her miscarriage in which Leslie had shared that Julia was on her list of potential baby names. She was trying to talk Cate out of using it. If she didn't already have empathy for Leslie's situation, she would've been annoyed. Couldn't people be creative? There were 50,000 names to choose from, and they were scared to death that Cate was going to pick the only one they liked.

Now she understood why Beth had chosen not to share the name of her child until he'd been born. Beth had avoided hearing everyone's claims and opinions. People seemed to mind their own business when everything was kept a secret.

The name came to them several days later. It was so simple, and they wondered how they had made it to the Ts in the baby-name book without thinking of it earlier. Annie. It was going to be Annie Constance.

Friends and Enemies Everywhere

Planning a shower always sounded easy. Send out some invitations and serve quiche and iced tea. Not much to it, right? Wrong. Shortly after Cate sent out the invitations she felt an old feeling of duty from her bridesmaid days. She had to buy favors and decorations, plan a menu, and get prizes for the games. Since Janet was as useful as a bum after three bottles of whiskey Cate made most of the arrangements by herself.

The hardest part was getting a head count. The few friends and relatives that Denise had invited were terrible about RSVPing. For a while Cate wondered if people had received her invitations because, except for Rita and her mother, no one replied.

So as she headed to the mall for favors she had no idea how many she needed to purchase. She'd dragged Ethan along with her. He was in dire need of new jeans and she needed his help carrying packages, too.

The beauty of North County shopping center was that they had parking places reserved for expectant mothers. These spots were near the main entrance and right next to a row of handicapped spots. It wasn't often that she actually scored one of the coveted expectant mother spots, but today she was feeling lucky. As she drove toward the aisle she thought she saw an empty one.

Ever since she'd come out of the pregnancy sickness she'd been easy to please. Finding a good parking place at the mall, hearing a song she liked on the radio, a soft pair of socks were all things that could make her day. She felt joyous when she realized she'd have a good parking place.

She was within feet when a Jeep Cherokee rounded the corner and darted into her spot.

"Shoot," Ethan said. "She beat you to it."

In all fairness Cate was still a little ways off and this woman probably hadn't even seen her coming when she'd come around the corner. She felt a little disappointed, but it wasn't a big deal. She was about to drive away when she noticed that the person emerging from the car was not pregnant.

Ethan shook his head. "What a dickhead."

A man had stolen her spot. A young lad with a baseball cap, and a heavy layer of arrogance. His legs looked skinny in his baggy jeans and he couldn't have been much older than twenty-four.

Cate revved the engine. She wasn't sure what bothered her more—the fact that he'd stolen a parking place from a pregnant woman, or the fact that he seemed proud of it. He didn't even appear worried as he slammed his door and set the alarm. She watched him, and for a moment actually thought she felt progesterone-laced smoke coming from her ears. She was fuming. What kind of a man steals parking places from pregnant women? She had every intention of finding out.

When she started driving toward him Ethan suggested she look down the next aisle. "I thought I saw someone leaving over there," he said with fear in his eyes.

First Comes Love   219

She drove toward Mr. Flossy Legs and rolled down her window. The parking space thief was straightening his baseball cap as she pulled up next to him. "Excuse me," she said. Ethan groaned and sunk down into his seat.

The crook looked at her through sunglasses. He had the look of a man who had no idea what was about to hit him. "Do you realize where you just parked?" she asked.

"Ummm . . . oh . . . uhhh . . ." Then he mumbled something that was indecipherable.

"What kind of man are you?" she asked. "Stealing parking places from pregnant women. Is something wrong with you? Are you crippled?"

For a moment he looked like he wanted to run. "Uh . . . no."

"Do you have a penis? You must not. Because a *real* man would never act like such a slob. I can't imagine that you must have one. And you know what? I feel sorry for your mother," Cate said. "She must be ashamed that she raised such a selfish, lazy thief. You should be embarrassed. What would your mother say if she knew you were stealing parking places from pregnant women? Huh? What would she say?"

"I'll move. I'll move my car. All you had to do was ask. You can have my spot, okay?"

"Good!" she snapped.

He climbed into his Jeep as if he were in a hurry. His tires spun over the concrete as he threw the car in reverse and fled from the spot. "Well, here we are," Cate said as she pulled into the space.

Her thick middle had become a full-blown potbelly. As she moved around the mall, looking for shower favors, she realized that she needed to tack on a half hour to every single errand she ran. She made friends everywhere she went.

"When are you due?" the salesman asked as he yanked a Velcro sneaker onto her bloated foot.

"June." She was in the shoe department of Nordstrom. Ethan was in the men's department trying on jeans.

"I knew it was safe to ask when I saw your belly. Once got myself in trouble though." He glanced at her stomach. "But you're pretty obvious."

"There is no hiding it now."

"How do those feel?" he asked as Cate walked around.

"Good. I'll take them." She liked the idea of Velcro. No more bending over to tie shoelaces.

"Have you had an easy pregnancy?"

"I was miserable the first three months but it's getting better now." She slipped the shoes off.

"Yeah, my wife threw up quite a bit in the beginning. Then toward the end she swelled up like a corpse. I literally thought her feet and ankles were going to pop."

Great, she thought. So this is what she had to look forward to. After being poisoned by hormones until she thought she would wither away she'd bloat up like Elvis in his prescription-drug-use days.

"It's so worth it though," he said, a twinkle in his eye. "Once you have that baby you won't remember any of this. My wife hated being pregnant and a week after we got home from the hospital she was like, 'I'm ready to do it again.'" He got a faraway look in his eyes, one that suggested he'd momentarily been taken to a place of fond memories. Lately, she'd seen the same look in a lot of people.

"There is really nothing like it." He put her shoes in the box. "Oh, and my kids were both breast-fed. They're six and four now and they've never once had to take antibiotics. You plan to breast-feed?"

"That's the goal. It doesn't always work out that way though."

"You have to go buy lanolin before you give birth. It really helped my wife. She'd rub that on and it would relieve some of the pain.

They gave it to her in the hospital, but just in case they don't you should definitely pack some to take with you."

Ethan walked up, carrying a shopping bag. His hunt for jeans must've been successful. "Did you hear that, honey?" she said. "We need to get some lanolin before we go to the hospital."

It was strange that she was talking to a shoe salesman about rubbing ointment on sore nipples. But this is the way things had become lately. Something about the bulge in her belly made everyone want to talk to her. Men, women, children.

That morning she'd gone to the grocery store for vitamin C. She'd felt a strange pain above her left eye and wanted to prevent the early stages of a cold.

En route from the car to the entrance of Vons she listened as a homeless man collecting coins in a tin can called out to each person that passed by.

"Can you spare a man some change? I gotta get on the bus to Fresno." She listened to this at least five times before he shouted, "Hey yo! Expecting mother! You! Expectant mother, you got compassion in yo heart. Bringing a baby into da world. Can you spare a man some change?"

How could she say no? With the whole parking lot of Vons watching her she'd be a heartless mother. She threw a buck into his can.

"When you due?" he asked, all smiles.

"June twenty-sixth."

"June twenty-sixth! That's my birfday! Maybe you should name the baby after me!"

She laughed. "Okay, what's your name?"

"Seymour."

She chatted with him for a few more minutes about what it felt like to be a Cancer before being cornered by a woman with gold teeth and the worst hair extensions Cate had ever seen in her life. She asked Cate to sign a petition to get a proposition on the ballot that would preserve land north of Escondido. She signed the petition and was just about to make a clean getaway when the woman began sharing every detail of her child's birth with Cate.

When she'd returned Ethan had been annoyed that it had taken her so long to get one single item. However, after spending a couple of hours in public with her he realized why.

"It seems like you're running for mayor," he said as they left Nordstrom and headed to See's Candies. "You're the most popular person at the mall."

As they rode the escalator she felt a dull ache in her eye again, as if it were bruised. "It feels like I got punched in the eye," she said. "I hope I don't have pink eye or something."

"I'm sure it's just your sinuses or a cold. Did you take the vitamin C?"

She nodded.

The woman behind the counter at See's took one look at Cate's belly. "When are you due?" This was always how it began. One simple question, and she knew it was only seconds before the following questions came.

"What are you having?"

"Do you have a name picked out?"

"Are you scared?"

Sure enough the conversation proceeded as Cate predicted and she knew what would come next. She would hear the tale of this woman's labor and delivery.

"My son was almost born in the back of my boyfriend's car," she said. "My water broke and my boyfriend said you just hang in there and relax. Don't stress. You just breathe and relax. And lemme tell ya, I just relaxed and then I got the epidural and that baby came right out. Ten-pound, three-ounce boy, and two pushes and that baby was out. Are you gonna get the epidural?"

"Yes." Cate had been asked this a million times also. She knew that there were a handful of women who turned down modern medicine and opted to face labor and delivery with a lot of courage and some breathing techniques. Personally, she had no idea why anyone would turn down a safe option to alleviate pain in the face of torture.

She would be on the phone with the anesthesiologist en route to the hospital. She wanted him and his five-inch needle waiting for her upon check in. No one had warned her about pregnancy sickness. However, she'd had a fair warning about childbirth. She'd seen *Gone With the Wind*. And nearly every person with a vagina over the age of forty had warned her. There was no way in hell she was making a conscious and sane choice to suffer through childbirth. This was not the 1800s. They had modern conveniences now and she planned to take full advantage.

Apparently she and the candy salesgirl were on the same page with this one. "Anyone who turns down the epidural should have their head examined," she said as she packed two dozen butterscotch squares for them. "My second one, there wasn't time for the epidural and lemme tell you, just trust me on this one, you don't wanna do that."

Cate paid for the candy and figured if she'd bought too many for favors Ethan and she could eat them.

She'd remembered Sarah warning her about all the attention. "Everyone wants to talk to you and touch your belly," she'd said. "And they'll talk to you forever. It's so annoying."

Cate didn't find it annoying. She kind of liked it. The baby was on her mind twenty-four-seven. She enjoyed talking about Annie, and she couldn't imagine how lonely it would be if no one was interested in her pregnancy. She was able to relate to people she wouldn't normally share a common ground with.

After See's they headed over to Bath & Body Works and bought candles for shower game prizes. They were leaving the store when Cate's phone choked.

> Hi C8. Just so you know. I don't want any of those dumb shower games at my shower. I h8 the games. And Keith's mom is coming. She's bringing Keith's Aunt Rhonda too. Luv, D

Oh, she was getting games. Everyone had games at their shower and every bride had suffered a little humiliation. Just for that she was getting every bad shower game Cate could think of, and she knew them all. She'd have Denise wrapped in a bridal gown made of toilet paper and a crown made of paper plates.

Wait, on second thought, great! Wonderful if she didn't want games. It meant less work for Cate. Seeing how she wasn't getting any help from Janet it was good news. It was perfectly fine with Cate if Denise wanted a dull afternoon with no icebreakers. Everyone could sit around eating finger foods and struggling for conversation with a bunch of strangers who all shared one thing in common—total boredom from watching Denise open boxes with plates and silverware inside.

She looked inside her Bath & Body Works bag. If Denise wanted to be that way, she'd keep the candles for herself.

·32·

Just You Wait

Cate woke during the night with a pain unlike anything she'd felt in her life. It was in her eye. It was every type of pain possible—stabbing, stinging, pinching, pounding, throbbing. Looking at the fuzzy green glow on her alarm clock was like throwing water on the Wicked Witch of the West. She thought it would kill her.

She'd underestimated the bruised feeling she'd felt earlier. In a moment of fear she realized that this wasn't a cold. Not only did the glow of her alarm clock hurt her eye, but she felt as though she could hardly see from her painful eye. She covered her good eye and looked at a green blob. She couldn't even make out numbers in the clock.

All she could think of was toxoplasmosis. What if her mother had been right? She'd read the brochure her mother had dropped off. The disease was no joke. Not only did it cause blindness but brain damage, too. She began to cry. She couldn't help it.

Ethan woke up, startled. "What's wrong?"

"My eye, it's so bad," she said between tears.

"I'm calling my parents," he said. "They'll know someone. I'm sure they know an ophthalmologist."

"It's two in the morning," she said. "Even if they do know someone, what will they do right now?"

"We can have someone paged. They can at least talk to us."

He stood up and went to the kitchen in his underwear. It seemed like an eternity before he came back. When he finally returned, the pain hurt so bad she couldn't move her head. Each time she changed positions or rolled over the stabbing became worse. It not only felt like an ice pick was being driven into her eye but a brick was resting on the left half of her face as well. He was talking to someone and she could tell it wasn't his parents by the tone of his voice.

He pulled the phone away from his ear for a moment. "Cate, when did this start?"

"I noticed the pain a couple days ago. I just thought I was getting a cold. I thought it was my sinuses."

"A couple days ago," he said back into the receiver. "Uh-huh." Pause. "Yes, she can't look at any light whatsoever." Pause. "Uh-huh. Yeah, okay. Sure. We'll see you then. Thank you. Uh-huh. Good-bye.

"That was Dr. Morgan. He's an ophthalmologist. He wants to see you first thing in the morning."

"What did he say?" Cate asked.

"He said to put ice on it and take Tylenol."

"I've taken four."

"And it hasn't helped?"

"It hasn't done a single thing."

He flipped on the light and she winced. "Sorry." He shut it back off. "I'm going to make you an ice pack."

She never went back to sleep. Not only was the pain unlike anything she'd ever experienced but she was scared to death. This was her eye—her vision. But the most frightening thing was that she was pregnant. All she wanted was a healthy baby. She thought of every single time she'd complained about morning sickness and felt guilty. This was the most important time of her life. She was responsible for another life. Ethan didn't get much sleep either. They were supposed to meet the doctor at seven.

Upon stepping into sunlight she realized that sunglasses weren't enough. The throbbing assaulted her as light filtered through the edge of her glasses. She crashed into the front door when she turned to head back inside, and hit her forehead hard against the doorjamb.

"Here," Ethan said, taking her by the arm. "Wear my sunglasses." He yanked hers off and quickly replaced them with his. They were large and she felt like they made Jackie O's look like goggles.

"Light is still coming through," she said, covering her face with her hands.

"Let's get you a baseball cap." He ran to the bedroom and returned with his Padres cap and a black sash she'd used a couple times as a belt. They wrapped the sash around the glasses like a blindfold, and then he tucked the hat onto her head. It was the only way to block out the sun.

"Are the neighbors watching?" she asked as he led her across the porch and down the steps. If they thought she was strange when she'd barfed on the porch, what must they think of her now with Ethan leading her around like she was Helen Keller?

"Who gives a shit," he mumbled.

"This must look so crazy," she said.

"I don't care." He helped her into the car.

The pain on the way to the doctor's office seemed to reach a new level. The light had set off something fierce. The ice pick was back, and the throbbing seemed stronger than ever. All she could do was shut her eyes and lean back. She felt like crying again.

"Will you grab my purse," she said as he helped her from the car. "I'm going to need my insurance card."

Even though she couldn't see a thing she could tell everyone was watching her in the waiting room. The doctor shared his practice with two ophthalmologists, so she figured it had to be crowded. A silence fell over the room when Cate had entered. She could only imagine what they must look like to all the strangers in the waiting room. Cate still in her bedroom slippers and a blindfold, and Ethan carrying her purse. The nurse must've sensed the awkwardness because she offered Cate a private room to lie down in. Cate lay down on a cot and Ethan sat next to her rubbing her back. The lights were off and there were no windows, so Cate removed the blindfold. A small amount of light came through the doorway so she left the sunglasses on.

The examination was hell. The only thing that helped her through it was the drops they applied to her eye to relieve some of the pain. "You have iritis," the doctor told her. He explained that it was a virus that attacked the iris, making it extremely sensitive to light. According to him, scientists had yet to discover a cause. It wasn't caused by germs or infection—that much they knew. The good news was that the baby was fine. She didn't have toxoplasmosis and the virus was not related to her pregnancy. Furthermore, with the doctor's strict treatment she should begin feeling better by the end of the day.

The bad news was that it might take weeks before she could see clearly again and there was a slim chance her vision might be slightly damaged. The treatment was specific and aggressive. Ethan had to apply one kind of drops to her eye every fifteen minutes for the rest of the day. They also had to apply another kind of drops every half hour and still another twice a day.

"I'd like to see you tomorrow," Dr. Morgan said.

"It's Saturday." Cate felt something similar to a burn when she remembered Denise's bachelorette party. However, she quickly dismissed it from her mind. She was more concerned that the doctor wanted to see her on a Saturday. "Are you open on Saturdays?" she asked.

He shook his head. "No. But I still want to see you. My grandchildren are going to be in town but let's meet here at nine-thirty. Does that sound good?"

You knew it was bad when the doctor offered to meet on his day off.

The nurse came in with some of the best news Cate had ever heard in her life. "We called your obstetrician. He said it's okay for you to take Vicodin."

"That's good," Cate said. "Because I am in the worst pain I have ever been in in my life."

The nurse looked at her belly. "You might change your mind about that."

When Cate had her wisdom teeth removed she'd turned down pain medication. Prescription drugs had never appealed to her. They scared her. She'd rather take the pain than feel out of control or overly tired. However, if she hadn't been pregnant and they'd offered her heroin to ease the pain, she would've seriously considered it.

She looked at the doctor. "So you don't think I have toxoplasmosis?"

He shook his head. "Toxoplasmosis affects a different part of the eye. I think it's highly unlikely that you have it. I don't see any signs of it."

She wanted to believe him, but it was strange that she'd developed some random eye virus while pregnant. They had to be related.

"My purse," Cate said as Ethan led her to the car.

"I've got it. Don't worry. And by the way, you really need a new one. This thing is a rag. It took me ten minutes to find the insurance card. It's such a mess and it's falling apart."

On the way to the pharmacy Cate thought of Denise's shower. "How on earth am I going to throw Denise's shower tomorrow?" Cate asked.

Ethan shook his head. "You're not."

"I have to."

"You can't. I won't let you. My mom will do it. Your mom will do it."

"Ethan, she is going to shit a pineapple if I'm not there."

"Too bad."

She waited in the car while Ethan went inside for her prescription. While she waited she called her obstetrician's office just to make sure it was okay to take painkillers while pregnant. She still couldn't believe it and she wasn't going to feel comfortable until she heard it straight from Dr. Hatcher's mouth. After she got the green light from the doctor she called Denise. Getting out of the shower wasn't going to be easy so she figured she better lay the foundation now. Explaining the situation wasn't horrible. Talking to Denise's voice mail made things easy.

Cate phoned her mother. "It's toxoplasmosis. I told you to get rid of that cat."

"Mom, it's iritis. It has nothing to do with Grease."

"I would get a second opinion."

Cate turned the subject to Denise's shower. Due to the size of Cate's home, Connie had volunteered her house for the shower. "Don't worry," Connie said. "Rita and I will handle everything."

Cate felt bad. Her mother didn't really know Denise that well and now she'd been sucked in to hosting her bridal shower.

Ethan returned from the store with her prescription, two gallons of ice cream, and a half pound of salami and provolone. He stayed in bed with her all day, diligently putting the drops in her eyes every fifteen minutes. They ate ice cream from the carton and pigged out on salami and provolone.

Her phone choked and Ethan reached for it. Even if she could read, she wasn't in the mood for Denise.

" 'Cate.' " He read out loud. "She spelled your name wrong . . ."

Instantly, she knew it wasn't Denise. It was that Kimball woman—another one Cate wasn't in the mood for.

" 'We talked to your husband about catering another event for us, but he said you were going to have a baby. Is that still true?' "

"What? Does she think the pregnancy just went away on its own? Tell her it's true and no, we can't cater anything for her."

Ethan wrote back, complaining that he could never understand why people liked to text message.

She noticed a difference in her eye within a few hours. The Vicodin kicked in and the drops eased some of her flaring sensitivity to light. They drew the curtains and she watched television with her sunglasses on.

It had been a long time since they'd lounged around in bed all day and it felt nice to snuggle up next to him even if she was in her sunglasses. He kissed her on the forehead.

"You're a warrior," he said.

"The funny thing is—maybe I'm being naïve. But I feel like after the morning sickness and last night with my eye I'm ready to face childbirth. I'm not afraid. It can't be worse." However, on the other hand, she couldn't imagine anything worse than the pain she'd felt in her eye. If the pain had been any worse, she might have passed out. With that in mind, she was terrified.

·33·

Expertise from the Naïve

The following morning she reached for Ethan's sunglasses at the first crack of light, but most of the pain had subsided. A white fog still obstructed her vision, though. She put her hand over her right eye to test the vision in the bad eye. Ethan watched her. "Can you see?" he asked.

"I can tell it's you, but I can't see any details on your face. I can only make out shapes." She pulled her hand away from her right eye.

"The doctor said it could take several weeks for your vision to return."

"I should go to Denise's shower," she said.

"You sure?"

"Yeah, I'm sure. I'll have to wear my sunglasses the whole time, but I'll feel guilty if I don't go."

"She'll get over it."

Ethan not only had to play chauffeur but he'd become her nurse as well. He had to put drops in her eye every hour, and she'd need his help setting up. Having bad vision made it difficult for Cate to do almost anything without his help.

While she applied her makeup she squeezed her eye shut. She didn't want to know what it looked like. Ethan's description of her eye had been mild. He'd said it was bright red and her pupil was so big that it covered most of the blue in her iris. The way it had felt made her imagine something from a horror movie.

An hour before they were supposed to leave for Dr. Morgan's she remembered that she still didn't have a gift. They stopped at the mall on the way. Maybe it was her imagination but Cate felt people staring at her as they walked to the bridal registry kiosk. She was tempted to ask them if they wanted autographs.

In Macy's they printed Denise's registry. She definitely hadn't under-registered. There were plenty of things to choose from, and most were over $200. The few gifts that were in the shower-friendly fifty to a hundred range had been snatched up like nuts in a squirrel farm famine. The remaining gifts included fine china, a number of overpriced vases and platters, crystal glasses, and silver—not *silverware*, but silver. Silver was stuff Cate's grandmother pulled out on several occasions and came with a $250 price tag.

Who did Denise think was going to buy her this stuff? Cate wasn't going to be the one to break it to her, but all the expensive stuff she'd registered for was going to end up collecting dust and taking up space in her attic. Unless she planned on feeding Keith Junior and Ashlyn on fine china and hand washing their utensils every night, she'd never use it.

"Let's just get her a gift certificate," Cate said. "There isn't one thing on here for under two hundred dollars. Not one."

"Let me see that."

Ethan inspected the registry. "What the hell has she done?" He pointed to something. "Just get her that."

"That platter is two hundred and seventy dollars."

He shrugged. "Business has been going well. Just get it."

They had the platter gift wrapped, then headed for Dr. Morgan's. This time she could see him. He had a head full of white hair and was a tall man with a kind grandfatherly face and narrow glasses.

"Much better," he said as he looked into her eye with his long microscope. "I still see quite a few white blood cells, but it's getting better already."

He reduced the fifteen-minute drops to every two hours. The every-two-hour drops were now once a day and the twice-a-day drops could be eliminated. He wanted to see her again the following week. She thanked him profusely for seeing her on his day off. After the exam they went straight to her mother's house.

Since Ethan had played nurse to Cate the day before, he hadn't been able to prepare the food for Denise's shower. Rita and Connie had improvised and picked up several quiches and a salad nicoise from a French bakery.

The first thing Cate did was close a few curtains. Ethan was applying drops to her eye when Denise breezed in. She wore a brand-new suit with nylons and pumps that looked as if they were meant for a woman thirty years her senior. She didn't say a word about Cate's eye, or even acknowledge the fact that she'd managed to make it considering the circumstances. She looked around Connie's house. It was hard to tell what she was thinking. There was no praise for the decorations Rita had put up or the vases full of roses that Connie had arranged.

Instead she pulled out her binder and asked Cate's opinion on a veil she was considering. As Denise's guests began to arrive Cate greeted them. A little under a dozen of Denise's colleagues and acquaintances were expected to show. She didn't feel like explaining her eye over and over again, and let them draw their own conclusions.

She couldn't care less if Denise's friends thought she was pregnant and on drugs, or pregnant and suffering from delusions that she was actually a movie star, or pregnant with a black eye. Maybe she should drink nonalcoholic beer in a glass and really let them wonder.

Scary's mother had flown in from Arkansas for the event. Cate had been curious about the woman who'd raised Keith. Morbidly obese, she had just returned from a cruise up the coast of Mexico, and she had the sunburn to prove it.

Denise lit up when she noticed her. "Patty! I love your hair!" They hugged as if they were long-lost sisters.

"Isn't it cool? Everyone on the cruise had braids," she said. "Everyone is wearing braids in Mexico."

Patty wasn't talking about French braids or cornrows. In fact, looking at her hairdo Cate wasn't sure what kind of braids she was talking about. Braids that stuck out like worms? If her hairdo was the "in thing" in Mexico the entire country needed a makeover. To begin with, she had a mullet. On either side of her temples, she'd taken two skinny pieces of hair as long and thin as string beans and braided them. To pull her look together she'd managed to stick a few plastic beads on her braids.

Denise shoved a camera in Cate's hands. "Here. Will you take a picture of us?" They put their arms around each other and posed with Patty's five chins for the photo.

"Oh, Patty. Let me introduce you to Cate."

Cate reached over to shake her hand and Patty gave Cate her purse. The handle was loose and Cate had to hold the bag from the bottom.

"So you're the one who made the invitations?" Patty asked.

Cate smiled, remembering how much time she'd spent picking them out and then how cute they'd turned out. "Yes!"

"Your directions were *terrible*! I got *so* lost! I don't know what I would've done if I hadn't had Aunt Rhonda with me."

"Oh. I'm sorry. If you'd RSVPed, I could've given you better directions." Cate would've never responded this way prior to being pregnant. Pre-pregnancy she would've immediately begun worrying that everyone else was lost and sent Ethan out to hang signs.

Patty ignored Cate and continued ranting. "I would've never found it if I didn't have Aunt Rhonda with me. She saw *one* balloon. I would've *never* seen it. *Never.*" She shook her head. "I'll take a Corona," she said.

Cate looked at Ethan. "Do we even have beer?" Iced tea and mimosas were on the menu.

He shook his head. "Sorry, we don't have beer." Thank God someone had spoken because Cate thought if she was forced to answer she might have to tell Scary's mom to take her braids back to a Princess cruise liner headed for Baghdad.

Did they have beer? This wasn't an all-inclusive trip and she wasn't freaking Julie from *The Love Boat.* She could feel the pregnancy hormone levels reaching their limits and if she didn't move away from the Mother of Scary she was going to snap.

"You don't?" Her sigh was long and dramatic.

"I have a Budweiser in my garage," Connie offered. "It's warm though."

She thought for a moment. "What else do you have?"

"We have champagne and tea. Coffee. Iced water."

"Do you have anything harder than that? I wanted to show Denise how to do a Mexican Hat Dance. It's a shot I learned on the cruise. God, it's hot in here. Is anyone else hot?"

It was then that she stepped aside and revealed Aunt Rhonda, a smaller version of Patty with severely crooked teeth and more braids. Cate hadn't even known she was standing there. Aunt Rhonda held the gift. Cate could tell it was a bunch of stuff that Denise hadn't registered for by the flimsy oven mitt that had been tied to the bag with the kind of stringy ribbon that was supposed to curl when scissors were scraped down its edges. The ribbon looked as limp as a dead worm.

Her suspicions about the gift were confirmed when Rita reached in to take it and Aunt Rhonda said, "Do you think that an oven mitt from the Dollar Domain is safe to give to someone?"

Rita looked puzzled.

"I tried to tell Patty we should go to Wal-Mart but she said the dollar store is just as good."

Rita looked at the mitt. "Um, it's, well, I don't know. Are you afraid it will burn her hand?"

"Yeah, and all the potholders we got, too."

"Maybe you should warn her. Just to be safe," Rita said politely before she carried the gift into the living room.

"Cate!" Denise called. "I need you to take a picture of Miranda and me."

Cate quickly went into the other room and took a picture of Denise with each of her three real estate friends that had attended the shower.

Far be it from Denise to ask someone to take a picture of Cate and her. After all, why would Denise want a picture with the hired help? However, avoiding a photo was fine with Cate. She didn't really want her picture taken in Ethan's sunglasses and a sapphire maternity dress that looked like a tent. They didn't need to capture the moment on film.

However, her feelings were a little stung that Denise hadn't once said please or thank you or even lifted a finger. The least she could've done was brought Connie a hostess gift—a small plant or flowers in gratitude for offering her house to a bunch of Denise's friends that Connie didn't even know.

As Cate watched Denise slap on her phony, bridezilla, wedding-obsessed smile, Cate felt on fire with annoyance. Every nerve in her body burned with irritation. Who did she think she was? Fine, if she wanted to treat Cate like crap. But Connie? No one screwed with her mother. That was her mother. The woman who had made sure she got a peanut-butter-and-jelly sandwich with grape jelly in her lunch box for nearly a decade. Nobody else in the world would've cared what kind of jelly she'd had. She'd come to Cate when she'd had nightmares and held her when she was sick. She'd picked out prom dresses with her and helped her with homework. Suddenly, Cate felt like crying. She set Denise's camera on the coffee table and slipped from the room.

"Cate, wait!" Denise called. "I need you to get a picture of me with Aunt Rhonda!"

Cate pretended like she didn't hear. She'd had it. It was then and there that she decided she was finished with Denise. She didn't give a hoot if she married an ax murderer and his two bad seeds. She deserved them. She wasn't lifting another finger for the wedding and she sure as hell wasn't going to her bachelorette party. She went up to her old bedroom and closed the door behind her. She began to weep.

It was the pregnancy hormones again. She wasn't the type of person who cried easily, and she hated the fact that she felt so out of control. She'd been up there for a few minutes when her mother walked in.

"Are you crying again?" she asked.

"I just had to get away from Denise and those idiots she's about to be related to."

Connie made a face. "That woman is awful." She shuddered. "She just asked me for a clean plate for her cheese and crackers. She said the other one had a spot on it—as if this is a restaurant."

Cate cried even harder. "Mom, I'm so sorry. I feel so bad that you had to do all this and that they're treating you this way. Has Denise even thanked you?"

Connie shook her head, then smiled. "No. But she has lettuce in her teeth and I didn't tell her."

Cate's mouth dropped. "You didn't!" Then she laughed. It was so un-Connie. Her little Catholic mother who prayed to the saints on a regular basis had sinned?

"Just ignore her, Cate. Denise has the nice car and the ironed suit, but deep in there she's just a bad-mannered little twit who doesn't know any better."

"But I just can't stand to see them being rude to you. You don't even have anything to do with this."

"I'm fine." Then she leaned in and sniffed her. "You smell like the cat."

Cate sat up. "Mom!" Any feelings of sympathy toward her mother had just been squashed.

"Well, you do."

"Are you serious? Should I change clothes? I don't have any clothes here. Now I feel self-conscious. I can't go back down there."

"I guess it's not *that* bad."

"Obviously, it's bad if you had to say something. Otherwise, you wouldn't have said anything." Cate had quit crying and was now sniffing every square inch of her sleeves. "All I can smell is fabric softener."

"I'm just trying to tell you that the cat should go outdoors."

They were interrupted by the sound of Denise's voice. "Cate! The doorbell's ringing!"

Couldn't she just answer the damn door? Was Cate her butler now, too? Cate returned to the party with damp eyes and a complex that she smelled like Grease's litter box.

Janet was the last person to the shower, which shouldn't have come as a surprise. "I'm *so* hungover!" she said as soon as she noticed Cate. "I went to this new club, Firewalk, downtown last night and I am absolutely dying. The sight of food or alcohol is going to make me puke. But I'll help. What would you like me to do?"

"Just make yourself comfortable, Janet," Cate said. Janet didn't hesitate to plop her skinny self onto the most comfortable chair in the living room.

"Did you know your sunglasses are still on?"

Cate ignored her and went back to the kitchen. She passed Ethan on the way. "You doing all right?" he asked.

"I'm fine."

He looked at his watch. "It's time for your drops."

They snuck off to the bathroom and Cate held her eye open while Ethan applied the drops. "How 'bout Scary's mom?" he whispered.

"She's a nightmare. She wanted to teach Denise how to do some shot at her shower?"

"Sure does explain a lot. Doesn't it?"

Cate nodded. When she returned to the party Connie and Rita had begun serving lunch. Cate could feel a few of Denise's friends eyeing her. When she looked at them they quickly looked away. She found an empty space on the couch away from Scary's mom and was just taking a bite of pasta salad when Janet slid in next to her.

"So how is the pregnancy going? Have you been working out?"

Cate shook her head. "No. I've been sick for most of the pregnancy and it's hard to move when you're carrying all this extra weight. My back hurts. My calves are sore and I don't get much sleep at night. So, no, I haven't been exercising."

"I like Kelly Ripa's attitude about pregnancy. I want to be the same way when I have children."

"And how is that?" Cate asked.

"She loves being pregnant. She said it's the best she's ever felt in her life and she feels skinnier than ever."

"Well, everyone is different. That's for sure."

"My sister had a horrible pregnancy," a colleague of Denise's spoke up. Her name was Miranda and Cate had only spoken a few words to her since she'd arrived. "Then the delivery was so smooth. She had the easiest delivery. I think it's a trade-off."

Another friend nodded. "I've heard that same old wives' tale. A bad pregnancy means an easy delivery and vice versa. Personally, I'd rather take the bad pregnancy. It would be nice to have a good start to motherhood with an easy delivery."

Cate liked them. "At this point, I think I can handle anything," Cate said. "After puking and being bedridden for three months straight, twenty hours of pain seems like nothing. Labor and delivery is just one day."

"Are you going to get the epidural?" Janet asked.

"Sure. Why not?"

Janet shook her head. "I'm really opposed to that."

And please tell us why?

She crossed her skinny legs. "There are all kinds of side effects to those. They're really bad for you. You *can* do it naturally, you know? Getting an epidural isn't the only option to relieving pain." She paused. "I bet they don't tell you *that* in your childbirth classes. Do they?"

"Actually, we haven't taken our classes yet." *But why don't you tell me, skinny single girl who has never been pregnant or given birth. Please, inexperienced one, add your two cents. I haven't gotten enough advice, and seeing how you know nothing I really need to hear what you think.* Cate caught a glimpse of Denise's other friends, who were staring at Janet with amusement.

"Everyone is different," Cate said. "I've learned a lot during my pregnancy, but one of the biggest things is that everyone is different. Each pregnancy and delivery is really unique. What works for one person may not be right for the next."

"Well, I have a girlfriend who has given birth twice and she did it both times without drugs. And she is going to write a book on how to manage pain without injecting something into your spine. Because it *can* be done. They just encourage you to get epidurals because they need to keep the anesthesiologists busy."

Fortunately the conversation was interrupted by Connie. "It's time to open gifts."

Cate felt kind of sorry for Denise. All the importance she'd placed on her shower, and her gifts weren't even that great. She got a few things from her registry but most of it was stuff she probably didn't want and couldn't be returned.

Patty had made something she called a popcorn bowl in her ceramics class. Lopsided, it was orange with uneven brown polka dots and the glaze had already begun to crack. Cate imagined that if it could be used for anything it might be good for a dying plant Denise wanted to hide.

Aunt Rhonda had made a couple of things that were supposed to be mugs. Cate figured that cavemen probably would've found them useful. She kept her ideas to herself as she recorded Denise's gifts on a piece of paper. She could hardly see what she writing with her bad eye, but was kind of tempted to put *Aunt Rhonda and Patty—a pile of shit.*

Lucky for Denise, the mugs and bowl weren't the only gifts. Aunt Rhonda and Patty had filled a gigantic gift bag with microwave popcorn and instant coffee. Also inside the bag were tons of kitchen utensils they'd picked up from the dollar store. When Denise pulled a soup ladle from the bag the handle fell off.

"You might want to be careful of the oven mitts," Aunt Rhonda said. "Patty pulled the tags off them that said to keep away from heat."

Patty waved an arm and rolled her eyes. "They put that on kids' pajamas, too. I used to let Keith wear those flammable ones all the time. Even with a space heater right next to his crib."

"I wouldn't put the bowl or mugs in the microwave either," Aunt Rhonda said.

Maybe what she should put next to Aunt Rhonda and Patty was *explosives. Use at your own risk.*

Denise handled it gracefully. "These are gorgeous! I have to pass them around!" She gave the mugs to Janet, who didn't even bother looking and immediately turned them over to Rita.

In fact, Denise handled her crappy gifts so well that Cate wondered if she really did love the stuff they'd bought for her. She gushed over their creations as if they'd made a twenty-foot rug from imported materials on a loom. She thanked them so much that she even had Cate fooled. She was going to be ecstatic when she opened the platter.

She tore away the gift wrap and pulled the platter from inside. "Oh. My platter." She looked it over then passed it to Janet. "Thanks." She waited for Rita to hand her the next gift.

That was it? She'd acted like she owned the winning ticket over her highly flammable dollar-store loot. All the platter got was a blank stare and a quiet thanks? Why was Cate surprised?

As Cate sat there, recording Denise's gifts, a spine-tingling thought came to mind. They hadn't even discussed the bachelorette party yet.

Part Three

The Homestretch

·34·

Pricks and Needles

Hi C8, Now that the shower is over, I thought we could start discussing bachelorette ideas. I have lots. Call u later! Luv, D

The words felt like a surprise injection in the ass. Hearing from Denise was starting to feel prickly. Cate had postponed her own baby shower until the weekend before her due date so that it wouldn't interfere with any of Denise's events. Denise hadn't even thanked her for the rescheduling, yet she was more than eager to discuss anything that involved her wedding.

Cate dreaded this moment for many reasons, and was hoping by some miracle Denise would forget all about the bachelorette party. Something about pregnancy and bachelorette party just didn't go together, and she hoped Denise had enough sense to realize this. Cate couldn't imagine anything worse than sitting in a bar or strip club, eight months along, while Denise and whoever she invited to celebrate her last days of singlehood with drank themselves blind. Having

Braxton Hicks contractions while fake-tanned oily men in Speedos twirled past her sounded as appealing as sitting next to a colicky infant on a flight headed for Sydney. If this was the kind of night that Denise was dreaming of, Cate would be more than willing to do whatever she could to help. She'd send invitations. She'd buy favors. She'd even pay for cab fare, but she wasn't going along. The only thing worse that Cate could imagine was going on a cruise. Cate had avoided the topic the same way one would avoid their insurance company when they didn't receive a bill in the mail. Why remind them?

Cate decided to take the day off from Denise's wedding. She erased the message and put her phone in her purse.

She went to the medicine cabinet for her drops. Putting drops in her eyes had become routine. It had been two weeks since she'd been diagnosed with iritis and her eye felt better. However, she was still under strict orders to apply the drops three times a day to ensure that it wouldn't come back. Thank God for insurance because she felt as if she'd done nothing but visit with the doctor ever since she'd become pregnant. If she wasn't discussing a pregnancy concern with Dr. Hatcher she was having her eye examined by Dr. Morgan.

Today was no exception, as she had back-to-back appointments scheduled. Dr. Morgan and she would be discussing glasses. She went to his office first. She read about the latest Britney Spears gossip in *Us Weekly* before the nurse called her back.

"I'm so glad to see that you're feeling better," she said.

"Thanks," Cate said.

"You were the worst case I've ever seen and I've been here thirteen years."

Cate didn't know how to take that information. Being the worst of anything was never good, but in a way it validated her pain. If an experienced nurse said she was the "worst" case ever, then they had taken her seriously. All her pain and tears hadn't been in vain. "Really?"

She nodded. "I've seen some bad cases, but I've never seen someone that bad before. Not the way you were."

"Well, it hasn't been an easy pregnancy."

She looked in Cate's eye through a telescope. "With both mine I
had easy pregnancies, but it was afterward that was tough. With my
daughter, I had a C-section and my stitches got infected. Then I got
really bad baby blues. I guess everyone pays their dues—whether it's
during or after."

The doctor joined them and Cate went through a series of vision
tests before he wrote a prescription. "This should help you see better," he said.

"Will it ever be the same again?"

He shrugged. "Maybe."

"Maybe?"

"I'd say there is an eighty percent chance of full recovery."

The news didn't fall lightly. It wasn't that she'd have to wear
glasses that bothered her. It was just that she couldn't understand
how something like this could happen, and at all times during her
pregnancy. The only connection she could make to eye problems and
pregnancy was toxoplasmosis. She didn't care if her vision wasn't
twenty-twenty. She just wanted a healthy baby and she couldn't help
but worry when she'd been stricken with some bizarre eye disease
that the doctor couldn't explain.

"You're sure I don't have toxoplasmosis?"

He sighed. "The possibility is always there," he said. "I can't give
you a hundred percent guarantee. But it's *highly* unlikely. *Highly* unlikely."

Highly unlikely wasn't good enough for her. Highly unlikely
would keep her awake at night.

"If you're really worried," he said, "talk to Dr. Hatcher about it."

"I'll be seeing him in a few minutes."

She said good-bye to all her new friends at the ophthalmologist's office, then headed over to Dr. Hatcher's. He had a new receptionist. Her name was Trinelle. Probably around nineteen, Trinelle chewed gum and wore rings on almost every finger. When Cate asked if she had any information on toxoplasmosis to read while she waited Trinelle looked puzzled. "What? I don't even know what that is. Toxo what?"

"Never mind. I'll just grab the latest *People.*"

The waiting room felt exceptionally hot and the soft-hits station had been replaced. Country blasted from the speakers. There was a certain kind of country that Cate enjoyed, and it wasn't this. Listening to it made her nostalgic for Kenny G. Neither Dr. Hatcher nor Tina seemed like Alan Jackson fans, so the only one to blame for the change was Trinelle.

Cate was happy when Tina called her back. "You're going to have your RhoGAM shot today," she said.

"Excuse me?"

"Your RhoGAM shot."

RhoGAM shot? What the hell was this? No one had told her about any RhoGAM shot? She'd been well aware of the impending gestational diabetes test. She'd heard all about it from her friends, and from what she'd heard it wasn't fun. Her explanation was complicated, but basically when they'd taken blood in the beginning of her pregnancy they'd discovered that she was Rh negative. There was a chance her child could have Rh positive blood. If so, her body would view the fetus as a foreigner and begin releasing antibodies to attack it. It sounded frightening, but Tina assured her that it was fairly common and with a shot of RhoGAM everything should be fine.

"All right. It goes in the butt, so you can go ahead and lean over and lower your pants."

Cate followed the instructions, thinking how plump and pale her rear end had become since the start of her pregnancy. It seemed to take Tina a while to prepare the shot and they chatted about the up-coming Nordstrom sale while Cate waited for the injection with her butt exposed.

The shot was nearly painless and she headed off to the exam room where she pounded Dr. Hatcher with questions about toxoplas-mosis. "Shit happens," he said. "What happened to your eye could've happened at any time in your life. It just happened to happen to you while you're pregnant. If you're really worried about toxoplasmosis, I'll write you an order for blood work."

She accepted the offer.

"By the way, it's time for your gestational diabetes test, so Tina will get you set up for that."

"It's a good thing I'm not that afraid of needles anymore," Cate said.

"That's usually what happens during pregnancy. Women get over that fear."

From the doctor's office she headed straight for the lab. She wasn't exactly sure what the gestational diabetes test entailed, but she knew there was an hour-long visit to the lab and a horrible sug-ary glucose drink involved.

She signed in at the lab and waited her turn to be called back. Labs were always strange places. Everyone looked suspiciously over the brims of their magazines, wondering what everyone else was do-ing there. Then there were the people who worked at them. Collect-ing poop samples and drawing blood didn't sound like the most appealing career, and Cate wondered how many people were lined up to take the job. She swiped up a *People* she'd been reading at Dr. Hatcher's. Rarely did she have the luxury of finishing an article and she picked up right where she'd left off.

Several minutes later the receptionist called her name from the sign-in then handed her a cold fruit punch type drink. "Go ahead and drink that and they'll draw blood in an hour."

She'd heard horror stories about the glucose drink. How sugary and nauseating it was. Cautiously, she took the first sip. It wasn't that bad. She wouldn't order it at a restaurant but it wasn't the worst thing she'd tasted. She polished it off then returned to her magazine.

Her phone rang and the caller identification came up private. These types of calls always made her wary. It could be anyone on the other end. "Hello." Her voice was almost a whisper.

"So I decided what I want to do for my bachelorette party."

"Oh, hi, Denise."

She was blocking her number now? The girl was becoming a stalker. "So what did you have in mind?" Cate asked, dreading what came next.

"I want to go on a cruise!"

Now this is where she drew the line. A cruise? While pregnant? What if she went into labor at sea? It wasn't happening. She knew that many people lived for cruises. Frankly, she couldn't imagine anything worse. Really, what was the appeal of being trapped at sea with hundreds of other people for days on end? And what if everyone on the ship was obnoxious? Even if they did sail into a number of appealing ports, all she would think about the whole time she was visiting a city was getting back on the ship so it didn't leave without her. Who wanted to put themselves through that kind of torture?

"That sounds like fun!" Cate said. She had to play this one cool. Her first response couldn't be negative. Otherwise, Denise would blame Cate for spoiling the fun and thinking only of herself, which is what Denise believed had happened in the first place. Hadn't Cate gone off and gotten pregnant just to ruin her special day? "What a good idea. Where do you want to go?"

"Well, I really wanted to sail up the coast of Italy, but I figured with you being pregnant that might be a long journey, so I thought we could just book one for the coast of Mexico. I think they might even do ones that start in Los Angeles and head to Ensenada."

How did she think this helped? Did she honestly think that taking a pregnant woman who was prone to nausea and vomiting on a cruise was being considerate? "Oh, that will be a blast!" Cate said. Then she dropped her voice to a disappointed level. "But, oh, I better ask my doctor first. Gosh, I really hope he says I can go."

"Can't go? You think he'll say you can't go? Tell him they have doctors on the ship."

Cate had to play this one well, and if she played her cards right she might get out of any kind of responsibility for the bachelorette party. She'd wait until Denise had booked Janet and herself on a cruise to break the news that she wouldn't be attending. "I'll ask him. Why don't you go ahead and book it for you and Janet and I'll make my reservations after I see the doctor next week. Come to think of it, I don't see why he'd say no."

"Sounds like a plan!"

"Catherine Blakely?" The lab technician was calling her name.

"Oh, that's me! Well, Denise, they're calling me back to the lab so I better go. But we'll talk more later." Cate quickly hung up. She'd rather have blood drawn.

You'll Look Like an Idiot

1. *Heartburn*

2. *Pain in my V*

3. *Waking up on my back*

4. *Tuna*

5. *Teeth whitening products*

6. *Braxton Hicks contractions*

7. *Denise's bachelorette party*

She'd started writing down her concerns. As she waited for Dr. Hatcher she looked at her list.

Heartburn. Just as she thought it was safe to go in a restaurant again she was wrong. Now that the nausea and vomiting were gone their horrible cousin heartburn moved in. It was a shame, considering how often she was consumed with pregnancy cravings. She dreamed of eating zucchini, peanut butter, tuna sandwiches with mustard and pickles. It was impossible to enjoy these things when she dreaded eating. Water gave her heartburn, and her belches could be heard in Australia.

Pain in her V. It was yet another pregnancy symptom no one had told her about. However, each mother she'd mentioned her sore crotch to groaned upon hearing it.

"I forgot about that," Beth had said with dread in her voice. "Don't worry, it's normal though."

"I know. Sometimes I have to cut my yoga in half," Sarah chimed in. "It's just too sore. But don't worry. My doctor said it's natural. Everything is just changing for childbirth."

She felt as though she'd gone on the midnight ride with Paul Revere. This was not normal as far as Cate was concerned and she planned to mention it to Dr. Hatcher.

She was wondering what kind of damage she may have caused by continually waking on her back when Dr. Hatcher walked in. She expected him to run at the sight of her list. He was a very busy man and was probably tired of being stalked by hormonal women with lists. Instead he smiled. "Hey, Cate. Feeling like you're ninety years old these days?"

"Yes."

"I know. I wonder why women have babies. Why do you guys do this to yourselves?" He chuckled. She found it odd that a man had become her biggest comrade and possibly the most understanding person she'd been around since she'd started puking. "It's miserable," he said. "Everything has changed in your body. Things are changing every day."

"Well, I have a list of questions."

"Sure, go ahead." He leaned back in his chair.

"My heartburn is awful."

He nodded before she could describe sleepless nights and a chest that felt as though it were on fire. Though he was understanding and knowledgeable, Cate realized that Dr. Hatcher wasn't a faith healer. She was hoping for a miracle cure, and all he had was advice she'd already read about in her pregnancy books. "Try taking a liquid antacid. Those seem to help some women more. Eat small amounts. Avoid fat. Avoid eating late at night."

She moved down the list. It was awkward discussing her privates with anyone, even if he was a doctor. Was she supposed to say V? Or crotch? Or wee wee? Or hoo hoo? Was he hip with the slang for female genitalia? "I've been having some pain in my . . ."

"In your vagina?"

"Yes!" She was just glad she didn't have to say the word.

"Very common," he said. "Again, everything is changing. These are all things that are very normal. That's why I asked if you were feeling like a ninety-year-old woman."

"I've also been waking up on my back. I can't help it. I can't stay on my side all night. All the books say not to sleep on your back because it will cut the baby's circulation off."

"Don't worry. It's okay. It's not going to hurt the baby. Your circulation would get cut off before the baby's did and you would move. Next question."

She looked at the list. "Oh yes. Tuna. I know you're not supposed to eat sushi or a lot of fish but—"

He answered as if he knew what she was going to say before she finished. "Twice a week. Tuna is okay a couple times a week. The mercury content is not high enough to cause damage. Next."

"I'm in my cousin's wedding and my teeth are so yellow, and with all the pictures coming up I really want to whiten them and I was wondering if teeth whitening products are okay?"

"No! Why do you want to do that? Everyone will know you did it. That looks so fake. I can't stand it when people do that."

"Oh . . . well . . . er . . . is it safe?"

"Yes, it's safe. But it's so phony. Everyone knows when you do that. You'll look like an idiot."

His honesty made her laugh. "I guess you're right. But I don't want to look pregnant and dumpy."

"You look great," he said. "What else?"

"My Braxton Hicks contractions. I have so many of them."

"More than four in an hour?"

"No."

"Okay, as long as they're not extremely painful and more than four in an hour, then you're okay."

Braxton Hicks contractions were fake contractions that prepared women for labor. They were pain-free, but strange. Her stomach became as hard as a rock and they often made her stop whatever she was doing.

"What else?" he asked.

"Oh, well, I'm invited to go on a cruise for my cousin's bachelorette party and I was wondering if that was okay?"

"Do you want to go?"

"No."

"Then it's not okay." He smiled. "Tell her I said you can't go."

He looked at her chart. "Well, bad news."

Cate felt her heart sink. "It looks like you failed the gestational diabetes test."

Of course she had. Why would anything easy happen at this point? It would've wrecked the consistency of one miserable event after another for the entire nine months. Cate knew what this meant. It meant she had to go back to the lab with an empty stomach, drink double the glucose, and have blood drawn, not once, but four times—four times over the course of four hours. It sounded like hell. No sane woman would want to sit in a lab for four hours on an empty stomach while being poked and prodded with needles.

"I would say about a third of women fail the first test, and out of those most pass the second."

"And if I don't?"

"Then we have to treat you for gestational diabetes."

"More needles?" Cate asked.

He nodded. "Unfortunately, yes."

It was still better than going on a cruise.

·36·

Make Room for Baby

Cate had just finished a bottled water and a Rice Crispies treat when she pulled up to Target. She was supposed to be on her way to visit Sarah and Miles at the hospital. Their son, Gabriel Edward, had arrived. She realized that she'd run out of Tums, so a detour was in order.

As she went to the pharmaceutical aisle she felt the heartburn beginning. She felt as if her stomach was right beneath her throat and the awful burn that plagued her after each meal had started. She found the antacids toward the back of the store and felt her heart leap with joy when she realized the amount of flavors that Tums came in. She'd become very easy to please in her pregnancy and seeing the wide variety of antacids made her giddy. For the past month she'd followed each meal with a handful of Tums and was starting to get tired of mint and tropical fruit. Furthermore, Tums also came in small little bottles that she could carry around in her purse. She practically cleaned off the shelf. She suspected that the heartburn was only going to get worse in these final months of pregnancy. She may as well make the most of it and sample every flavor Tums had to offer.

The basket felt heavy, and she needed two hands to make it to the checkout. She unloaded on the conveyor belt. The woman behind her looked at the Tums then looked at Cate's belly. She flashed Cate a knowing smile. "Heartburn?"

"Can you tell?" Cate laughed.

"Mine was awful. Truly horrid." She shuddered. "God, I don't miss that." A little boy peeked from behind her legs. "The old wives' tale means the baby will have a lot of hair."

"I've never heard that one." And she'd heard plenty.

"Oh yeah. In his case it was true." She looked down at her son. "He came out with a full head of hair. Now my daughter, I never had heartburn with her, and she was as bald as can be."

"Huh." Cate was more intrigued with the fact that one pregnancy had been better than the other. This woman hadn't suffered with both children? Was that possible? "That's interesting. Would you say, overall, the pregnancy was better with your daughter?"

She nodded. "*Yes.* I was on bed rest with him, too. It was hell. I'll say this though, the day I delivered him that heartburn was gone. I remember eating my food at the hospital. I had forgotten what it was like to eat without getting heartburn. It was the best meal I've ever had."

They talked for several more minutes about pregnancy and childbirth. The checker joined the conversation and told Cate to drink a glass of milk with every meal to help the heartburn. Again, Cate felt as if she were making friends everywhere she went.

She took her year's supply of antacids and headed over to the hospital in La Jolla. Before heading inside she loaded up her purse with little bottles of antacids. On the way up to the maternity ward she popped three in her mouth.

Cate couldn't wait to be in Sarah's position, holding her baby and eating meals without feeling as if her stomach were resting beneath her collarbone. Cate had bought overalls and a striped onesie for their boy and carried the gift into their room. Unlike Beth and Isaac Sarah and Miles had been eager for visitors.

Perhaps it was because Sarah had scheduled a C-section. She'd gotten a good night of sleep, had bypassed labor, and had gone into the operating room mentally prepared. There was no guessing, or pushing, or complications.

The only reason for the surgery had been convenience. Miles worked in sales and traveled frequently. They'd wanted to assure that he wasn't on a business trip when Sarah delivered the baby. To some people, the decision had seemed ridiculous.

Emily, in particular, had felt that Sarah was cheating and Leslie had said that C-sections should only be used when medically necessary, and for no other reason. Cate thought it was perfect. It worked for them. She didn't plan on scheduling a Caesarean, but if it worked for Sarah, then who was she to judge. To each her own. Here in this millennium women had options. Cate was glad that modern times offered so many conveniences and safe ways to deliver a baby.

Miles was holding the baby when Cate arrived, and Sarah was combing her hair. "Cate! You made it." She looked tired, but happy. Her pajamas were cute and it looked like she'd started to do her makeup, but had been interrupted halfway through. She had foundation but no blush, and mascara but no lipstick.

"Look at him," Cate said as she leaned over Miles. "He's perfect. Absolutely adorable." C-section babies always looked a little older. Gabriel had escaped being squished through the birth canal like toothpaste. His head was beautifully shaped and he had bright eyes. She held the baby, and Sarah told her about the surgery. "I won't lie, I'm in a lot of pain. Just getting out of bed is nearly impossible.

And I can tell the second I need more pain medication." Sarah looked lovingly at her new baby. "But I feel like the richest woman in the world."

"I can't wait," Cate said.

Ethan's car was gone when she returned home, and she won-dered where he'd gone. She called his cell phone and was greeted by his voice mail. She was ready for a nap. She propped her pillows behind her back and dozed off sitting up. Obviously, sleeping on her belly was out of the question and the pregnancy books advised against back sleeping. Sleeping on her side only made her heartburn worse, so she'd gotten used to sleeping partially elevated.

She was awakened by the sound of her husband whistling. He entered the bedroom. "Hey, come look at the briefcase I just bought."

He had a briefcase now, too? What was the world coming to? Soon he'd be growing a tail. "You bought a briefcase?" she asked.

"Yeah, I keep forgetting things when I go down to the kitchen. I need to get organized. Come check it out."

She rolled over and heaved her legs over the edge of the bed. Ethan took her hands and tugged her to a standing position. She followed him into the dining room. A large shopping bag from Macy's sat on the table. She reached inside and pulled out a black leather Coach handbag. "Is this for me?" she asked.

He grinned. "Do you like it?"

"I love it! I've never had a nice bag in my entire life, I've never spent money on a purse." She was afraid to think of how much he'd spent. It was a bigger style with plenty of room for all the junk she lugged around. She didn't even know how much a bag like this cost. Leslie and Sarah would know. They'd been known to drop a pretty penny on handbags while Cate had been scouring the clearance rack for sacks at Old Navy.

"Don't worry about the cost," Ethan said. "Since you've had a rough pregnancy, and with everything that's happened to your eye, you deserve something nice."

She had married the nicest man on the planet.

"If you don't like it though, we can exchange it. I just thought with the baby and everything you might want a bigger one. You can fit diapers and a bottle in there."

"It's perfect." She looked inside. There was a pocket for her cell phone and her lipstick. "I can fit all my Tums in here," she said. She leaned over and kissed him. She hadn't asked for a new purse. In fact, the idea of getting one hadn't even crossed her mind. She loved the Coach handbag, but what really made her happy was knowing how thoughtful and sweet her husband was.

"I'm glad you like it," he said. "Now go and throw away that rag you've been carrying around."

· 37 ·

Going Down

The glucose test wasn't as bad as everyone had made it sound. In fact, it was probably the best blood-drawing experience she'd ever had. She lived walking distance from the lab so they let her go home.

Each time she returned she didn't have to wait because they had to draw blood on the hour every hour for three hours, so there was no waiting or anticipating in a germy waiting room. They took her right into the lab and drew her blood. In fact, she felt lucky when she cruised into a full waiting room and bypassed the sign-in sheet and old stacks of magazines.

She had to give herself credit. Pregnancy had strengthened her in many ways. If she could get through three months of morning sickness, an afternoon of lab work was no big deal. When they were finished she realized the worst part of it was the hunger. She felt slightly light-headed after the final drawing and the lab technician told her to wait fifteen minutes before she left. He was worried about her fainting. While she waited her cell phone rang.

"Hi, sweetie." It was Ethan.

"I'm just finishing my glucose test," she said. "Are you at home?"

"Yeah, I just walked in and I'm starving."

"Me, too. Come meet me at the lab. We'll go have lunch," she said. "I have to sit here for fifteen minutes. You can walk over here in ten and we can take my car to lunch. I'm feeling light-headed anyway. I probably shouldn't drive."

"All right."

He met her in the waiting room. After the lab technician gave her the green light to leave they headed to the third-floor elevator. While she waited for the elevator to arrive she fantasized about the Carl's Jr. drive-thru. She wanted a Santa Fe Chicken combo with a milkshake. Severe hunger had killed her aversion to poultry, and heartburn seemed like a faded memory.

The elevator doors opened and they stepped inside. Cate was about to press the number for the parking level when a tall man in his late thirties slowly backed into the elevator. He held the elbow of a woman who looked as if she'd survived the Civil War. Cate and Ethan both moved to back corners of the elevator to make room for them. It became clear to Cate that the man hadn't noticed them when he began to back up dangerously close to Cate. "Oh, excuse me," Cate said nicely. The man continued to back up, until Cate was nearly plastered against the elevator wall. He was a mere centimeter from crunching her toes and smashing into her belly. "There is someone behind you," she said. "There isn't much more room over here."

He looked over his shoulder. "Then move." His voice was firm and cold.

Cate caught a glimpse of Ethan's irritated face. Then she watched Ethan look at her. His face went from irritated to fear. Maybe it was the look in Cate's eyes that made Ethan mumble, "Oh no." Perhaps it was the memory of the parking lot thief that made him wither into the corner.

"Excuse me?" Cate said. "Did you just tell me to move?" As the invader looked over his shoulders Cate folded her hands over her belly. He was much uglier than the thief, but he wore the same confused expression of a man who had no idea what was about to hit him. "Just who the hell do you think you are?" Cate looked him square in the eye. The old woman, clearly deaf, was in her own world. Cate continued. "Do you own this elevator?"

"Uh . . . er . . . um . . . no, I was just—"

"That's what I thought," she snapped. "Wipe that smirk off your face. Huh? You surprised that someone finally said something to you? How long have you been walking around like you own the world? Pushing pregnant women around? I see you have an elderly woman with you, and that's nice, but you're not the only ones in the world. You got that?" She didn't know who looked more alarmed—Ethan or the buffoon.

"Uh, Cate?" Ethan whispered.

"Oh, I'm far from finished. What floor are we on? We still have two more floors to go." She turned back to the man. "You think it's okay to smash up against my belly? Well, maybe you do. Maybe someone did that to your mother when she was pregnant with you. Maybe that's why you're so damn stupid. Maybe the polite section in your brain was damaged."

The elevator door dinged when it reached their floor. The man looked absolutely befuddled.

"Sorry, man." Ethan shrugged. "Hormones."

"Sorry," he mumbled weakly. "I didn't know you were . . ." He looked at Cate's belly.

"Well, next time you should check before you just steamroll over people on the elevator. Oh please, go ahead." Cate motioned for the doors. "I wouldn't want to get run over by you on my way out."

"Oh . . . uh . . . okay . . . sorry." Cate noticed that his hands were shaking and sweat beads covered his forehead as he took the woman by the arm. His voice sounded shaky as he led the elderly woman through the doors. "Now watch your step here, Annie," he said.

Cate's mouth dropped. Of course the one name they had agreed on belonged to a key player in the worst elevator ride they'd ever had in their lives.

·38·

Amongst Friends

They spent several days debating whether or not they should change the name. Ethan felt a different name was necessary after he explained that he would never be able to forget that elevator ride for the rest of his life. However, once they began going over their old list of names they kept coming back to Annie.

They finally decided en route to their childbirth preparation classes that Annie would stay. They weren't going to change her name just because of some idiot on an elevator and Cate's short hormonal fuse.

The classes were held at Palomar Hospital near their home in Escondido. It wasn't the hospital where Cate would deliver, but riding the elevator up to the maternity ward made her anxious. Six more weeks seemed like an eternity and she longed to be checked into the hospital and holding her baby. She'd forgotten what it felt like to live a heartburn-free existence, or to walk from one place to another without feeling like she needed a cane. She longed to sleep on her belly or her back—to take a hot bath and sip a glass of wine. She fantasized about eating pizza in a pair of jeans and exercising.

Exiting the elevator, they passed a woman in a wheelchair. She held her bundle of joy in her arms while a nurse pushed them to their new lives and dad followed with the video camera. It was a picture-perfect moment and Cate felt sentimental for them.

They were the last couple to arrive to class. Upon entering Cate was reminded that they'd also forgotten to bring sack lunches. It was hard to ignore all their coolers lined up against the wall. The other couples had packed their iceboxes as if they were heading to the beach on the Fourth of July. All Cate could claim was a purse full of antacids. However, she looked around the room and felt right at home. Seated in chairs that were arranged in a semicircle were a dozen other ripe-looking pregnant couples.

Cate knew the instructor and she were going to get along real well when she overheard their leader telling another classmate, "Pregnancy can really suck."

Cate and Ethan took the only available seats left. They were farthest from the door and at the end of the group.

"Welcome." The instructor smiled at them. "I'm Karen, and now that everyone is here we can go ahead and start."

A registered nurse and lactation consultant, Karen was a no-nonsense type of gal and just the kind of company Cate needed toward the final weeks of her pregnancy. After listening to Beth, Cate had been worried that the leader of their class would be a granola-eating midwife who encouraged underwater labor and frowned on epidurals.

As an icebreaker, Karen asked each couple to share their biggest pregnancy gripes. Cate and Ethan went last, which was good because it gave Cate plenty of time to prioritize her long list of complaints. Pregnancy sickness, heartburn, peeing every five minutes in the middle of the night, pregnancy sickness, a crotch that felt like it belonged to Paul Revere, pregnancy sickness, flatulence that could put her in divorce court. The list went on and on, and she was shocked to find that almost everyone in the room had the same complaints and were just as eager to dish them out. One woman, due in two weeks, was still throwing up on a regular basis. Someone else had failed both gestational diabetes tests and had been pricking her fingers on a regular basis and eliminating carbs and sugar from her diet. Cate had received the wonderful news that she'd passed several days ago. Another had lost thirty pounds the first trimester and been visited by a home nurse equipped with IV fluids. When the rest of the class had gasped, this particular classmate explained that she'd been rather overweight to begin with.

For the first time since the start of her pregnancy Cate felt normal. She felt like she fit in. The glowing pregnant ladies were outnumbered and the miserable complainers ruled. There were only a couple of glowers and Cate spotted them instantly.

The first glower said her biggest complaint was gaining weight. "I just feel so fat," she said, looking as if she'd worked out daily since conception. Cate hated feeling fat, too. However, all her life she'd dreamed of eating for two, only to find those dreams shattered by a temperamental digestive system that controlled her existence and was ruled by strong odors and hormones. She wanted to tell this girl that there had been three months when she would've been happy just to lift a fork to her lips. *Weight gain? Ha! Rookie.* If that had been Cate's biggest complaint she would've been thrilled. *Then again, it's all relative.* If Cate hadn't experienced pregnancy sickness, she probably would've thought weight gain was the worst thing ever. The girl had no idea what she'd escaped and Cate only wished she'd been as lucky.

There was one unique little individual who had no complaints and described "the best nine months" of her life. Another classmate chimed in and said very seriously, "You must've had a horrible life."

It was several minutes into the course when she discreetly, or so she thought, pulled out a bottle of cocoa and creme Tums and popped a handful into her mouth as if they were popcorn. When she looked up almost every woman in the room was watching her as if they were little orphans and she'd just eaten a handful of candy.

"Anyone?" she asked as she held up the bottle.

Nearly everyone raised their hands. She passed the bottle around like it was Jack Daniel's at a campfire, and she'd never felt closer to a group of women in her life.

After the icebreaker Karen began showing diagrams of the internal aspects of a female body before pregnancy and the female body during pregnancy in the third trimester. It appeared that her intestines, once comfortably tucked in her abdominal region, were now smashed somewhere near her collarbone. Thus the explanation for the heartburn. Cate wondered if she would ever be the same again.

After explaining the physiological impact pregnancy had on the human body Karen went into describing the early signs of labor. A week or so before giving birth one could expect serious bouts of PMS-like behavior and diarrhea. Cate would greet these symptoms with open arms if it meant labor was imminent.

An hour into the lecture she heard the noise. She'd been so absorbed in Karen's lecture that she hadn't really noticed it. She knew the sound had been there for some time, but she'd been too fascinated to find its source. For a moment she wondered if it was janitorial equipment, or some kind of hospital machine. Hopefully, it wasn't keeping anyone alive because it sounded horrible. It was snorty, and unstable. She turned her head to the direction of the noise. There was Ethan, head wilted over his right shoulder like a tetherball. He was snoring. Panicked, she looked around to see if everyone was staring. The answer was no. Everyone else's husbands were taking notes. The second glower—the one with the perfect pregnancy—was the only one who seemed to notice. She threw a curt smile in Cate's direction, then turned her attention back to Karen.

Cate elbowed him, hard. He didn't even stir. "Ethan," she whispered. She pinched him, and quickly realized it had been a mistake. The pinch startled him and he jumped.

"What?" he yelled, unaware of where he was or why he'd been pinched. She watched the realization wash over his face that he'd dozed off. Cate didn't need to look around the room to know that every single set of eyes was watching them. Ethan had a mark as red and deep as a scar from the zipper on his hoodie running down the side of his right cheek. There was no question that he'd been dreaming only seconds before. The class burst into laughter and Cate couldn't help but chuckle, too.

"Maybe we should take a coffee break," Karen said tactfully. She looked at her watch. "Why don't we regroup in about fifteen minutes?"

Cate joined Ethan in the hospital cafeteria. "Sorry," he mumbled groggily as he poured himself a cup of black coffee. "I cannot keep my eyes open."

"That's okay. I'll just deliver this baby by myself." With her husband missing most of the class Cate could only imagine what it would be like when she went into labor.

"C'mon. You're not going to deliver the baby by yourself."

"You're right. There will be nurses to help."

Ethan must've sensed her annoyance because he paid such close attention after that, he became the annoying classmate that bombarded the teacher with questions. Every ten minutes he was raising his hand.

The rest of the class went smoothly. However, Cate feared that most of what she learned had gone in one ear and out the other. The baby wasn't due for a couple of months and so much information about breathing techniques and preparing for the hospital had been presented in such little time.

After they returned home Cate checked her e-mail. She was surprised to see that she had a message from Denise. Cate had practically forgotten that it was Denise's bachelorette weekend. She figured they would've been having the time of their lives lying by the pool and gambling, and had never imagined that Denise would e-mail her while on a cruise. Who sent e-mails on their bachelorette weekend? It was unheard of.

Afraid of what lay inside, Cate kept her hand still over the mouse. Her better judgment told her not to read it. The moment she opened the e-mail she would be sucked in. She could no longer claim ignorance. Whatever it was she'd have to be a part of it. Saying that she hadn't received the e-mail would be lying. There were ways people could tell if their e-mail had been opened and she figured Denise was the type of person who knew all these tricks. Whatever lay on the other end of that e-mail would soon be her responsibility. Nonetheless, she was the maid of honor and she'd promised she'd be in touch. With her eyes closed she clicked.

Within seconds the worried faces of Janet and Denise popped onto her screen. They stood in front of a slot machine, holding cocktails. They looked as though they'd just seen a ghost. The color had drained from their faces and their smiles appeared forced. Maybe they were seasick? Cate scrolled down the screen and looked at a few more photos. Janet and Denise at a roulette table. Janet and Denise by the pool. In each photo their smiles seemed forced, their shoulders stiff. Frankly, they didn't look like they were having fun. They looked scared. Cate wondered if there had been some kind of bomb scare on the ship. Maybe they'd been arguing?

She scrolled down to the message.

Hi Cate, So far the cruise has been okay. The food is good and our room is nice. A large club of lesbians booked for the same weekend and there are two hundred and twenty lesbians on

board. Everyone thinks Janet and I are gay. If we pretend like
we're a couple no one hits on us, except for one rude woman.
Anyway, I just wanted to say hi. I'll talk to you when I return.
Luv, D

She hardly noticed Ethan's footsteps behind her.

"What's going on?" he asked. "If your jaw drops any lower it
will be touching the keyboard."

"Read this," she said.

He leaned over her shoulder. "Denise and Janet are at sea with
two hundred and twenty lesbians?" As he read the rest of the e-mail
his laughter became contagious.

Cate began to chuckle, too. She couldn't help it. They both
laughed so hard that they fought for breath. "Here she was probably
hoping for a male stripper to show up at her stateroom and instead
she's pretending to be Janet's partner," Ethan said.

"Poor Denise," Cate said. "It's not the first thing that comes to
mind when thinking of bachelorette parties. Hopefully, she's making
the best of it."

"Yeah, hopefully."

·39·

A Ray of Hope

Picking up a bridesmaid dress designed for a body in its ninth month of pregnancy wasn't exactly like shopping for, say, a wedding gown. Cate wasn't expecting an *ahhhh* moment when she slipped into it. She knew anyone who told her that she looked good would be lying. It was what it was—a pregnant bridesmaid dress. She'd pretty much realized when she'd gone in for the first fitting that it wasn't going to be the fashion peak of her bridesmaid days.

Denise was going with her to pick up the dress and she was waiting outside her condo when Cate pulled up. Seeing her and her briefcase actually came as a relief. This meant that Cate didn't have to get out of the car to go get her. In these final weeks of pregnancy getting around had become difficult. Each time Cate took a step she felt like she had a watermelon in between her legs. Every square inch of her back hurt. She waddled, and in just a few days she'd be waddling down the aisle in a yellow tent they were calling a dress.

She waved to Denise as she pulled up to the curb. Denise blew her nose. It was one of those spring days when pollen was ripe in the air. Cate's eyes had itched that morning as well, and she'd sneezed when she walked past their emerald jungle. Denise had better get help for her allergies in a hurry. The last thing she wanted was hay fever on her wedding day.

Cate was dying to know how the rest of the gay cruise had gone. As Denise slipped into the passenger side of the car Cate realized that she didn't have allergies. She was crying. She looked as if she'd just spent the last two hours with a box of Kleenex. Cate suddenly felt an overwhelming sense of guilt. She knew the pregnancy was reason enough to miss the party, but deep down she'd been glad and maybe even a little relieved that Denise had chosen to go on a cruise. It had given her the perfect opportunity to get out of celebrating with Denise, and even if she'd been allowed to go on a cruise during her eighth month of pregnancy, she hadn't wanted to go. She hadn't wanted to be around Denise or Janet, and she suddenly felt like a poor sport, as if she were responsible for Denise's misery. She closed the door then pulled her seat belt over her chest.

"What's wrong?" Cate waited before driving. "I'm so sorry I missed the cruise. I feel terrible. As soon as I have the baby we'll do something fun."

"The cruise was fine." In between her tears she managed to chuckle. "Actually, it was kind of funny to be on board with a bunch of lesbians at my bachelorette party. They were all nice and bought us shots and toasted me for getting married. We actually had a really good time."

"Good. So what's wrong?"

"I don't know." She began to sob again.

"Did the wrong napkins come in? Were the flowers cancelled?" Cate tried to think of things that were important to her.

"I don't know what's wrong with me," she said in between sobs.

She glanced at the clock. "But we better go. We'll be late to our appointment."

Cate put the car in gear and headed out of Denise's neighborhood.

"I can't explain it," Denise said. "Ever since I got back from the bachelorette party I've been so overwhelmed with all these feelings. Sometimes I just feel like I don't even know what I'm doing."

Denise was getting cold feet. A ray of hope had just been cast over the wedding. There was still hope that she would come to her senses. "Are you confused?" Cate asked, quietly.

"Yes." She sniffed. "I don't know if I'm doing the right thing. I mean, I love Keith but seeing all those women together on the ship. They were so happy. Not that I'm gay, but the way they looked at each other and touched each other. Keith and I don't look at each other that way. Then I thought of you and Ethan and what you guys have and I just don't think Keith and I have the same thing. I don't think we're best friends. He hates my cats and we can't agree on paint colors and he doesn't have friends or ever really wants to spend time with my friends or family. I know these things all sound like they're no big deal, but what if there is someone else out there for me?"

Cate tried not to respond too quickly. She wanted to tell Denise that there was someone better for her, but she didn't want to sound like she was dying for Denise to call off the wedding. "Everyone gets a small case of cold feet. It's normal. Your life is about to change completely. Really, life as you know it will never be the same again. So it's only natural to have some fears." Cate paused. "With that said, you have to think about what's important to you. Your cat and the color of your walls are important things. Those are the things you love. You deserve to spend your life with someone who appreciates all the same things."

"But I'll never find the perfect person," she said. "And I don't want to start all over again."

Cate thought about how lucky she was to have Ethan, and how she often took for granted all the simple pleasures that came along with being married to him. He was the kindest person she'd ever known, and they had a lot in common. As she talked to Denise she realized how important the simple things were. Foods they liked, television shows, animals, how they spent their Saturdays—paint colors. All these things seem trivial, but when two people sleep next to each other every night and wake to each other's faces each morning, life could be miserable if they didn't have a common ground. She'd never thought about all the compromises she'd have to make if Ethan didn't appreciate and value all the things that were important to her. Having this conversation with Denise made her love her husband even more.

"Denise, there is no such thing as a perfect marriage. There will definitely be hard times, and days when you don't agree on things. But if you don't go into the marriage with a solid foundation, the good days are going to be scarce and the bad days are going to be hard. Think about it. Do you want to live like that?"

The only sound in the car was the low hum of the radio. Then Denise spoke. "I don't want to be alone. And I want children."

She felt as if Denise were teetering on the edge of a diving board above a pool without water. Cate wanted to pull her back—to save her from jumping in and ruining her life. She didn't have to settle. Unfortunately, she'd seen a few friends settle for the sake of their biological clock. As far as Cate could tell they seemed to be making the most of their marriages. They seemed content. These couples weren't miserable, but they didn't seem as if they were bubbling over with love either. They were fine, but who wanted to be fine? Who wanted to make the most of something?

They had no idea what they were missing. Cate still felt excited when she saw Ethan's phone number on her caller ID. She still craved the warm feeling of his chest against her face. They had fun together.

"Denise, I can tell you firsthand that pregnancy was nothing like what I had imagined. I am excited for the end result. I truly can't wait to have my baby, but it's been hard. If I wasn't in a good marriage it would've been a lot worse. Sometimes Ethan knows what I need before I do. I don't know if that makes sense, but I couldn't have gotten through all this if it wasn't for him. And we haven't even started raising the child yet. I've been around kids long enough to know that we're going to face obstacles. I can't imagine going in to parenthood with someone who didn't share all the same values I did. If he doesn't want to spend time with your family, what is your life with him going to be like? If he doesn't understand how much you value your family, then what is raising a family with him going to be like?"

They arrived at the tailor's and Denise put her Kleenex in her purse. "I'm fine," she said. "You're right. I'm just getting a little case of cold feet."

Cate waited until Denise opened her door to pull the keys from the ignition. She could feel the opportunity slipping from her grip.

"Denise, wait," she said.

She was halfway out of her seat and looked over her shoulder at Cate.

"I just want you to be happy. But . . . I think . . . I think you're making a mistake." It was hard to say it, and Cate could feel her heart pounding. The silence that followed seemed to last forever.

"Cate, I appreciate your concerns. But I'll be okay. We can talk more about it later. I don't want to miss our appointment." She stepped out of the car.

When the seamstress held up the bridesmaid dress Cate's first thought was that it was too big. There was no way it would fit. Even the arms looked too big, as if they'd been cut from a man-sized pattern. Sure, she'd gained thirty pounds. However, she wasn't Santa Claus. Cate watched Denise's face as she and the seamstress zipped up the back of the dress. Her eyes were red and she still looked troubled.

Denise's cell phone rang. "It's the band," she said. "They need the names for the grand entrance. I'll be right back."

Cate didn't know if she should feel relieved that the dress fit or not. Her size was alarming. She'd never had big arms. The seamstress stepped back and looked at her. "It looks cute," she said in her Russian accent.

Cute is what Cate had become in the third trimester. She was beginning to think that *you look cute* was really just a way of saying *you don't look terrible*. It was a way of saying that her appearance would pass. She didn't look horrible. But sexy, pretty, and stunning were words that didn't belong anywhere near her. She longed to be sexy again. In fact, she'd just be happy if she could slip into a pair of jeans. In all her life, she never dreamed that she'd long for a day when she could zip up a fly.

Cate turned to look in the mirror and covered her mouth with her hand. Rather than heading down the aisle with her elbow linked to a groomsman, her escort could roll her down the aisle. She had become a barrel—a big, yellow barrel.

"It looks so cute!" Denise said when she returned. A smile had replaced her sullen look and a twinkle had cast out the red in her eyes.

"You like it?" Cate asked.

"I love it. And I think the fabric will match Janet's perfectly."

Denise's opinion was really all that mattered. Lord knew, Cate wasn't wearing the dress for herself.

Cate slipped out of the dress and back into her maternity sweats and blouse. In the final weeks of pregnancy very few things fit her. If she'd known she'd be relying on two pairs of gaucho sweats and a couple of blouses from Old Navy, she would've bought them in every color. At this point spending money on clothes seemed like a waste. So she'd recycled her minimized wardrobe daily in the washing machine. As for the rehearsal dinner, she'd be dressing up her sweats and blouse with a pashmina, a cute pair of ballet flats, and a broach.

While she wrote a check for the dress Denise took a call from the florist outside. Cate carried the gown on a hanger. Denise wrapped up her phone call as Cate unlocked the car.

Once inside, Cate looked at her. "How are you feeling?" she asked Denise.

"Fine. I'm fine. Really, it was just pre-wedding jitters. I appreciate you listening."

Cate felt her heart sink. The wedding was still on.

·40·

In Reverse

Cate had been a bridesmaid so many times that she'd practically made a career out of walking down the aisle. She'd been reduced to the lowest levels of bridesmaid hell possible. She'd sported the bad hair, worn the hideous dresses, walked in uncomfortable shoes. However, nothing could have prepared her for being a pregnant bridesmaid.

Everyone had called what she was wearing a gown. However, it looked like a yellow tent that hung to her knees. Her ankles were swollen. She hardly recognized her calves. Her face was bloated, and her hair looked like crap. When she'd gone to the salon that morning she'd asked for a chignon, a nice little knot at the nape of her neck. Strangely, all her hair had ended up piled like rags atop her head. The updo was rough to the touch and if she hadn't already been through Hair Hell and back so many times she would've feared that the hairdo would never come out of hairspray sedimentation.

She stood in front of the mirror before they left for the church.

She didn't know if she wanted to laugh or cry. She tried not to do either. Ethan already thought she was going crazy. He might have her committed if she became hysterical.

"You look cute," he said.

"I look like a pregnant prom queen."

He threw his head back laughing. When he caught her stoic gaze in the mirror he stopped. "You look great! You do! Pregnant prom queen? You? No way."

He was a horrible liar. Cate grabbed her purse. "Let's go," she said. "I just want to get this over with."

When they arrived at the Hotel Del Coronado Cate hoped that Denise wouldn't be there. She hoped the coldness in her feet had gone to her head, and she'd made the abrupt yet rational decision to run for her life. Denise's room was on the first floor, and Cate made her way through the hotel grounds. The weather wasn't ideal for a wedding, and Cate felt kind of sorry for Denise and Scary. A heavy blanket of gray covered the sky and the air felt muggy.

Unfortunately, Denise was in her bridal suite. A look of terror occupied her eyes. It was the same expression that could be found inside the eyes of most brides minutes before they headed down the aisle. Cate recognized the fear that resulted from thinking of 200 friends and acquaintances watching your every move. The fear stemmed from worries over tripping down the aisle or forgetting critical parts of vows. Despite the look in Denise's eyes, she looked pretty. Her dress had sleeves that fell over her shoulders and a full skirt. The gown was flattering on her figure. Her hair was pulled into a classic French twist, and her makeup made her dark eyes pop. The photographer was taking some photos of her in front of the mirror.

Cate did a double take when she noticed Janet. She'd expected something X-rated. Her boobs weren't hanging out of her dress and the material seemed thicker and more satiny than what Cate remembered from the picture. The dress looked completely different.

"We match well," Janet said.

"We do?" Cate looked at Janet's dress. It was more a canary yellow than a pale yellow. Had Cate lost her mind? The dress seemed so different from the one Cate remembered. She was losing it. The pregnancy hormones had finally taken control. She was officially delusional.

"Yeah, good job matching," Janet said.

"Yours looks so different from what I remember."

Janet lowered her voice. "Actually, I had to buy a different dress yesterday. I spilled a Coke on the other one, and I had this one FedExed from J.Crew." She looked down at the skirt. "Don't tell Denise though."

Cate bit her bottom lip. She'd promised Ethan that she would control her hormonal outbursts today. She wanted to wring Janet's neck. All that fuss over the dress, and she didn't even end up wearing it.

Fortunately, for Janet's sake, the wedding coordinator, a well-manicured woman wearing a sharp navy-blue suit entered the bridal suite. She held a walkie-talkie. "All right. We're almost ready."

"I just need a moment to myself," Denise said.

"Do you need any help?" Cate asked.

She shook her head. "No. I'm fine."

They all watched her walk to the bathroom in her hotel room.

"I'm going to go check on Keith," the coordinator said. "I'll be back."

As soon as she was gone Rita turned to Cate. "You look adorable."

"Thanks," Cate said. "It's not my best moment as a bridesmaid, but I guess things could always be worse, right?"

Rita laughed. "You look cute."

Cate looked at the bathroom door. "Is she nervous?" she whispered.

"She seems very calm. She hasn't said much, but I guess that's how most brides are the day of the wedding."

Janet sat on the bed, text messaging, while they waited for Denise to return. The baby kicked, and Rita placed her hand over Cate's belly to feel. Lately it had felt as though a small baseball was swinging up against her ribs every time Annie kicked.

Several minutes passed. The coordinator returned. "Well, I just saw Keith. And he's doing great." She spoke of him as if he were a normal person. Cate didn't know what Keith doing "great" was like. She'd never seen him in a good mood. Maybe getting married was bringing out the best in him. Or maybe the coordinator was a really good liar. It was her job, after all, to keep things running smoothly. It's not like she would come in and say, "That Keith is such a dickhead! Someone is actually marrying him?"

The coordinator pointed to the bathroom. "How's Denise coming along?" she whispered.

"It's been a while. I'll check on her," Cate said.

She waddled to the door and tapped on it. "Denise, do you need anything? It's Cate."

There was no reply. Cate looked at Rita then shrugged. "Maybe she didn't hear me." She knocked louder. Something inside the bathroom fell and she heard the sound of silk rustling. "Denise, are you okay?"

Still nothing.

Cate turned the handle and found Denise climbing out the window. The dress was a mountain of white on the floor and Denise had wrapped herself in a robe. Cate slammed the door behind her then ran for Denise's ankles. Her nylons were slick beneath Cate's hands. "Denise! What are you doing?" One of Denise's pumps fell off.

She looked over her shoulder. A tear trickled down her cheek. "I can't do this."

"Okay, well, get back in here. Running away isn't the answer."

She began to cry. "I can't face Keith or the kids. I just can't. Or Patty. They're going to hate me."

Cate could hear the sound of waves crashing outside. She'd for-gotten how close they were to the ocean. "They're not going to hate you. And you can't run away."

"Okay, then I'll do it." She began to reverse her body back in through the window.

"Do what?"

"I'll get married."

She was irrational. "Denise, being afraid of facing people is no reason to commit *your life* to someone."

She didn't answer.

"You can't hide from them forever."

Denise sat down on the toilet. In spite of everything, not a single hair from her French twist was out of place. If Cate hadn't known better she would've thought that the wedding was still on, as if Denise was waiting to put on her gown. It felt as though events were in reverse. She looked up at Cate with long eyes. "Will you tell them?"

Cate shook her head. "I won't tell Keith. I'm sorry, Denise. But you owe him that."

Denise began to weep again.

"I'll tell all the guests if you'd like. I'll make the announcement." And to think, she'd been nervous about the toast.

"What will everyone do? They're going to think I'm nuts." She shook her head and went to the window again. "It's the only way."

"Denise, get back in here. It's going to look worse if you disap-pear."

This time she had one leg out the window. She turned to listen to Cate.

"Look, most of those people out there are your friends. They want you to be happy. Do you think anyone who cares about you wants to see you walk down the aisle and commit your life to someone you're not happy with? Do you think your friends and family want to see you divorced?"

She shook her head. "No."

"Then don't you think they'll understand?"

She nodded.

It was Ethan who broke the news to the guests. Denise found Scary Dad, and in the privacy of his hotel room called off the wedding. Cate hadn't heard the whole story yet, but according to Rita the meeting had resulted in the destruction of a patio chair and a table lamp.

Neither Keith nor Denise had chosen to be present during the announcement. Cate watched from the back of the veranda. All the guests waited in fold-out chairs, fanning themselves with programs. Ethan walked up to the altar, looking pensive.

A hush fell over the crowd. "Hello, everyone," he said. "On behalf of the bride and groom, I'd like to tell you all how much it means to them that you came to celebrate with them today. Your friendship and support means a lot to them, and they hope that you can continue supporting them in their decision to cancel the wedding." There were a couple gasps and then only the sound of waves crashing. "Right now Denise and Sc—Keith . . ." He'd almost called him Scary. Cate thanked God that he'd stopped himself. ". . . Really need some time alone and hope that you will understand their decision."

He walked away from the altar like Michael Jackson's publicist after a press conference, only he wasn't going to be available for questions. As Cate looked over the sea of puzzled faces she could imagine the rumors that would ignite, the overwhelming sense of curiosity the guests must feel.

It really didn't matter what they thought. It didn't matter that a $2,000 cake was going to waste or that 200 entrees would go cold. It didn't matter that bouquets would never be carried and champagne would never be cracked. The bouquets would be wilted by tomorrow, and people would forget about the food anyway. The only thing that mattered was that Denise had done the right thing. Cate couldn't recall feeling more relieved.

· 41 ·

What Happens When Men Nest

What the pregnancy books failed to mention was that husbands experience the nesting instinct as well. Just a week after Denise's nonwedding Ethan woke at the crack of dawn. He jumped out of bed, reached for a dirty pair of jeans, then pulled an old T-shirt over his head with the kind of enthusiasm that could only belong to someone who had plans.

"Where are you going?" Cate asked, groggily.

"The Home Depot."

"The Home Depot?" She snapped out of dreamland. The last time her husband had gone to the Home Depot first thing in the morning she'd spent half a year on an island known as The Bed. That was after camping on the kitchen floor beneath exposed ceiling beams for weeks on end. "For what?"

"I want to remodel the bedroom closet today."

She knew this idea had been ticking inside his head like a time bomb for several months now. It wasn't a bad idea. Lord knew they needed the cabinet space. Opening their closet door was dangerous. Exposing the inside of the closet even a few inches could cause an avalanche. Shoes, clothes, books, gift wrap, spare sheets, towels, blankets, a set of dishes, their blender, several cookie sheets, their tax return, and God only knew what else was crammed inside a space meant for a wardrobe belonging to one person. Their historical home only had two tiny closets, and very limited kitchen space. They'd shoved whatever they could into that closet, and the unspoken rule was that if you could smash it in there, put it in there. She'd fantasized about shelves.

However, three weeks from her due date was not the time to embark on a task that could involve a semi truck from the Salvation Army and a table saw. "You want to do that *today*?" she asked.

"Yes, I think I can crank the whole thing out in one day."

"Ethan, have you lost your mind?"

"What?" He pulled on socks.

"Our baby could arrive any minute."

"It won't." Grease jumped on the bed and rubbed his body across Ethan's back.

"That's not what Dr. Hatcher said. Dr. Hatcher said the baby could come any time."

"Wasn't your mom three weeks overdue with her first?"

"Yes, but that doesn't mean anything."

"I'm telling you, I can do the whole thing today."

"Ethan, I doubt if Bob Vila could do the whole thing today."

"You said yourself, we don't have any space for the baby. This will make more space, and we can get rid of all that crap we don't need." He leaned in and kissed her on the forehead. "I'll bring home breakfast." He grabbed his keys off the top of the TV and headed out the bedroom door.

"Ethan, wait!" she called. She felt desperate, as if her lover was heading off to battle without a weapon. "Please don't do this!"

"What do you want for breakfast?" he called.

"I want you to get my suitcase out of the garage for me. I haven't even packed for the hospital yet. I want to go to Costco to get frozen food so we don't have to cook when the baby comes. I want to make a list of people we need to call when I'm in labor. I want you to stay here!"

"See you in an hour! I'll get your suitcase down from the rafters when I get back! Love you!" She heard the front door close behind him.

An hour later he returned with enough lumber to frame a gas station and a quiche from the French bakery down the street. Within minutes he began his project. The sound of saw blades spinning was familiar and frightening.

She sat backward on a chair and watched while he worked like a man on a mission. First, he pulled the closet doors from the wall and stood back as the avalanche crashed onto their bedroom floor. He moved every item from the closet into the dining room. As she picked at her breakfast she became enclosed by mountains of clothes, blankets, towels. A hill of shoes began to obstruct her view.

There were things she'd forgotten she'd even had in there. A baseball hat she'd picked up on a trip to Mexico they'd taken. A few CDs she'd forgotten about and a set of napkin rings they'd received as a wedding gift. She watched as the mountain range of junk formed in the family room. She wondered how they'd ever fit even half the stuff inside the closet.

She knew the man was nesting because she could see it in his eyes. She'd worn the same expression when she'd scoured the spice rack and laundered every piece of the baby's clothing a week before.

She picked at her quiche, but didn't feel very hungry. She felt tired and a little queasy and prayed that she wasn't getting the flu. Could she just make it another three weeks without getting sick? Chronic heartburn was bad enough.

She tried to keep things neat and tidy as Ethan raced from table saw to closet, dropping swear words on the way, and leaving a long trail of sawdust behind him.

Oscar and Grease had made themselves comfortable on their spare sheets and a cashmere sweater that Cate paid way too much for. She gently nudged them off and found them ten minutes later resting on their towels and Ethan's only good suit. By three o'clock Cate was starting to worry. An inch of fur and sawdust covered almost all their bedding and clothes and Ethan wasn't even halfway finished.

The following day was Monday. That meant Ethan would be back to work and God only knew how long they would live in squalor. She'd seen this happen before. It had started with putting new texture on their walls and had turned into an extremely long episode of *Flip This House*.

"Ethan, honey, do you think you could get my suitcase from the rafters?" The least she could do was pack.

"I have two more shelves to put in and then I will. I promise."

Two more hours passed and Cate got an overwhelming craving for cake. White cake with thick, sugary frosting. She went to the grocery store and found a chilled coffin full of big slices of all kinds of cake. Her cravings got the best of her and she not only bought white cake but carrot cake and German chocolate as well. She knew Ethan would be annoyed if she brought home cake for dinner, so she waddled down the aisles looking for something more substantial. She had a Braxton Hicks contraction that stopped her in her tracks. As soon as it passed she headed to the deli. She ordered some chicken strips and potato wedges and listened to the woman behind the counter share every gory detail of her birth.

"You look like you're due any minute," she said.

"Three weeks." Cate rubbed her belly. "I'm having a Braxton Hicks contraction. My stomach is as hard as a rock."

"I had so many of those with my son. Have you packed yet?"

"No, I've been nagging my husband all day to get my suitcase down but he's remodeling our closet right now."

"Remodeling your closet?" She handed Cate a jalapeno popper. "Here, have a sample," she said. "It's on the house."

Cate nodded. "Yeah, I told him not to, but he insisted."

She laughed. "Watch, the baby will come tonight."

Cate laughed even harder. "Wouldn't that be funny? I don't think so though."

She thanked the woman for the sample, then returned home. She made Ethan a plate of food. Sawdust stuck to every square inch of his sweaty body like feathers on glue.

"How much cake did you get?" he asked, looking at the three plastic containers full of cake on the kitchen counter.

"I've been craving it. I can't help it." She stuck her fork into the white cake first. Ethan ended up eating a couple of chicken strips and a few fries, then joined her for a dinner of cake as well. After they were finished she cleaned up the plates.

"The suitcase?" she said as she put the leftover cake in the fridge.

"Okay, I have one more shelf. But come see what I've done so far."

She followed him into the bedroom and looked at his work. "Wow!" she said. "You did all this?"

He nodded. "Once I get the last shelf in and slap a coat of paint on there it will look wonderful."

"Are you going to do that tonight?"

"I'm not going to paint it tonight, but all the shelves will be finished. I'll paint it tomorrow."

She knew better than to get sucked into this trap. Tomorrow could mean weeks, even months from now. She couldn't live with the house looking like the back room of a thrift store. "I think we should put everything away as soon as you're finished with the shelf and when you're ready we can take everything back out and paint."

"No. I promise. You have my word. Tomorrow after I finish working I'll paint. Everything will be finished tomorrow night."

She gave him a skeptical look. "Ethan, you know how these things go. You'll finish working, and you'll be too tired and then you'll just want to watch *Wife Swap*."

"This time I swear."

"What about my suitcase?"

He squeezed her shoulders. "Lemme finish this shelf, and then I'll get your suitcase."

The shelf ended up taking three hours. He miscalculated when he was sawing and cut the wood too short and had to start over. Cate laid out clothes for the baby that she wanted to pack. She had no idea how long she was going to be in labor so she picked out three DVDs she wanted to take to the hospital. Her other pair of sweatpants was in the hamper with the pajamas and nursing bras she wanted to take to the hospital. She'd pack those after they were clean. She threw a load of laundry in the washing machine, then took a shower.

At eleven o'clock Grease and Oscar were still asleep on Ethan's suit. Sawdust covered their pets and Ethan was dragging in his table saw from the back porch. "Listen, honey, I promise I will get your suitcase first thing in the morning."

"All right." She was annoyed but too tired to argue and climbed into bed. She had a hard time keeping her eyes open while she waited for Ethan to take his shower and join her in bed.

Ethan smelled clean when he slid into bed next to her. They flipped off the lights, and he put his arm over her back. "Come here. Let's spoon for a little while," he said. "We haven't spooned in such a long time."

It was true. Cate had felt too uncomfortable to spoon or snuggle and she'd forgotten what it felt like to have his body pressed against her back. He was warm, and she could smell his Irish Spring soap. "I love you," he said.

"Ethan?"

"Yes?"

"I think my water just broke." If it had happened any quicker she wouldn't have felt the little popping sensation. She would've only felt the fluid on her inner thigh.

He laughed. "Real funny. Good night."

She jumped out of bed. "I'm not kidding. My water broke." He flipped on the light and they watched as a puddle formed around her feet. "Ethan, call the hospital. Tell them we're on the way. We're going to have a baby."

·42·

Alas

"You are definitely in labor." The nurse smiled. Her name was Rachel and she had just clocked in for her twelve-hour shift. She wasn't much older than Cate and had light brown hair that was pulled back in a loose ponytail. "You're already four centimeters dilated and about eighty percent effaced. One way or another, this baby will be here within twenty-four hours. Congratulations."

Ethan leaned in and kissed Cate on the forehead. She hoped he was comfortable in his dirty jeans and old T-shirt. Unless Rachel gave him a hospital gown that's all he'd be wearing for the rest of the night. There hadn't been time to pack, and they'd both shown up in pants he'd dug out of the hamper and old T-shirts.

In spite of this, she wasn't angry. How could she be mad? They were having a baby. Annie was coming and the excitement was enough to kill any *I told you so* feelings she had toward him.

"How are you doing?" he asked as he pulled a strand of hair from her forehead.

"I feel good."

Rachel came around the side of her bed to adjust the strap around Cate's arm that monitored her blood pressure. "Are you planning on getting an epidural?" she asked.

"I don't know if I really need it right now," Cate said.

"If getting one is in your delivery plans, we should call the anesthesiologist now. By the time he gets here, your contractions will probably be stronger. And you don't want to wait too long to get one."

Cate nodded. "Okay. Go ahead and call him."

She should've known by now that any preconceived notions she'd had about pregnancy and childbirth should've been erased from her brain. For the most part, nothing had gone as expected. Morning sickness—she'd been clueless. Heartburn—completely ignorant. Going into labor—totally in the dark. For the first time since she'd conceived, something had turned out better than she'd thought. So far, she had no real complaints. The worst pain she'd felt had been when Rachel shoved an IV into the back of her hand.

Their room at Pomerado Hospital felt like a suite. Immaculately clean, it was larger than their master bedroom at home. The polished floors felt homey and a gigantic spa-sized bathtub took up one corner of the room. They had cable, a DVD player, and a refrigerator. When she was finished delivering she had the luxury of ordering room service from a menu next to the bed.

Her contractions had started in the car. Less than a minute, they felt no worse than bad menstrual cramps. What she hadn't expected was the wave of vomiting that took her by surprise. The vomiting snuck up on her so quickly that she hardly had time to call out for a trash can. Rachel explained that this was normal for labor and would pass soon.

Several minutes after Rachel left to call the anesthesiologist her contractions became worse and Cate was thankful that the epidural was on the way. She now understood why women on *A Baby Story* looked like they might pass out while in labor. By the time he arrived they were painful. A few had taken her breath away, and she could definitely see how things could go downhill from here. God bless any women who braved it from that point without pain medication. As far as she was concerned, numb was the way to go.

The injection felt like a frosty bee sting. It was cold and startling before it shot up her back bringing a tingly sensation with it. Several minutes later her legs felt like tree stumps, and contractions were a distant memory.

Cate looked at the clock as soon as he was finished. It was three in the morning. She turned to Rachel. "When do you think I'll have the baby?" she asked.

She shrugged. "It's hard to say because it's your first. But if I *had* to guess . . . I'd say the baby will be here by . . ." She glanced at her watch. "Lunchtime."

She'd waited nine months, and now these final hours seemed like they would never end. Lunchtime seemed like years from now. She couldn't wait to meet her daughter, and felt as if she'd never wanted anything more.

"You should try to get some sleep," Rachel said. "You're really going to need energy for pushing."

How could she sleep at a time like this? She was too excited to sleep. Her husband, Ty Pennington, welcomed the suggestion and stretched out on his fold-out bed. He fell asleep like a man who'd done manual labor all day.

The room was dim, and she watched CNN *Headline News* with the volume turned low. It was hard to pay attention to all the top stories when her daughter was about to arrive. She wasn't worried or scared—just excited. One hour passed, then another. Rachel came to check on her a couple times. With each visit, Cate was a little more dilated. They were a little closer.

Eventually she must have drifted off because the next thing she saw was her mother's face looming over her bed.

"I had a feeling this baby was going to be early," Connie said.

"I wish I had. What time is it?"

"Seven."

Ethan rolled over on his cot. A streak from the plastic mattress covered the side of his face. He yawned. "How are you doing?"

"Good. I can tell when I'm having a contraction because of the pressure, but I can't feel anything."

"I just talked to Rita and Charles," Connie said. "They're on their way. And dad will be here soon, too." Ethan had called all their parents on the way to the hospital. Connie made herself comfortable in a chair near Cate's bed. "I hardly slept at all last night," Connie said.

Cate was dying to know how much her labor had progressed since she'd fallen asleep. She waited for each visit from Rachel the same way a child waits for his turn to see Santa Claus. Fortunately, it wasn't long before she returned. "Did you get some rest?"

"I slept a couple hours," Cate said.

Rachel lifted the sheet that covered Cate's lower half. "Looks like you are . . . you are pretty much ready! You are fully dilated. I just need to go grab a couple things and Dr. Hatcher should be here any second to check in. After that, you can start pushing."

Ethan squeezed her hand. "It's almost time."

Rita and Charles arrived, and Cate's dad followed shortly after. She called a few friends on her cell phone to tell them she was in labor.

"Things are quite a bit different from our day, aren't they?" Connie elbowed Rita. "Getting epidurals. Talking on cell phones."

"Oh my gosh, I know. I would've never been able to make a phone call during labor. I was in so much pain. *So* much."

Rachel returned and all the parents left to set up camp in the waiting room. One by one they kissed her good-bye, wishing them luck. Cate and Ethan had decided they wanted to be alone with the nurse while they pushed. Cate didn't really want her in-laws, or her own parents for that matter, seeing her naked from the waist down. Really, she wasn't even sure if she wanted Ethan to see her crotch at its goriest during childbirth. If he wanted to look, it was at his own risk.

Rachel refreshed their memories from childbirth class and gave them a brief demo on pushing. Just as she was finishing up Dr. Hatcher joined them. He was dressed for the office in his slacks and lab coat.

"Well, here we are," he said. "Let's have a look." He lifted the sheet. "Looks like this baby has a lot of hair."

Cate felt a surge of excitement course through her veins. Any information about the baby was welcome. "Really? What color?"

"Dark. Come here, Dad." He motioned for Ethan. "Take a look."

She felt a little left out that they were all looking at her baby's hair and the only thing she could see were her feet in the stirrups. She watched Ethan. He got the same look in his eyes that had been there when they'd seen their daughter's heartbeat on the screen for the first time. He looked awestruck.

"What does it look like?" she asked.

"All you can see is one tiny spot of hair—no bigger than a penny. But her hair is pretty long and dark brown."

"All right." Dr. Hatcher stood up and pulled his gloves off. "You're going to have this baby today. Rachel will call me when you get closer."

Cate pushed for three hours. She wanted to find out the name of the person who had invented epidurals so she could write and personally thank him or her. Though exhausting, the entire pushing experience was pain-free. In fact, she must've asked Rachel a million times if she was really pushing because she couldn't even feel it. After a while the only things she felt were tired and hungry. She felt her stomach growling while simultaneously feeling as though she would doze off right there in the stirrups with Ethan and Rachel on either side of her.

"As soon as this baby is out you can order food," Rachel said.

Around eleven Rachel called Dr. Hatcher. Cate thought that getting him out of his office would've taken another hour but he appeared within minutes. While Dr. Hatcher prepared for the delivery Ethan ran to the waiting room to tell the grandparents the baby was coming. After Ethan returned the grandparents stood vigil outside her room.

"This baby will be out in ten minutes," Dr. Hatcher said.

The following ten minutes seemed like a blur. They flew by but at the same time seemed to take forever. First the head was out, and Ethan left her side to watch. Then the body. Then the sound of newborn cries, loud, hiccupping cries that filled the room like a symphony.

Dr. Hatcher held Annie up and Cate looked into her daughter's blue eyes. He placed the baby on her chest. There was no way to explain how Cate felt as she held her baby, listening to the sound of her quick, strong cries. It was instant love and a sense of protectiveness. She wanted to warm her bare body, and hold her as close as she could so she would feel safe in this strange place. In Annie's face she saw Ethan's forehead and her chin. Annie had inherited her father's dark hair and their blue eyes. Cate couldn't tell whose nose she had, but her mouth definitely had come from Cate's side of the family. She was beautiful. For a long time mother and baby gazed at one another. Cate felt like they had been walking down the same path and had just met. It was as if they'd experienced all the same strange things and had been aware of each other's footsteps but had never come face-to-face. Even though they'd just met for the first time Cate felt as if they'd known each other much longer. They'd felt each other's every movement for the good part of a year. Annie had been listening to her heartbeat since her ears had developed, and Cate had known each time she'd had the hiccups. Cate sensed that they were going to get along just fine.

·43·

A Family

"She looks like Ethan," Leslie said.

"You think?" Connie asked. "I see more of Cate in her."

"I can't tell," Rita said. "She just looks like Annie."

Ever since Annie had joined them Cate's hospital room had been full of people. In the five hours that Annie had been on earth there had never been a shortage of arms to hold her. Emily had stopped by and Chuck was driving down from Los Angeles to meet his niece. Sarah came with a few sleeping gowns and a stuffed animal for the baby. Beth dropped by without her baby and it had been inspiring to see that her figure had already started to return. Cate hoped that she was just as lucky.

Now Leslie was meeting Annie for the first time. She'd shown up with a bouquet of roses and a gift bag full of pink baby clothes. Cate had loved the steady flow of visitors. Even though she felt exhausted she was excited and eager to show off her daughter. She'd never felt such a sense of pride.

Connie passed the baby to Leslie. "I think I'm going to head home," Connie said. "But I'll be back first thing in the morning."

"I think I'm going to leave, too." Rita stood up. "Call us if you need anything." Cate's father and Charles had left with Ethan to help clean the house. Cate and the baby were being discharged from the hospital the following day and it didn't seem right to bring Annie into a world of squalor.

Cate kissed her mom good-bye. Then Rita leaned over the bed and hugged Cate.

Cate looked at Leslie, sitting in the glider at the end of her bed. Annie slept in her arms and Leslie's face looked soft as she admired the baby. "She's perfect, Cate. Absolutely perfect."

"Thank you."

She took her eyes away from the baby. "So I think Russ and I made a decision."

"Really?"

"Yeah, we'd really like a child of our own eventually, and I think with in vitro we'll have success—"

"I do, too," Cate said. "I've heard so many success stories."

"*But* . . . I don't think we're ready for the financial impact. We'd have to take out a loan, and we just refinanced the house last year so we could pay off Russ's student loans. It just doesn't seem like it's meant to be. With in vitro there are no guarantees. We need some time. So for now, we're going to foster a child."

"Really? That's so cool. I think that's great, Les. Someone out there needs you and you're going to make one little child very happy."

"I hope so. We've signed up for a program, and we've requested children under the age of two with the possibility of adoption."

"Les, that's amazing! I'm so proud of you for doing this."

"It seems like the best option for now. And we have so much to offer a child. It just doesn't make sense to go into debt trying to have one."

"I think that's a wonderful decision."

"Thanks."

Her cell phone choked and she grabbed it from her nightstand, daring to read the message.

C8! Wow and ahoy! I just got the news about Anie at sea. Rita and Chuck e-mailed me aboard my Singles at Sea Cruise Liner! I am having the time of my life and becoming quite the Texas Hold Em Champion on board the ship. Some of the other women are jealous of me becuz I'm so good at poker and I'm really connecting with the guys becuz of it. I do feel a little bad about taking all the attention away from the other women, but who cares? My next door neighbor, Miguel, says those other women are boring anyway! Ha! Miguel does home loans in San Diego so we have a lot in common. He also loves cats and is looking for someone to take ballroom dancing with! Well anyway, congratulations! Talk to you soon!

Luv, D

Interesting, very interesting. She read it twice. Cate hoped that it wasn't just Denise succumbing to her delusions again. She'd keep her fingers crossed.

Leslie stayed for a little while. Before she left she placed Annie in her bassinet so Cate could sleep. Her exhaustion was becoming hard to ignore. After Leslie left it wasn't difficult to drift off. When she woke, Ethan had returned. He was sprawled out on his cot, holding his swaddled daughter against his chest. His hair was a mess, and he was still wearing the same clothes but he looked so peaceful. She'd enjoyed having visitors but she was glad they finally had a moment to themselves. The hours following Annie's birth had seemed busy.

First, she'd needed food. After three hours of pushing and nearly eighteen hours without a meal her appetite had grown ravenous.

Ethan had been starving, too, and the grandparents had fought over who was going to hold Annie while the new parents wolfed down room service.

As soon as they'd finished eating Cate's epidural had worn off. Nothing could have prepared her for the pain that followed. It felt as though a boulder had exited her crotch. Here, all this time, she'd thought she'd been escaping a pain-free childbirth experience. She'd had no idea what she was in store for. Just putting her legs over the edge of the hospital bed was enough to draw tears to her eyes.

Peeing for the first time after childbirth had been more complicated than anything she'd faced during labor and delivery. After a long trip to the restroom with Rachel she'd realized that going to the bathroom could take up to a half hour. Toilet paper was out of the question and her new routine involved a squeegee bottle, Tucks medicated pads, a cleansing foam, and a sanitary pad so thick it could safely collect rain during a hurricane.

Then there had been breast-feeding. Annie's first experience at the breast had been challenging to say the least. For one thing her tiny little heart-shaped mouth felt like it belonged to a piranha. The nurses explained that the baby wasn't latching on correctly and that it was going to take some work before breast-feeding went smoothly. The second feeding had produced a hickey on Cate's nipple, which she later learned was not normal.

"Breast-feeding is supposed to feel good," the lactation consultant had said. "You shouldn't have bruises or cracking or chafing of any kind. It should be a very enjoyable experience."

It seemed hard to believe that anyone enjoyed having their nipples feel as if they were being torn apart, but women had been doing it for forever so it had to get better.

In spite of all Cate's aches and pains she was in baby heaven. She didn't care that her entire crotch region throbbed or that it would be weeks before she used the restroom like a normal person again.

Feeding her daughter hadn't been a dream experience but they were learning together and she was optimistic that Annie would be latching on correctly in no time.

Her happiness didn't come from the fact that she'd enjoyed a meal without facing a single symptom of heartburn or that she didn't have to sleep sitting up anymore. She felt like she was on a second honeymoon. The only other times she recalled feeling equally as happy were when she fell in love with her husband, then two years later when they committed to each other for the rest of their lives. She had her healthy baby and her husband by her side. What more did she need?

·44·

In a Heartbeat

They were visited by many friends and relatives after Annie arrived. However, no one visited as often as the UPS man. He came almost daily. Packages from relatives that Cate hadn't spoken to in years arrived. Friends of her parents that she didn't even know sent baby gifts. She now understood why people got so excited over babies, why every single parent she'd passed in public had stopped her to chat during her pregnancy. It wasn't just because things in small sizes were adorable. She knew it sounded corny, but having a child was, for lack of a better word, magical. She understood why people called it a miracle.

It was hard to explain but the love she felt for her baby was the most intense thing she'd ever felt in her life. Of course, her love for Ethan was as deep and strong as anything could be. In fact, her love for her husband had only grown since Annie had come into their lives. They were a family, and without each other they couldn't function. But being a mother was different than being a wife. Instinct was involved. Something deep inside the core of her existence made her bonded to Annie. It ran deeper than love. There was a protectiveness.

She knew why even the most hardened criminals had mothers who still loved them. Scott Peterson's mother had stood up for him even after his siblings had turned against him. Not that what his mother had done was right, but Cate understood her a little more now. It was because a mother saw all the vulnerabilities in her baby. Mothers saw their children at their weakest, at their neediest. Maybe somewhere in those adult faces they still saw that vulnerable little infant that relied on them for survival.

Now she understood why everyone wanted to chat with her, because being a parent was special in a way that only other parents could understand. It sounded weird but having a baby had really changed her view of the world. No matter where you were from or who you were, mothers and fathers all had one thing in common. They had experienced that miracle. Of course, there were exceptions. There were a handful of creatures that couldn't be explained—those who rejected their children and did unspeakable things to them.

Ethan and Annie accompanied Cate to her six-week checkup with Dr. Hatcher. Cate was breast-feeding and didn't want to be too far from the baby. It was a warm day, the kind of warmth that beckoned everyone outside. Soft breezes tickled the tree branches and Ethan decided to wait outside with the baby.

She waited in Dr. Hatcher's office wearing jeans. Her figure was far from back and whoever had said the pounds would just melt away from breast-feeding must've also been taking TrimSpa. She would hardly call the extremely slow process of losing weight melting off. Her belly button looked like a small canyon and her stomach muscles were so flimsy she wondered if she would ever touch a bikini again. The funny thing was, she didn't really care.

She looked around at the other women all waiting their turns, bellies bulging. They had no idea how much they would love their babies.

When she was called back into the exam room she realized this would be her last visit to his office. She'd gotten used to seeing Dr. Hatcher and Tina on a regular basis. She'd have to start watching *Extra* if she wanted all the celebrity gossip. She thought she *might* even miss the light-hits station. She'd looked forward to her doctor's appointments. Each time she'd seen Dr. Hatcher she'd learned something new about the baby. She had a lifetime of things to look forward to with Ethan and Annie, but she felt a little sad. She never thought she would say this but she realized that there were things about pregnancy she would miss. She would miss having a due date. It was kind of fun having a countdown. She would miss all the surprises that came along with learning more about the little stranger inside her.

"How's the baby?" Dr. Hatcher asked as he entered the exam room. "The love of your life?"

"I knew I would love her, but I had no idea how much. I can't explain it."

He nodded. "I know. Go tell your mother. She'll understand."

The examination went by quickly, and he told her everything had healed well. "You have a good summer, Cate." They shook hands.

The sunlight was bright when she came outside. She saw Ethan and Annie waiting on the bench. Her heart still skipped a beat each time she saw her daughter in her husband's arms. She felt like she was falling in love with him all over again every time he sang to their baby or rocked her to sleep. They looked like they belonged together.

Life was different now—waking every two hours with a screaming baby and sore nipples. They never made it anywhere on time, and spontaneous dinners or movies were history. But life was good. She couldn't imagine what it had been like without Annie.

She ran her fingers through Ethan's hair.

"You ready?" he asked.

She nodded.

"Everything okay?"

"Everything's great."

He stood up and kissed her on the forehead. "Would you do it again?"

"Yeah, I would do it all over again. It was definitely worth it."

"No, I mean, will you do it again?"

She smiled, then looked at her daughter. "In a heartbeat."